The Hex of Blackbriar Academy copyright © 2019 by Olivia Ash.
Covert art commissioned and owned by Wispvine Publishing LLC.
Book design and layout copyright © 2019 by Wispvine Publishing LLC.

This novel is a work of fiction. Names, characters, places and incidents are either products of the author's imagination or used fictitiously. Any resemblance to actual events, locales, or persons, living, dead, or undead, is entirely coincidental.

All rights reserved.

No part of this publication can be reproduced or transmitted in any form or by any means, electronic or mechanical, without permission in writing from Wispvine Publishing, L. L. C.

www.wispvine.com

978-1-939997-92-0

1st Edition

BOOKS BY OLIVIA ASH

Dragon Dojo Brotherhood

Reign of Dragons

Fate of Dragons

Blood of Dragons

Age of Dragons

Fall of Dragons

Death of Dragons

War of Dragons

Queen of Dragons

Myths of Dragons

Vessel of Dragons

Gods of Dragons

A Legend Among Dragons

Blackbriar Academy

The Trials of Blackbriar Academy

The Shadows of Blackbriar Academy

The Hex of Blackbriar Academy

The Blood Oath of Blackbriar Academy

The Battle of Blackbriar Academy

The Nighthelm Guardian Series

City of the Sleeping Gods

City of Fractured Souls

City of the Enchanted Queen

Demon Queen Saga

Princes of the Underworld

Wars of the Underworld

Sentinel Saga

By Dahlia Leigh and Olivia Ash

The Shadow Shifter

STAY CONNECTED

Join the exclusive group where all the cool kids hang out… Olivia's secret club for cool ladies! Consider this your formal invitation to a world of hot guys, fun people, and your fellow book lovers. Olivia hangs out in this group all the time. She made the group specifically for readers like you to come together and share their lives and interests, especially regarding the hot guys from her novels.

Check it out! Everyone in there is amazing, and you'll fit right in.

https://www.facebook.com/groups/LilaJeanOliviaAsh/

Sign up for email alerts of new releases AND an exclusive bonus novella from the Nighthelm Guardian series, *City of the Rebel Runes*, the prequel to *City of Sleeping Gods* only available to subscribers.

https://wispvine.com/newsletter/olivia-ash-email-signup/

Enjoying the series? Awesome! Help others discover Blackbriar Academy by leaving a review at Amazon.

BOOK DESCRIPTION

THE HEX OF BLACKBRIAR ACADEMY

Each new term at Blackbriar Academy is a new beginning—but this year, my new beginning could be the end of everything I love.

I'm settling into my new routine, and everything in my second year at Blackbriar seems great—until it is very suddenly not.

What's supposed to be a fun school-wide trip ends up being a huge betrayal by my own flesh and blood. I barely escape with my life. Now I'm out for revenge. The bloody kind.

The Order is close—and they're watching my every move.

They want the very magic that courses through my blood. They won't stop until they have it all: my magic, my power, my meteorite. And they'll kill anyone that stands in their way.

But I won't go down without a fight. They don't know who they're messing with. And when I'm backed into a corner, I'm deadly.

They say blood is thicker than water. Whoever "they" are, they never met *my* family.

With my men by my side, I'll fight until my last breath to keep what's mine. And if they dare touch the ones I love—there will be a bloody reckoning.

I'm done playing nice. If the Order wants a war, I'll *give* them one.

THE HEX OF BLACKBRIAR ACADEMY

BOOK THREE OF THE BLACKBRIAR ACADEMY SERIES

OLIVIA ASH

CONTENTS

Chapter 1	1
Chapter 2	13
Chapter 3	21
Chapter 4	29
Chapter 5	35
Chapter 6	47
Chapter 7	55
Chapter 8	67
Chapter 9	79
Chapter 10	85
Chapter 11	91
Chapter 12	99
Chapter 13	111
Chapter 14	123
Chapter 15	135
Chapter 16	145
Chapter 17	157
Chapter 18	167
Chapter 19	173
Chapter 20	183
Chapter 21	191
Chapter 22	199
Chapter 23	211
Chapter 24	219
Chapter 25	229
Chapter 26	237
Chapter 27	243
Chapter 28	261
Chapter 29	273
Chapter 30	289

Chapter 31	297
Chapter 32	303
Chapter 33	309
Chapter 34	321
Chapter 35	329
Chapter 36	341
Chapter 37	347
Chapter 38	355
Chapter 39	369
Chapter 40	381
Chapter 41	395
Author Notes	401
About the Author	405

CHAPTER ONE

I'm surrounded by golems.

I dodge a blow from a rigid fist and roll to the side to avoid another attack. That one was *close*.

I cast a quick glance at my father. His expression is a stony mask of determination and cold distance. He stands stern and unwavering with his arms crossed over his chest, observing my training. I search his eyes for an inkling of approval, but his silent stare tells me to keep my gaze on my foes.

All summer long, we've trained almost daily with these creatures. Today is no different. And he always has the same stone-like features of a man who is focused on tactical advantage and strategy. This is his serious side. There is no hint of his love for his only daughter in his deep brown eyes. Only studious examination of my every move.

I'm not used to this side of him. And I'm not sure I ever will be.

At first, it was difficult to overcome. But as soon as training was over, my father was right back to the man I know and love. The man from my childhood who would let me ride on his shoulders. The man who cradled me during severe thunderstorms. The man who I clung to after my mother died.

I return my attention to the task in front of me as the remaining five of ten golems move quickly through the large open field surrounded by giant sycamores, maples, and pines with points stretching high toward the sky.

They are out for blood.

And they're fighting *dirty* to spill mine.

Gryffons lounge in the grass in the shady corner of the field, sleepily watching the display as I maneuver between the golems and take one down using a swift sweep of my leg and blasting it in the heart with my magic. It dissolves into dust as I quickly stand and face the last four golems.

The gryffons are Gideon's. Well, sort of. He saved the King's mate and heir once. And they've been loyal to him ever since, taking up residence on his own estate that has become the safehouse for my father. For now.

My father's name still needs to be cleared. Though no official charges have come against him from the council, or magusari, he's still a suspected criminal. His reputation has been tarnished, thanks to the Order.

Meanwhile, the gryffons help safeguard my father from unwanted visitors, should anyone manage to slip through the wards set to keep this whole estate hidden.

Though I've had plenty of practice with the golems over the summer, these ones are particularly difficult to take down. Each week, my father has increased their numbers and upgraded their skills. Today, I'm sweating despite the cool seventy-six-degree weather. I'm just a hair faster than them, and they are slightly stronger than me.

Challenge accepted.

As I destroy another golem with fire, one immediately takes its place and in one swift motion hits me square in the stomach. I double over as the wind is knocked from my lungs and my movement becomes difficult. My magic floods through me as anger from my distraction fills me. My skin starts to burn. I can't even take in a deep breath to calm myself because of the stabbing pain that ricochets through my torso. I have to calm down or I'll lose control of my magic, disintegrating everything around me. With my father so close, I can't risk that.

"Stop!" My father's voice rings through the air. The fight is paused, and the golems back off as though they heard a silent command from him, returning to their starting location just a few yards away from me.

I look at him as the last remaining specks of dust from the golem I destroyed falls to the ground.

He points a stiff finger at me. "Keep your head in the game, not in the clouds."

I nod, though I flinch a little at the sternness of his voice.

He approaches me and helps me to stand straight. "Never have your back to your enemy, keep them in view. Angle yourself like this." He demonstrates by twisting just slightly at the waist. "If you let yourself get distracted, you can die."

I gulp.

"And never let your enemy see your weakness." He nods toward my stomach.

I take in his dark eyes and the slight frown that pulls at the corners of his lips as he stresses each word. His color has returned now, and his strength, but he still shows the signs of his captivity every so often with the fleeting shadows that cross over his eyes.

I know he's trying to make me stronger. I know he loves and cares for me. But right now, he's not my father. He's my teacher. And his job is to teach me how not to die.

He stands in front of me, back straight and shoulders angled back, like a soldier. "You must be aware of your surroundings. Don't focus on them, but be aware. Your attention should be on your enemy."

He's good at confusing me too. I shake my head as a pinch forms in my forehead, wondering how I'm supposed to do all that and win.

"Again!"

He moves out of the way as the golems advance. And I just can't stop trying to figure out what the hell my father means by being aware of my surroundings without being focused on them.

Though I'm frustrated at the confusing direction, I do my best at making do with what I can understand of his words. I feel like this whole daughter thing is new, and I want to please him, somehow. Make him happy with me and my progress. Call me crazy, but I just can't help caring about that.

Living with trolls for six years taught me to depend on me, and me only. Fight for myself. Fend for myself. Avoid attention, because attention often led to punishment. In that time, I forgot about a lot of what it takes to be a part of a family. Now I'm relearning it.

Slowly.

A slight, cool breeze picks up from the east, blowing against the canopy of trees. As it brushes against the golems, I notice they move to the west just a fraction of an inch more.

Hmm... interesting.

Their steps clump and crunch against the grass that's turning brown and yellow with the coming cooler months. Their lifeless eyes zoom in on me like lasers as they spread a little farther out, trying again to surround me. Some of them ball their clay fists, a promise of pain if I don't take them down first.

Behind me, I barely hear the whispering breaths my father takes. Behind him is the house, guarded by four of Gideon's most loyal guards. The gryffons stand and stretch their backs and wings, moving to a sunnier spot in the field.

As I keep my attention on the golems, I'm slowly figuring out what it means to be aware of my surroundings without focusing on them. I can almost feel where everything is without having to look.

Balls of burning white light fill my hands, the

flames kissing my forearms as I move into my ready stance.

One by one, the golems charge.

I follow my father's directions, twisting and taking out each featureless mud creature, disintegrating them into clumps of dirt and dust. I attack two simultaneously, sending a punch to the torso of one, blowing a large hole through its middle. I side kick the other. It topples off balance and takes a couple steps to recuperate, but I'm already facing the third golem. I form a large ball and release the blast into it, and without so much as a breath leaving my lungs, spin to face the final one. I jump in the air for a spinning roundhouse kick, and my foot delivers a blow to the fragile connection between the golem's head and neck, severing the head as it flies through the air and nearly bumps into a gryffon.

To finalize my fight, I blast the body with electricity. The body explodes.

I take a deep breath and face my father for his final critique.

Per usual, he nods, relaxes his arms to his sides, and turns for the house.

We'll talk about everything over lunch.

We normally do.

But as we silently make our way into the house, my

father immediately walks through the kitchen, disappearing behind the corner and down the hall. The twist of a doorknob echoes toward me just before the squeaking of the hinges. Moments later, my father returns with paper and ink pens.

He sets them on the table in front of me and gestures for me to take a seat.

I slide into the chair and settle my gaze on him. "What are these for?"

"You haven't learned how to send letters. I'm going to fix that. This way, we can stay in contact with each other throughout the school year and you'll get to practice doing something I should have taught you a long time ago." His voice is softer now. The stern tone is replaced by a gentler, loving one. The one I remember from my childhood.

My eyes widen as a jolt of excitement rushes through me. "Really?"

Suddenly, I'm a little girl again, hanging onto every little moment spent with my father, absorbing all the information he feeds me as though it is more precious than gold.

I have to say, this is all still a little weird and a bit awkward, but I love it.

I watch as he takes a page and folds it in half, creasing the paper firmly before opening the flaps and jotting down a few quick words. His eyes lift to mine and he nods. My silent go-ahead to do the same.

I do.

"The symbol I am about to draw means hidden secrets and is what keeps the letter encoded. My intention is you. So only you can unlock it."

I nod.

Beneath his words, he draws an intricate symbol with two slanted lines standing parallel. Both are joined by a half circle and a crescent moon shape attached on the end of the second line. It looks like a strange musical note. It's a simple design, but I pay careful attention to the detail as I draw the same symbol. I place my intention on my father, keeping his image in mind as I draw each line and angle with perfect precision.

"Of course, you've already discovered how to decode these," my father adds, a tone of pride in his words.

I smile.

"Now, for the location part..." He folds the letter closed and begins to fill in another design. I recognize each rune as he draws it. Ansuz, the broken "F" with the top and middle line pointing down, Yr, the slanted looking letter "A" with a "T" at the base, and Raido, an open-looking letter "R."

As soon as he finishes, he uses his magic to burn the letter. It disappears into nothing. Not even a single ash remains.

"Whoa."

He chuckles. "Go on, I sent it to your room."

I jump up from the table and rush to the room I have been sleeping in over the summer. Sure enough, the letter rests on my bed with not a mark on it. The symbols on the front are gone and as I open the page to read what is written, the page sits empty.

At first, nothing happens. Within seconds, the letters start to take shape, and the words: "Are you ready for this?" appear. I smile and giggle and rush down to the table with the letter in hand.

My father smiles, his brown eyes crinkle at the corners as he beams at me. "Very good. Now, you try."

I nod and repeat the motions on the top of my letter. I decide to focus on him and his room for the letter as I etch the runes in the same way I saw him do it.

Lastly, I use my magic to burn the letter. It disappears with little evidence of it having been here. I frown as I settle my questioning gaze on my father.

"Don't worry, it'll still work. The ashes will disappear the more you practice. Where did you send it?"

"Your room," I say and watch as he stands from the

table calmly and walks with confidence toward his room.

As soon as he leaves the room, I notice that it's sitting on the stove. I gape. Something went wrong here. Soon, my father returns, and I point to the stove.

"Ah." He picks up the letter and reads the letter. "Good. Very good."

"It didn't go where I wanted it to," I mutter, disappointed in myself.

He shrugs. "Practice." He nods to the stack of papers and I begin again.

CHAPTER TWO

By the end of the day, I'm a pro at sending letters like the ones my father sent me when I first arrived at Blackbriar. Although we had missed lunch, we got to sit down for a mouth-watering meal of roasted chicken and vegetables. With the sweet tooth that I have, I waste no time in finishing dinner and grabbing an ice cream cone before accompanying my father for a stroll around the estate.

I race him to the top of a small hill overlooking the grounds. I catch a glimpse of him wearing a smile as we catch our breaths. This is one of the relaxing moments of just being with my father that I've longed for. I love reconnecting with him. I feel like a little girl again, and memories from before everything went wrong play through my mind. I take another lick of my ice cream as a small river of melted, creamy goodness slips down the side of the cone.

Those were the days that kept me going through some of my most trying moments when I was with the trolls. Now, I finally have my father back, and I can also finally slip into some semblance of normalcy. Be a normal girl.

If there is even really such a thing as normal anymore.

We reminisce about the adventures we've had over the summer. We're having such a good time talking, I forgot to keep eating my cone. I take an absent minded lick of the marbled chocolate and vanilla substance as I settle my gaze over the gryffons stretching their wings. And they return my curious gaze.

"You've done excellent over the summer," my father says pensively. "Soren has trained you well."

"It was a team effort really." I take a bite out of the top of my somewhat soggy cone.

He nods and becomes silent. There is something about the silence between us that unsettles me, and I feel inclined to ask what's bothering him.

"What are you thinking about?" I ask.

His eyes are focused on the forest below, stretching out as far as my eyes can see. The weight of the tension settling between us becomes almost too much to bear, and in these final moments I have left with my father, I don't want things to end on this note.

He shakes his head and sighs heavily. "The trees."

I look at them and back to him, turning so that I face him head on. "Okay?"

"The harsh winters you had to endure because you were sent to the wrong person."

My eyebrows knit themselves together as I once again discard interest in my melting ice cream cone for what is weighing so heavily on my father's shoulders.

A young gryffon makes his way up toward me and as soon as he is close enough, I toss my cone to him. He eats it up in one gulp, and I break a smile. If only for the moment, I'm caught by the enchanting magnificence of the creatures.

"I blame myself for the things you had to go through. The person you were sent to." My father's words are tinged with regret and anger. He's beating himself up, and that's not okay with me.

"Dad, don't. You didn't have a choice."

"Doesn't change the fact that I almost lost you because I trusted my sister."

"Aunt Patricia?" I ask. "Why?"

He shakes his head. "I overheard a conversation I wasn't supposed to. I almost didn't. Having been beaten into submission again, I barely clung to what consciousness I had. When Deacon and one of his accomplices thought I was out cold, I heard him say her name." He faces me, and the haunting look in his eyes makes my heart skip a beat. "I assumed they were planning to go after her because they saw her as a threat or maybe even take her hostage. But when I learned how she was freely traveling the world and even visiting you at Blackbriar, I wasn't sure what to make of it. I had chalked it up to her just being well-protected."

"When did you become suspicious of her?" My question comes out in a low voice. I can see where he's going with this.

He lets out a long breath. "Just a few days ago, as I was trying to piece together who would even think to spread rumors about me and my so-called unsanctioned magic. It would explain why the council and magusari have no charges on file. I analyzed a hundred times how my sister remained untouched as you were conveniently snatched from her home. And why would Deacon mention her but take no action against her? Maybe I was blinded by emotion to not have seen it sooner, but Patricia is up to something. She's involved with the Order somehow."

"Do you have proof of this?"

This could be it. That thing that stands out to me. The lack of emotion she seems to have toward me every time Aunt Patricia is around. Even though, at times, she shows glimpses of warmth and promises to keep me safe. I'm inclined to side with my father, but without proof, it's just speculation.

He huffs another sigh and shakes his head, breaking eye contact with me as though he feels ashamed of himself. "Unfortunately, I wasn't able to find any evidence. I can't say for sure that she's a member of the Order, she could be a sympathizer or an unwitting pawn. But what I can say with certainty is that she can't be trusted. Not until there is proof of innocence."

"Why would Aunt Patricia be involved with them?" I ask, hoping to know more. Maybe glean a bit more information to coincide with my own list of things.

"I don't know. All I know is I don't trust her."

Okay, maybe I need to try a different tactic. He should probably know what she has said about him, anyway.

"Dad... she basically told me the same thing about you."

He looks up to the sky and a sarcastic chuckle whispers from his mouth. "Of course, she did."

"What do you mean?" Okay, I'm genuinely

confused. "She said you were always trying to get her in trouble when you were kids. You were never close, and you were always up to no good. You were a criminal on the run when you disappeared, which is why you are stuck here until we can clear your name."

He faces me, resting his hands on my shoulders as he stares deep into my eyes. "She was obviously certain you'd never see me again and learn the truth, but I assure you, those are all lies. We were quite close growing up. She even encouraged me and worked with me on some projects, helping me push and test magical limits. We only had a falling out when I married your mother."

"None of this is making any sense." I shake my head. I want, for once, for things to be evident and clear.

He pulls me into him, tucking me close to his chest, leaving a gentle kiss on the top of my head before releasing me. "I wish I could tell you more, but I'm afraid there's not much left to tell. Just be careful, please. Keep your eyes open."

I nod.

My magic flares with strength and force.

"Am I interrupting something?"

Gideon.

I turn my gaze to him and nearly rush into his arms. He smiles at me as he approaches.

"Nothing at all. Just spending some time with Wren before she leaves." My father steps toward Gideon and gives him a handshake in greeting.

"I understand." Gideon smiles warmly at my father, like they're old friends and just catching up on shoptalk before getting to the nitty gritty. He faces me after taking his hand back and says, "Miss me?"

I smile as my heart races. "Maybe."

He chuckles and turns his attention to my father again. "I have some updates."

My father faces Gideon with a serious expression. "Fire away."

"Though there still aren't any criminal charges or warrants, you remain a person of interest, which is only made worse by the rumors encouraged and spread about you. I will keep checking, but for the meantime, I think it's best you hold up here a bit longer. The Order is still after you. We've been monitoring their movements and word is, they are organizing a manhunt. There's not a price on your head, but I suspect there will be soon."

My father nods. "I'm not worried. I'm well aware I may have to remain in hiding until the Order has what they want, and maybe not even then." He glances toward me. My intuition flares. I know my father wants to say more, but he won't because he knows whatever it is, it will worry me.

If only it were that easy.

"Let's hope it doesn't come to that. We're doing everything we can to settle it." Gideon shifts his attention to the gryffons approaching. "My friends!"

He approaches the largest of the small group. It's cute to watch as the gryffon nudges his hand and bumps into Gideon lovingly. Gideon lets out a chuckle and scratches the creature's head.

Before long, Gideon returns to my side. "Ready to go?"

"Just a moment." I rush to my father and throw my arms tightly around him. "Thank you for the summer."

He chuckles as his arms tighten around me. "We'll have more time. I promise."

"I'm so going to hold you to that." I pull away and join Gideon's side.

My father nods. "You better."

I smile as the portal forms between us. Gideon and I step through, and within seconds we're back on Blackbriar Island. My home.

CHAPTER THREE

I've missed this garden.

It's one of my favorite places to just sit and absorb the island sun and air. Breathing in the ocean and listening to the lullaby of the waves crashing against the base of the island that has become my favorite song.

Sitting with one of my favorite people adds icing to the cake.

Savannah busies herself with adding two French braids to the sides of my head as I fill her in on my time with my father.

"I miss him already." A warm, salty breeze brushes against my cheek. Sitting here with Savannah helps ease my mind as I wrestle with the question of Aunt

Patricia and where her true loyalties lie. I hope my father is doing well back at the safehouse.

"Of course, you do. He's your dad!"

"So, enough about me. Tell me about your summer."

She sighs. I want to turn and see the look on her face. I'm sure it's a disappointed one. But no sooner than I try to turn, she forces my head back.

"Spill the beans," I say.

"I'm almost done, then I will." And with a few more tugs, the last braid falls along the back of my shoulders. She flips it over to the front and I twist to face her. She smiles at me. "You're so freaking pretty. You know that?"

I giggle. "Nice change of topic, but thanks. I have your help to thank, after all."

"Oh, please." She waves the sentiment off as she settles onto her rear on the grass and kicks out her feet in front of her, crossing her feet at the ankles.

"Savannah…" I let the word hang there. She knows what I'm looking for.

"You're not going to like what I have to say." She settles her amethyst eyes on me.

I level my gaze on her in the way that says, *enough delays, spill*.

"During some of my down time, I've been keeping a journal, documenting everything we know so far about the Order and their possible dealings. And only after I sort of overheard a conversation my dad was having with my brothers, I knew I had to do something."

"And?" I sit up straighter, giving her my full attention.

She shakes her head. A frown pulls at her lips and I know it's bad. "Some things need to be shown rather than just told."

Before I can respond, she rests a hand on my shoulder, and I'm pulled into a vision.

I suck in a breath as the images blur through my mind with their sudden appearance.

"Sorry. It can be a bit much at first."

"It's fine." I shake my head and wave away her worry. It doesn't really surprise me that she can do this. Savannah is a powerhouse of her own right. "I like it."

"I knew you could handle it." I hear the smile in Savannah's voice. And I smile too.

Instantly, I'm in a hallway, darkened by the storm rolling outside. The curtains at the end of the hall are drawn, and a small wedge of light shines on the floor at the base of a slightly opened door. Savannah enters my view, and she leans against the door jam, out of sight, as three men discuss something of importance with tense words.

Savannah's voice drifts over me, like a warm breeze. "They were discussing some illness that presents with flu-like symptoms. But for some reason, nothing they are doing to combat it is working. On top of severe dehydration, they spoke about the veins in some of the patients becoming almost black. There were other strange symptoms that they believe are magical in essence."

Images of a woman, struggling for breath, pale and coughing up blood, sweating as she lays bedridden while an older gentleman lays a cool cloth over her forehead. The image switches to a child, no more than five or six as another younger man is trying to get the child to take small sips of water.

"That's horrible. How did they find this out?" I ask as the images continue to shift through man, woman, and child, all in various stages of the illness with the three men standing off to the side shaking their head as they struggle to out figure what is ailing these people.

She shrugs and removes her hand. "They always go to the poorer communities around the country and help out local clinics with supplies and healthcare. They said they'd never seen anything like it before. It's not a normal virus. In fact, they don't think it's a virus at all."

My eyebrows raise high up on my forehead as the sheer horror of what she shared settles around us. "That's so horrible. What are they going to do?"

"I'm not sure. They caught me after that and made me swear not to share that information with anyone. They don't want a mass panic on their hands. But I at least had to share it with you. It feels like there's more behind it, and I've read historical accounts where epidemics like this wiped out entire communities and were played off as an unfortunate accident."

"We can't just let innocent lives be taken. Especially if this is a magical malady afflicting people. If the illness becomes widespread, it could endanger hundreds and thousands of lives. Maybe even come here to this island."

My mind goes full tilt with the idea that the Order is behind this. I feel it deep in my bones. There is so much more behind this than we can even begin to comprehend. And I can't just sit back and allow innocent lives to be claimed so unnecessarily. We need to do something. Anything.

"You're right." Savannah nods. "We need to do

some digging into this. Think your men should know?"

"Yeah, probably. We need to make sure we have more than suspicion when going to them though."

"When will they be back?" Her eyes become lost in thought, like she's processing more information than she is sharing.

"Tonight," I say through a wistful sigh. "I miss them too."

"Don't forget, we're doing the introductions for the initiates tonight." Savannah bobs her eyebrows. "Fresh meat!"

I laugh. This girl is something else. I love it though. "What else happened over the summer?"

"I spent a lot of it helping out with my sister. She's strong, Clarrissa. She tries to hide the fact that she's constantly in pain." She sighs. "I talked about you and your men. I think she likes to live vicariously through others."

I chuckle softly. "Maybe she won't have to someday."

"That's the goal." Savannah smiles. "I'm hungry. How are you feeling?"

I narrow my eyes thoughtfully as I look into the sky. "I could go for some food."

"Fantastic. Let's raid us a kitchen." She hops up and brushes herself off.

"Well, since you put it that way." I jump to my feet and walk with her toward the kitchens to steal a snack.

CHAPTER FOUR

For the first time, I'm sitting with my house for the initiate ceremony. I'm seeing it from the other side, and I'm enthralled with the looks on the faces of the initiates. They file in and set their gazes on each of the four magical house banners that are situated along the left wall, we are all seated in front of our own houses, facing the faculty sitting at a long table with ten chairs. Balls of light encased in glass orbs hang from the high ceiling giving off a warm glow that fills the arena transformed for this ceremony.

First house inside the arena is my house. House of Phoenix. Just like when I first came here. And it only instills the idea that Blackbriar is very much so dependent on their traditions and routines. Next is House of

Drakon, then House of Kraken and House of Winterwolf.

From here, I catch Gideon, sitting in the center of the line of professors. A seat remains empty next to him, and I wonder who it's for.

Gideon stands, and as he waits to make his announcement, all the chatter throughout the arena settles into a hush.

"Welcome to another year," he begins. Hoots and hollers fill the air and he holds up his hands to quiet down the room. "As you can tell, most of our fourth-year students are especially excited as this marks the closing of a chapter for them, as well as the opening of another at the end of the year."

More applause.

"With that said," Gideon gestures to the door of the arena. "One of our graduates from last year has accepted a position as our new professor of Magical Defense."

The door opens, and Soren walks through. My heart skips a beat at seeing him, and I'm still waiting for the new professor to walk in. No one follows. Instead, Soren approaches Gideon and shakes his hand.

"Professor McCallister, ladies and gentlemen." Gideon's voice makes the fact official, and I shake my head at the audacity of them keeping this from me all summer long.

So, this was the surprise.

Assholes.

Ridiculously adorable assholes.

Soren catches my gaze as he takes the seat next to Gideon and winks at me with a satisfied smile stretching his lips.

I bite the corner of my lower lip and join in the applause.

Okay. I forgive him.

A little.

Still, I'm happy I don't have to live without him. I wasn't sure how I would make it through the year without him being around. He's become an integral part of my life and not having him would feel like a gaping hole. However, as soon as I can get him alone, I'm going to let him have a piece of my mind for keeping me out of the loop. One that perhaps leads to a celebratory romp between some sheets. Just so he knows how serious this is.

After Gideon goes through the rules for our new initiates, he moves down the row, introducing each. Every initiate stands proudly. Some of them I can tell come from wealthy mage families or a long line of mages, while others are shy or fidgety. The shy and fidgety ones I sympathize with. It wasn't too long ago I felt out of place and stuck out like a sore thumb. I too felt nervous about what laid ahead for me.

I barely pay attention to the names. I don't want to remember them because I know there is a very real possibility that they won't make it through. However, one name does stand out to me and it's because she's staring at someone in the House of Kraken. I follow her gaze and realize it's Milo.

"Agatha Collins."

She looks utterly mesmerized by him. Anger suddenly boils inside me.

It's a new sensation. Foreign and uncomfortable. I force myself to take a deep breath, because, after all, this is Milo. He's mine. Besides, she may not even make it past the trials.

I shake off the feeling and scan the crowd of initiates. Some of them will make it, and a few of those may join House of Phoenix. Soon, I'm overcome with absorbing how different it is to be on this side of this scenario. Not too long ago I was an initiate myself, seeing everything Blackbriar had to offer for the first time, and being on this side now brings me a sense of pride.

I join in on the chant with the rest of my house as the phoenix is reborn again. "Fire, death, rebirth, life."

And the feeling is *powerful*. Almost like our own words brings forth the new life of our house mascot. I can't help the smile that stretches my lips as my eyes settle on the initiates' wide eyes and mouths gaping in awe.

I know the feeling quite well.

Excited chatter erupts through the room from the initiates and before long, Gideon introduces House of Drakon.

I watch in wonder as the faces of the initiates take in every moment from each of the demonstrations. Seeing the hope and wonder alight in their eyes brings me a sense of belonging. I know I'm home here, and I can tell they want to find a home here too. If even, a home away from home.

As the waves for the demonstration for House of Kraken first crashes against the table, I have to stifle a chuckle at the way some of the initiates jump. There's a bit of fear in their eyes that makes me wonder if they think they're actually going to be taken by the great sea creature, pulled so deep into the experience that they forget it's only a demonstration.

This entire ceremony brings me such joy to see the hope and wonder on the faces of our new recruits. It saddens me a little that some of them will not make it through their trials. They'll have their memory of this place and all they learned and experienced taken from them like a dream that is swept away.

Somehow, my mind returns to what Savannah shared with me earlier of the plague. I wonder if the initiates will be afflicted by this illness and what could the Order possibly hope to accomplish with such dangerous experiments.

I hope Savannah and I can find time soon to dig deeper into this. So we have something concrete to share with the men and find a way to stop the Order from inflicting undue pain and suffering on such innocent lives.

Before long, the demonstrations are over, and the initiates are dismissed. As soon as I get the chance, I pounce on the opportunity to corner Soren.

I try to flag him down, but he escapes the arena without notice.

Touché. Two can play this game.

He's playing with me and judging the smile on his face as he left, he thinks he's winning.

Well, game on then, Soren. Game on.

CHAPTER FIVE

The sun is so *warm*.

Which is a good thing, considering how absolutely frustrated I am. So far, we have found nothing to tie the Order to the illnesses. Go figure. I know it's them though. My intuition is rarely, if ever, wrong. I just need to find something concrete.

The new school year begins in just a few short days, and I've spent a majority of them in the library, sitting here in my favorite garden, or hanging out with my men. Except Soren, who is the reason why I'm so frustrated. He manages to keep himself out of sight, busy with doing who knows what.

I just want to see him, touch him, feel him. And every time I catch a glimpse of him, he has that same cocky smile on his face. Most times, he winks. Other times, he just evades me and disappears moments before I finally catch up with him.

I'm so going to give him hell for this. The ideas are plentiful and downright torturous. He's playing cat and mouse with me, and I plan to do the same to him. Once I have him in my arms, that is.

I darkly laugh to myself at some of the thoughts rushing through my mind. Teasing him, making him inch ever so close to getting me between the sheets and dragging out that blissful need for as long as I can possibly stretch it out for. I'm not trying to be cruel now. I need him just as badly. But I want to show him two can play at this game.

An ocean-filled breeze brushes against my cheeks, cooling them from the rays of heat, and I sigh wistfully.

I soak in the peacefulness of the day until a sound grates on my nerves and pierces my ears, pulling my attention to Milo slowly making his way toward me.

But he's not alone.

Agatha.

Gah! That girl gets on my last nerve.

Sadly, she passed her trials. I mean, good for her, but she is pushing all the wrong buttons hanging around Milo the way she is. Even now, as he tries to make his way toward me, she's walking with him, giggling and chatting in a tone that just makes me hate her all the more.

I frown.

Poor Milo is oblivious to the way she makes googly-eyes at him. She touches him on his arm and laughs at something he says. "Oh, Milo. You're so funny."

He shrugs and tries to tell her in his overly polite way he needs to go. But she doesn't seem to take the hint.

This feeling that boils inside me isn't entirely anger. It's a sensation of warmth, but my stomach feels like it's twisting in knots and becoming heavy at the same time. Suddenly, I'm aware it's jealousy, and that's not a sensation I'm used to experiencing. It's uncomfortable and almost makes me feel sick.

She's flirting with my man. My Milo. And that's just not okay.

I hear the steps of someone approaching, and before I look, my magic tells me everything I need to know about who's coming.

Jesse.

He plops down on the grass, bending a knee and resting an arm around it as he grins at me with that mischievous smile of his. "Looks like someone has a bit of competition for our dear Milo."

I glare at him. "Not. Funny."

He leans back and narrows his eyes on me thoughtfully as a knowing smile stretches his lips even wider. "Someone is jealous."

I punch him in the arm. Not hard, but more like a love pat.

"Damn it, woman. I told you I'm precious cargo."

I chuckle. I can't help it. No matter how much I fight it, he just knows how to get me to lighten up. Damn his beautiful self for that.

"That's much better," he says, nudging his shoulder against me. "Besides, she's got nothing on you. She'll eventually get the hint he's not interested and move on."

"Or she'll get a clear indicator from me." My voice comes out dark and full of the promise I plan to deliver on if she doesn't back the hell off.

"For her sake, I hope it doesn't come to that. You, my dear, are a force to reckon with." He points a finger at me. "My money is on you anyway."

"Oh good, we can sell tickets. Split the winnings."

"I like your thinking." He beams at me in his devilish way that makes pressure build between my thighs and pleasant delightful chills snake through me.

I playfully push him as I chuckle. "You're not helping."

"You're laughing, aren't you?" He leans back on his arms, crossing his legs at the ankles in front of him.

Thankfully, Savannah walks up and pulls Milo away. The girl just shrugs it off and waves at Milo.

"Catch up with you later, Milo." Her high-pitched voice really grates on my nerves.

No, the hell, you won't. I'll make sure of that.

As the two approach, I clear my throat and stretch out my neck and shoulders to release the tension pinching the muscles. As Savannah sits in front of me, I mouth thank you.

She nods and smiles. "How are we doing this fine afternoon?"

Milo sits on the other side of me. "Ready for the year to start."

"Run out of projects? Or is the latest one particularly difficult to solve?" Jesse's eyes settle on Agatha as she sits on a bench, looking wistfully toward Milo. She doesn't even meet my glaring eyes. I wish she would. Perhaps she'd get the point that she's playing with fire.

Milo follows his gaze. "Huh? Oh, Agatha? She's just the latest member of my house." He shrugs it off like it's nothing.

I smile as I lean into him and rest my head on his shoulders. Good man.

He chuckles and rubs my back gently before I pull

away. I don't even look in Agatha's direction. Milo told me everything I need to know. He's mine. I'm his. End of story.

Before long, we're all laughing as Jesse talks about some of the pranks his brothers pulled on him from over the summer. He's shared a few of them with me already, but I listen intently to his story.

"The monsters did something to the pool. The pool! I mean, I'm impressed, don't get me wrong." Jesse animatedly throws his hands into the air. "But still."

"What did they do?" Savannah asks, leaning in as though she can't wait to hear the story.

"Cursed it. Well, the water anyway." He holds up his index finger. It's tinged orange with splotchy red patches. "Point is, my entire body looked like this. Can you imagine the horrifying picture this creates?" He gestures to his finger. "This perfect body marred as though a toddler got crazy with a few crayons." He shakes his head.

I stare at him for a moment as I picture Jesse colored head to toe in orange and red. Snorting, I let out a loud belly laugh.

"She gets it." Jesse adds with a nod in my direction. "It was hilarious."

"How long did it take for the rest of you to return

to normal?" Milo asks leaning forward and adjusting his glasses for a better look. "Interesting color choice."

"Try wearing it," Jesse quips. "Two weeks, and luckily this is all that's left. I hope it's not permanent." He frowns as he rubs at the skin as though friction is all it takes to remove the odd coloring.

He sits back and his eyes shift out of focus as though he is reminiscing about them. "I love them though. The little bastards know how to keep things interesting. But enough about me and my summer blues. What have my wonderful fellows been up to?"

We all exchange glances, waiting for someone to speak first. When no one does, we all break out into a loud peal of laughter. Finally, Jesse nudges me. I set my gaze on his beautiful face full of curiosity.

"What? You want me to follow your tale?" I wink.

He nods. "Your audience is waiting." He gestures to Savannah and Milo, who are each sitting back with patient expressions."

I shrug. "I spent the summer training with my father and Gideon at his estate."

"Oooh, tell me more!" Savannah bobs her eyebrows as I chuckle.

"Spare the dirty details, though." Milo adds shaking his head.

I quirk an eyebrow as I study him. His cheeks redden a little as he gulps.

Well, well... look at Milo being jealous himself.

I could play with him and make some stuff up, but I feel like it wouldn't be fair to Gideon or Milo.

"Don't worry, nothing happened like that. It was all platonic." I lay a hand on Milo's thigh.

He chuckles under his breath, and I detect a hint of nervousness within the soft sound. I smile for good measure.

"Your turn," I add.

He shoves his glasses farther up his nose and resettles in his spot. "I went to an alchemy convention."

"That's interesting," I say.

"Yes, very," Savannah agrees.

"Interesting is definitely one word for it, but not the word I would choose," Jesse says, poking fun at Milo.

"Behave," I say, shooting him a playful glare.

"That's no fun either." He winks.

I shake my head and look at Milo. "What else?"

He shakes his head. "Nope. It's Savannah's turn."

She smiles, amethyst eyes almost glowing in the sunlight. "I had fun with my family and entertaining my sister." She winks at me knowingly, and I give her a slight nod. We know more than that happened, but until she has more to go on, more proof, she's keeping that bit to herself. Besides, she wasn't even supposed to tell me.

I look at Jesse. "Seems like you win for having the most fun."

"Naturally."

"So, what do we want to gossip about now?" Savannah asks.

"Soren teaching." Jesse snorts. "This is going to be epic."

I stare daggers at him, hoping he takes my silent cue to explain himself. When he doesn't, I bite. "How so? This is Soren. He's an asshole. Class is going to be a nightmare. And believe me, I know."

His lips break into a mischievous grin.

That look says so much, and I know this is going to be *fun*.

"The idea here is to give Soren as much hell as possible to welcome him as our professor." He holds up two fingers on each hand, pumping them twice. Beaming at his own cleverness, he leans back on his elbows and gives a half-hearted shrug. "So, we all know how he is going to react to that, and therein lies all the fun." His eyes widen at the last word, glittering gleefully in the sunlight.

"And how does this masterplan work?" Milo asks.

Jesse turns his attention to him, all serious. "Professor McCallister."

Savannah and I snort and laugh. Milo eventually joins in. Jesse chuckles to himself as he gestures between us.

"See? I don't think any of us can fathom our seriously stubborn friend as being in charge of us. We're too close and know too much. Thus, my—as you so appropriately put it—masterplan."

"That's going to take too much effort getting used to," I say referring to Soren as Professor. I almost lose control of myself to the laughter again. Taking in a controlled breath, I ease the urge away. Just a little. "I have a plan of my own, using that title to my advantage."

This is going to be so much fun. My mind goes full tilt in all the wonderful ways I could use this to tease him. Behind closed doors of course. I can get under his skin just as well as he can get under mine. And I fully intend to exploit that as much as I can.

But Milo doesn't seem convinced.

"Seems a bit lackluster to me. We need to step it up, but not to the point of undermining him in front of our peers. First class, we let him have it. He loses control, perhaps gets a little payback, then we dull it down, give it some time, and just when he thinks this is behind us—*BAM!*"

Jesse's eyes narrow on Milo with a sense of curiosity mixed with pride. "Well, well. Milo has more tricks up his sleeve than I gave him credit for."

"Thanks. I think..." He shoves his glasses up his nose as his eyebrows furrow with confusion.

"Oh it, indeed, is a compliment." Jesse grins. "Let us begin with filling in the rules of our little game."

Excitement pulsates through me as we all huddle closer together and formulate the details of our plan to give Soren hell for becoming a professor. Before long, our plan is set, and we all leave to go back to our houses and prepare for the new school year to officially start.

CHAPTER SIX

I'm still reeling from the amazing, mind-consuming kiss Gideon left me with after our early morning training session. My mind feels fuzzy, buzzing with the way he makes me feel. Those small stolen moments we share behind closed doors seem almost dreamlike.

For now.

Once I'm showered and dressed, I head to my first class for the day. Magical Defense, taught by Soren, who won't be able to escape me today, finally.

I giggle as my team's plan to give Soren hell for being a professor comes closer to reality.

As soon as I'm through the classroom door, I catch sight of Savannah, Jesse, and Milo sitting at a table, saving me a seat next to them. Soren isn't here yet, but

I'm not worried. He wouldn't miss his first day of official teaching, and I can't wait to see his face.

Jesse waves me over and I join them with a smile. "Good morning, fabulous peeps."

Savannah lets out a breathy laugh. "What happened to you this morning?" She winks, and I feel my cheeks warm as heat rushes down the back of my neck as the recollection of Gideon's mouth on mine, moving his tongue in ways that makes me weak in the knees, fills my mind.

I take my seat and rake my gaze around the room's setup.

A collection of posters take up space on the walls. One resembles the Vitruvian Man with brightly colored circles at sensitive places on the body that shows pressure points. I commit a few of the more intricate places to memory. Hitting those spots with magic could deal a lot of damage and easily render any opponent ultimately useless. Good information to keep in mind anyway.

Another poster that stands out is one of colorful crystals that almost seem to pop out from the wall, shimmering and moving in angles as I shift in my seat. According to the title, these are crystals especially known for their defensive and protective purposes. In the whole collection of six different crystals, the ones I keep note of are the light blue one, aquamarine, I believe, which is used to protect against potential spells designed to drain strength, and the greenish color one, alexandrite, used to draw strength from others.

Despite the horseshoe shape of the room, where the desks take up the back of the class, an aisle divides the desks into two groups. In the center, between the students and Soren's desk, is a giant black circle painted on the floor with an equally large silver rune painted in the center. It shimmers within the light of the room.

A dummy, like the one I fought in Gideon's secret training room, stands guard in the left front corner of the room. And in the other corner, between the entrance and our desks, is a rack of weapons from staffs, swords, bos and pikes.

Soon, Soren enters the room through the back door. My magic burns through me as he draws closer and only barely lessens in heat as he passes by. He makes it to the front of the classroom and takes a stand front and center. He settles his gaze on each of us, hovering just slightly longer on mine before digging into his spiel.

"I'm Professor McCallister." His voice is deep, full

of command and authority. "I'll be teaching you the fundamentals of defensive magic."

Jesse breaks out in a belly laugh, which makes me, Savannah, and Milo join in with our own. Soren glares at us for a moment, impatiently waiting for us to get this out of our systems. But it only makes things worse. Our laughing gets harder and louder. The entire classroom of thirty some-odd students is staring at us like we grew extra heads.

The joke is lost on them.

Just before Soren loses his patience, Lady Alene enters the room, gracefully floating along the floor as if she were weightless and not made of incredibly heavy stone.

She addresses the classroom, her voice floating over our group's laughter. "Forgive those students. Professor McCallister is a close friend to them, and this is a surprise for all of them."

"I should've told them sooner," Soren growls.

"Yeah. Probably," Jesse says. "We could've had more time to come up with something extra special for you."

Soren's gaze levels on Jesse's as he takes a deep, calming breath. His anger is getting the better of him though. Steam nearly leaves his nostrils on the exhale. I tap Jesse on the arm and shake my head as my snicker starts to fade. Jesse shrugs and leans back in his chair.

"It's not like he didn't see this coming." Milo rests an arm over the back of his chair, relaxed as ever. I smile at him. Handsome nerd.

"Are you done?" Soren's voice snaps our attention to him. "Good."

"In this class... you will learn the difference between defense, offense, and when to use both to your advantage in a fight." He begins to pace the floor in front of his desk. His arms are behind his back, and as he speaks, it's full of militant authority. "We will practice using elemental magic as well as hand to hand combat for physical fights. These tactics will protect and aid you should you find yourself in the midst of wild animals, hungry for your flesh." He pauses in his pacing to settle his gaze on a few of the students. "You will also learn how to recognize other attacks, such as hexes, curses, and how to slow your breathing and pulse to prevent poison from coursing through your body. The meditations you learn in this class will also help you to reach the deepest recesses of your magic so that you reach your full potential." His eyes catch mine and holds me in his gaze for a breath of time.

"Lady Alene," he gestures to her. She bows her head regally in acknowledgment, "is simply here to help see things run smoothly and provide assistance on occasion. You will direct all your questions to me."

Jesse immediately raises his hand. Soren glares at him. He shakes his head.

"But it's a good question..." Jesse says as he slowly lowers his hand. "Party pooper."

"Gather your things, we're moving to the arena." Soren turns and follows Lady Alene out the door at the front of the classroom.

Each of us in my group snickers under our breaths as Jesse stands up, tosses his satchel over his head and over-exaggerates a marching cadence, mocking Soren. "Follow me, troops."

Milo walks next to Jesse while I walk behind them with Savannah. She leans in close and talks low. "What do you think this is going to do for your relationship?"

I shrug. "I honestly don't know. I'm sure it will be fine though."

I have thought about that fact, but I was waiting to hopefully discuss it with Soren. I intended to have that conversation before now, but Soren has slipped through my fingers time and time again. Now he can't. If I have to stay after class to get a moment of his time, I will.

"You're right." She beams and bobs her eyebrows. "Kinky."

I laugh and shake my head as she nudges me with her elbow. Jesse falls back to throw an arm around my shoulder. "She has me to keep her warm now."

I smirk. "You wish."

"That's not what you were saying before."

I elbow him in his ribs. He grunts against the force. "Behave."

"How? Especially when you know I like it rough."

Milo glances over his shoulder, switching his eyes between me and Jesse. "You created a monster."

"You're just jealous you haven't sealed the deal with her yet."

"Yeah. Totally correct." His words are clearly sarcastic. He faces forward and keeps walking.

I shrug Jesse's arm off and catch up to Milo. I slip my arm around his waist and smile lovingly at his beautiful face. His lips stretch wide as he hangs an arm over my shoulder. "Ignore him. He makes it sound worse than it is."

"Precisely. He makes *everything* sound worse than it actually is." His voice comes off lighter, and I lean my head against his shoulder as we arrive at the arena.

CHAPTER SEVEN

Once we all file through the large doors and into the room, Soren and Lady Alene have us gather in a wide circle around them.

"Spread your arms out and give yourself an inch between fingertips." Soren's voice echoes a bit in the room, somehow amplifying the seriousness in his tone. He's definitely showing his true asshole self as some students roll their eyes but still do as they are told.

I chuckle under my breath. Poor souls. They haven't seen anything yet.

I think back to when Soren and I first met. He's an asshole still, but he seems to soften toward me, and only me. Sure, he gets along with Gideon, Jesse, and

Milo. But he and Jesse especially push each other's buttons.

Like now, as Jesse stands non-committedly, arms crossed over his chest and most of his weight resting on his right leg, whereas the rest of us all stand straight.

"You're really milking this for all it's worth," I mutter toward him.

He smiles mischievously. "All part of the fun."

I shake my head. "Your funeral."

He snorts. "Even he knows I'm too pretty to hurt this beautiful masterpiece." He gestures to his face.

I look at Milo, following directions, though there is a devious tilt to his lips.

"What are you doing?" I ask.

He casually shrugs. "Acclimating. At least, I'm trying to. But damn it all… it's not easy."

"That's also part of the fun, though," Savannah adds. She sets her amethyst eyes on me and winks.

"Or part of the hell," I add as Soren glares in our direction again. He studies us and I can tell the gears are turning. He's forming a plan. One I'm not sure either of us are going to like.

"I firmly believe in demonstrations. We learn best by doing. In learning what you do wrong, you can then correct those issues and learn what to do right.

Thus, learning by doing." His eyes settle on mine and I barely shake my head.

"Mr. Taylor," Soren's voice booms.

Jesse hams up a flourishing bow. "At your service, Professor."

I shake my head and bite my lips to keep from letting the bubble of laughter in my throat from escaping my mouth.

Soren simply points to a spot about three feet in front of him, lips in a firm line and his amber eyes alight with fury. Jesse salutes him and walks forward, stopping on the very spot Soren has indicated. I shake my head as he walks, Jesse is a glutton for punishment, and I have half a mind to not feel sorry for him later. The other half of me of course wants to keep this joke going. But the last thing I want is for the students outside of our group to get any ideas. Insubordination is a thing Soren just won't allow.

"Jesse, you idiot, what are you doing?" I mutter under my breath.

Milo leans in and whispers, "Showing off."

That may be true, but still. I have a feeling this demonstration he's putting together is going to show just that. And I can't protect Jesse from Soren's wrath.

My eyes widen as my heart hitches in pace as Soren takes his place just in front of Jesse.

Oh, no. Not good.

If Jesse is at all worried, he's not showing it. He stands with his hands relaxed at his side, a smirk toying at the corner of his lips. I shake my head, caught between wanting to squeeze my eyes closed and being unable to look away. It's like watching a train wreck happen.

Both of my men get into a fighting stance and prepare.

The students surrounding the circle shift their weight between their legs as their worried expressions won't allow them to look away from what is about to happen. Lady Alene moves back to just in front of the circle of students and the lights cut out. A single beam shines on the two and it looks like this is going to be a lot worse than I originally anticipated.

Soren nods to Jesse, who returns the gesture. A gong resounds through the room and the fight is on.

Soren charges. Jesse heads him off, and is flipped onto his back, arm twisted and pinned behind him. Jesse slaps the floor and Soren releases the hold, allowing my poor illusionist to stand from the ground, rubbing at his shoulder and bicep.

"What did he do wrong?" Soren asks the class.

Mutters fill the room, but Milo's voice carries above them all. "He was too cocky."

Soren's attention snaps to Milo. "Excellent, Mr. Moreau. Take his place."

My eyes widen. "Be careful."

He winks. "Don't worry. I know what I'm doing."

Milo is brilliant, but he has yet to face Soren's wrath. It's not pleasant. I worry for him as he takes his place in the center of the circle. Jesse makes it back to my side with a satisfied smirk.

"You really enjoy being tortured," I say.

He shrugs. "I knew he wouldn't damage the goods."

I shake my head. "Not the point."

My attention is once again claimed by the sparring session in the center of the room, already in full swing, but Milo is keeping up.

My jaw slacks as I stare at the way Soren and Milo are moving together and I realize he's learned a lot more than he let on during our team sparring sessions. Milo is able to keep up, and though Soren gets in more shots, he still holds his own with brilliant moves. I smile at how powerful Milo is.

Powerful, sexy, and very intelligent.

Soon, a bell chimes as the lights switch on and the two bow with respect to each other.

Once the applause dies down at Soren's beckoning, he announces, "That is how you properly spar. Excellent work."

"Thank you, Professor." Milo's lips quirk at the corners and his Adam's apple bobs a bit, but his back is already turned toward Soren, so he doesn't see it.

Once he takes his place next to me, I bump against his shoulder. "You did well. You'll have to spar with me soon."

He smiles, narrowing his deep brown, gorgeous eyes on me. "I may have to take you up on that."

The words come out deep and almost growly, like there was much more to sparring in his mind than what he just demonstrated, and heat flushes through me as pressure builds between my legs. I take in the fullness of his lips and I bite the corner of my lower lip in anticipation of what it would be like to have my legs wrapped around my alchemist as he grinds against me, sending me through waves and waves of pleasure.

Shaking the tantalizing thought from my head, I return my focus to the class.

"Next, we'll be practicing lightning strikes." Soren nods at Lady Alene.

She nods in return and floats to the center of the room, turning to set her gaze on each of us students as she speaks. "In my prime, I was known as the greatest elementalist alive. Holding power over the elements may seem easy to some, but no. It takes a great deal of practice and concentration to master all of them and conjure them at will. Sometimes in conjunction with other magics."

The wonder-filled faces make me smile as I take in all the students who listen to each word Lady Alene speaks.

"Long ago, I was considered one of the greatest warrior mages of my time. One doesn't reach that level without extensive training. Thus, another reason why I am here. You must learn to protect yourself and learn when to recognize the signs of an attack before a fight becomes imminent."

Nodding heads bob throughout the room.

"Lightning can be your greatest defense. It is the quickest and most efficient form of defense in your arsenal. However, it is also the most dangerous."

Lady Alene demonstrates a collection of lightning without so much as a blink of an eye. It booms and crashes around her, splintering out in brilliant white lines bordered by light blue darkening into purple.

Awes break out through the room once silence falls and it's almost deafening as she rakes her gaze over the room. When her eyes fall on mine, she gives a nod and a slight smile almost unnoticeable. But I caught it.

"Any questions?" she asks the class.

Silent murmurs answer, and when no one raises

their hand, she bows her head to Soren, passing off the reins.

Soren takes over the class and has us find a partner for the next part. I partner with Savannah, and Jesse partners with Milo. He then has us all line up against the far wall of the arena. He walks us through the steps of performing lightning magic. Stepping behind me, he whispers in my ear. "Pretend this is your first time." His breath sends rivers of warmth through me, coupled with the way my magic reacts to him, and I'm close to melting into a puddle at his feet.

"Hands out to the side, feel for the power of lightning. It should tingle, maybe even feel warm."

All of the students around us do the same, and if he wasn't moving my hands for me, I would be too distracted by how close he is to pay attention. I've used lightning before in the past. Not often, but I have. He's never demonstrated this skill to me before.

Sparks appear on my fingers. Pink and purple and blue.

"Careful," Soren softly warns, and my body instantly wants to fall into him. Give in to the need that he drives through me so easily.

I rein it back as much as I can. "Hard when you're this close."

He laughs quietly to himself but doesn't move away

from me. I feel his head look down the line on both sides of me and with a nod he brings my hands together in a loud clap. Lightning shoots from my hands in a jagged line toward the other end of the arena, sparking and absorbing into the far wall until it fizzles out in beautiful veins of light, leaving behind smoke and char marks.

The class follows suit, and the room erupts in thunder as the electric strikes of lightning in all colors of the rainbow slam against the wall. Soon, the wall is blackened and covered in soot.

Soren releases me and moves to the front of the class once more. "Continue practicing. Really focus on feeling the energy more than setting the room on fire." He smiles to himself and I can't help but do the same.

Just when I thought I was getting the motions down, Soren calls the class to an end.

"For the next class, come straight here. We'll recap everything you learned through demonstration. Miss Blackwood, a word?"

As everyone else heads out, I smile to myself and turn on my heels to face him. "Yes, Professor?" I don't dare add his last name to the title. I almost can't keep my face straight even now. It's too hilarious.

He points at the ground in front of him, keeping his amber eyes on mine. I walk up to him and stop at the place he's pointing at. I lift an eyebrow in question, still trying to keep a straight face, but it's so difficult. Eventually, my body wins out and I smile.

As soon as the last student leaves the arena, Soren flicks his wrist and the doors shut and lock. He pulls me forcefully into him and slams his mouth against mine. I want to play hard to get and break the kiss. I can't. It feels too good to be wrapped in his arms, pressed so tightly against his chest, letting his mouth expertly move mine.

Heat floods my body, pooling between my legs as need rises within me. Just before I lose all self-control, the kiss ends, and he rests his forehead against mine. "I've missed you."

I chuckle. "Oh really? Well, it must not have been that bad."

He groans. "Damn it, woman. Can't you let me enjoy this moment?"

"I don't know, Professor. Don't you have a class to get to?" I bite the corner of my lower lip and try to pull away. But his arms tighten around me.

"I'm not in class, Soren will suffice."

"Mmhmm. But you are now faculty, so…" I let the last of that thought fall silent.

He shrugs. "Doesn't really change much."

My eyebrows shoot up. "Oh?"

He shakes his head. "We were in a relationship before I took the position. We just can't flaunt it. No PDA, especially during instruction hours. But I'm not ashamed to love you. I won't act like it now."

Whoa. He just said love. Like it was nothing. A cold, hard fact.

I smile. "I love you too, Professor."

He groans. "Keep it to the class only, please." He pulls away and I fight against the chill that surrounds me with the absence of his warmth. "Get to class."

"Yes, Professor McCallister." I wink and rush toward the door before he can say another word to me. I look over my shoulder and catch him shaking his head with his gorgeous, heart-stopping smile.

CHAPTER EIGHT

After dinner, I make my way to the library and take a seat at my favorite table. I haven't had much time with Milo and I'm looking forward to getting some in with him in the place where we first met.

The soft squeak of wheels hits my ears just before my magic starts to rush through me with a hint of an icy chill, cooling me from the inside out. I smile as Milo pushes a cart full of books into view, stopping next to the table.

"Care to help me put these books away? We may be able to steal some alone time." Milo pushes his glasses up on his nose. His deep brown eyes take in mine, and I'm enveloped inside his gaze.

"I'd love to." Now *this* is what I call spending time

with my sexy nerd. I stand from my seat and approach him. He faces me, eyes never wavering from mine. I lift up on my toes and plant a peck on his lips. Setting my feet firmly on the floor, I gaze up at him as his eyes narrow with need, focused on my lips. I bite the corner of my bottom lip and grip the handles of the cart, pushing it forward. "Where to?"

Always leave him wanting more. It's more fun this way.

He clears his throat, and I don't have to look over my shoulder to know he runs his hand through his hair. "Two rows down and to the right." His voice is deeper, more gravelly, and I chuckle to myself.

I follow his instructions, turning the cart between two tall bookshelves. "So, when did you start working in the library?"

"I actually volunteer, and about a month after school ended. One week after the convention. My parents were vacationing in Europe and I didn't want to stay home. So, I came here. After my parents returned home, I chose to spend the last week of break with them."

"Still proud of their son?" I ask as I pick up the book and glance at the spine for the author's last name.

"Always." He comes up behind me as I scan the

shelves for the book's home. My body feels drawn to him and I automatically lean into him. His arms wrap around my waist and I breathe in his intoxicating scent. He presses his lips on the sensitive spot on my neck, and I instinctively grab the back of his head as his warm breath rushes along my skin.

"What do they think of your job?" I'm almost breathless as need pools between my legs. I barely pay attention to where I place the book. I twist to face him, sliding my arms around his back.

He shrugs. "They wanted me to go with them. I told them I had things here I needed to take care of."

I narrow my eyes at him. "Like what?"

"You. Well, for you, anyway." He kisses the top of my nose and I giggle under my breath. That was such a sweet move. It makes me giddy. My heart flutters in my chest. I adore this man and all his little quirks.

Milo grins and releases me as he also grabs a book. Still beaming, I reach for another book on the cart.

"Like what?"

"Stuff," he says, and I can tell he's trying to play coy. I love it.

But it doesn't stop me from digging deeper.

"Stuff doesn't sound important enough to miss out on a family vacation to Europe, Milo." I still smile when I say his name. It's so easy, flows off the tongue, and I love the way it feels.

"Yes, but first, we have to help this extensive cart of books find their shelf mates."

I laugh at the notion as I find the empty spot where my book belongs, sliding it into place. However, there is a point I want to make. The idea that he is skipping out on time with his family for some project that has something to do with me is a bit unsettling and feels unfair. "Please don't blow off spending time with your family for me. I appreciate the effort and I adore you for it, but you shouldn't miss out on an amazing vacation with them."

He faces me, beaming like a kid on Christmas. "Relax. I already told them everything about you. They love you already. Besides, this was important stuff. You needed to spend time reconnecting with your dad and training. I took care of the research stuff. Isn't that what being a part of a team is?"

He's not wrong. But it still doesn't erase the small pang of guilt that is in my heart.

"Since you put it that way… but please don't miss out on future vacations."

He shrugs and turns his back to me as he replaces another book. He turns back to the cart and moves it into the aisle. "Relax, Wren. I didn't miss much. It was supposed to be their second honeymoon. I really didn't want to be a part of all *that*."

Oh.

My eyes widen.

Oh!

My cheeks start to burn, spilling down into my neck. "Yeah, that was probably a good call. But you do understand where I'm coming from, right?"

"Wren, seriously." He leaves the cart to join me. "Relax, damn it." He pulls me into him, pressing his mouth against mine and I'm lost in all that he is. I can't help it. It's almost spiritual, the things he does to me.

My soul seems to stir within me, and I feel so free with him. Most of all, I *feel*.

Milo opens me up to new ideas. A fresh look at things. He challenges me to broaden my knowledge and expand on old ideas. He fills me with a desire to learn and grow and be open to new possibilities.

Even love.

Which is a big deal.

Don't get me wrong, I adore all of my men. But Milo has a way with me. He touches me in ways no one else can. I'm vulnerable, but I'm free to be me. And the more time I spend with him, the more of my past falls away into just that. My past. I'm slowly learning to let go of all the horrible things I went through, no longer letting it define me but rather shape me into a woman that's stronger than the things that has happened to me.

With him, I can overcome anything.

We reluctantly break away from the kiss and share in small talk as we continue to put the books away.

"I bet you're loving this work," I say as we clear off the top of the cart and start working on the bottom shelf.

"I do. It helps me with that research I was telling you about." He pushes the cart into a closet and closes the door. Facing me, he holds out his arm and I slide mine into the crook of his elbow. "Shall we sit at our table for a bit?"

"I thought you would never ask." I'm beaming, and it's because this feels right. Walking with him arm in arm. It's natural and comes so easily. Being with him is like being with a life-long friend. We could unveil each other's secrets and not bat an eye at them or feel ashamed. I probably won't right this moment, but it's a truth that fills my soul with joy.

In seconds, we're in our chairs, sitting where we normally do. Him on one side and me on the other. He reaches below the table and pulls out his notebook from his satchel I hadn't noticed was sitting there all this time.

He flips a few pages and brushes his finger along the text until he finds what he's looking for, which he indicates with a tap. "Ah hah! So, I did a little digging for you regarding the prophecy of the meteorite and what the Order could possibly want with it."

"Okay, what did that big brain of yours conclude?"

He shrugs. "There's a lot of different information regarding stones of power. Not much in relation to the prophecy, but there were things I found that relates closely to what you are experiencing."

"We, technically," I add. It was such a relief when I told the men about my powers reacting to their presence, because I learned that I affected them as well.

He lifts his gaze to meet mine. "True." He continues on his notes. "I discovered that there is an ancient tome that describes a fable about a rock of power that became the origin of magic."

I lean in, aching to know more. A part of me feels pulled into what Milo is telling me, and it resonates within me. A piece of truth and history that fills my heart with knowing. My intuition is flaring at this.

This is it.

This has to be.

"It was believed to have been sent by the gods of old, to deliver mankind into a new era of prosperity." Milo continues his story, reading from the notes, while I become sucked into the imagery his words create. "You see, all of us resonate at certain frequencies. Those who resonated higher absorbed the power."

"How long ago was this?" I hear myself asking.

"Think back to the time of the dinosaurs. The meteor that hit Earth and wiped them out?"

I nod.

"That one."

"Wow…" It comes out breathless, barely above a whisper.

"This was the birth of all magic. It's said that people flocked to the rock. There were some who touched it and absorbed some of the power within it, giving birth to a new age and era of magic. Not everyone who touched it was given powers, however. Those gifted with the power of foresight and prophesy developed the stories within this book. Within the pages of this ancient tome, a story foretold that in a moment of desperate need, when the balance between light and darkness is shaken, another rock of power would appear, sent by the gods."

He lets that nugget of information settle between us as I sit back and process the profound possibility of what he's leading into.

Honestly, as much as I don't want to admit it, it all

makes sense. But a sense of dread takes over and I find myself shaking my head. "I can't save the world, Milo."

He shakes his head. "You may not have to. You only have one piece, right?"

"Yeah, and the Order probably has the rest of it."

He waves his hand over the table as though he's dismissing that fact. "No, I'm referring to the fact you fused with a piece of it, right?"

I nod, waiting to see where he's going with this.

"You resonated at the right frequency for it. There's nothing to say that there's not others out there who resonate at the same energy."

I pause to mull that over, and I have to say, my body floods with relief. It's a task in and of itself just to get through my four years of schooling, escaping the Order's sight, and keeping myself out of fights to the death. Save the world? Me?

Nope.

I'm just a girl who fused with a meteorite when I was five, lost my mother and father, and practically grew up with trolls. The fact I'm here right now is a miracle.

"So, there may be others?" I ask.

Milo slowly nods. "Theoretically, since I, Jesse, Soren, and Gideon also have similar feelings with our magic in your presence, it's possible we are all destined for the meteorite."

"But what if you're wrong?" My voice is distant, almost a whisper, like I'm afraid to acknowledge the pulsing magic within me that knows there's so much more behind me having the meteorite than what is being said right now. This goes deeper, and part of me is wary about digging further into this.

I don't want to save the world. I just want to be as normal as I can be, have a family, my team, and get through these next few years without much incident.

Is that too much to ask for?

Possibly.

"I'd be surprised." He sits back, proud of himself. He becomes serious again after a few moments of silence. He reaches for my hand, covering my skin with his warmth. His voice is soft as he says, "Regardless of the rock being all yours or not, you would never have to face the world alone. Not anymore."

I smile at his sentiment and cover his hand with mine. "I appreciate that Milo. I just don't know if this explains everything. Something inside me stirs at the story. We're getting closer, but there's more to this.

He nods. "Of course. You have magic. That's a miracle in itself. The gods blessed you with that.

There's a plan for you—for all of us—and it will take more time and a little more digging to figure it all out."

"If that ever happens," I say.

He shrugs. "The gods are mysterious. However, for the chosen few, things tend to have a way of revealing themselves." His lips stretch into a gentle smile as his thumb rubs along the skin of my hand. "I promise Wren, we'll all do whatever it takes to keep you safe. We're your team. We all love you."

CHAPTER NINE

I know in my heart, I'm falling for Milo Moreau. More and more each day. And with the information I had just learned, I'm beside myself. It makes sense. And that confession of love from him, by promising to always be with me, renders me speechless.

Finally, I smile. "Oh, Milo. What would I ever do without you?"

His bashfulness shows through a little as he looks away and shoves his glasses up his nose. My shoulders shake with laughter. That move of his means so much to me. I love it.

"I'm here for you," he adds. "I mean it."

"I am extremely grateful for you." I smile. "I mean it. Truly."

He hums to himself as he gently grins. "I feel the same way with you. I mean, I truly *feel*. It was noticeable the first time we met. I tried to figure out what that meant, and when you revealed that your magic reacts to us in Gideon's office that one time, I knew that was it." He shakes his head. "But it's so much more than that."

His eyes become distant as if he's recalling a memory or figuring out something complex in his brain. "It's like a cool breeze on a hot summer day, when I'm with you. You're my shade, my comfort. That's what fills me."

I smile. "That's the same for me. It almost rushes like currents through me."

"Exactly." He beams.

The door to the library echoes as it shuts. Before long, Agatha, of all freaking people, appears from behind the shelf and smiles as she sets her eyes on Milo.

"Milo! I thought I would find you here!" She sets her gaze on me. "Oh. Who's this?"

Her tone when she mentions "this," coupled with the dark shadow that crosses her eyes makes me clench my hands into fists and bite against the retort resting on my tongue. Instead, I say, "His girlfriend." I add a little look of my own.

Challenge *that*.

She deflates a little but quickly recovers. "Aww, that's sweet."

I quirk an eyebrow and set my gaze on Milo, silently pleading for him to get her out of the way and quick.

"What do you need, Agatha?" he asks, and it almost sounds like he's getting annoyed with her.

That thought makes me smile.

If she hears anything offensive in his tone, she doesn't show it. Instead, she soaks up each word he speaks to her like manna from the gods. "Oh, nothing! Just bored. Thought we could hang out." She casts a quick glance toward me as she mentions them hanging out.

Like, what? I'm not leaving. He's mine. Go get your own boyfriend, thank you very much.

"We're spending time together," I say, and the girl has the audacity to act like I didn't speak.

Finally, Milo interjects. "She's right, Agatha. I'm spending time with my girlfriend. If you need anything, see the House Leader for it."

Agatha frowns at me. I straighten my back and square my shoulders. If she wants to push her luck, I have no qualms with taking care of business right now. The only issue I have is the books that would get destroyed.

She's jealous. That much is certain. She's oozing it into the air. Milo, doesn't seem to notice. But I do.

And thus, why there's a problem.

"I don't need anything, silly," she says, flipping her curly blond hair over her shoulder. "I only wanted to hang out. You've been so sweet and helpful to me, and I just thought I'd repay the favor."

"Oh, that's not necessary," he says, holding up his hands. "I was just doing what I was asked to do."

I look at Milo. "What is she talking about?"

He sighs. "The House Leader assigned me to help show her around the house and to her first classes. He seemed to think we hit it off and insists that I help her when she needs anything."

"Even though that's *his* problem?" I ask.

Milo shrugs.

Poor guy looks very uncomfortable right now. I take a deep breath to release the building tension in my muscles, so he doesn't get the impression I'm blaming him for all of this.

"Look…" Agatha says, sounding wounded.

Sorry, not sorry.

"I don't want to get into the middle of you two spending time together. Like I said, I just wanted to hang out and show my gratitude for his help." Her blue eyes start to take on a glossy sheen as she settles them on me. "You have a really great boyfriend."

I smile. "Thank you. I am lucky to have him."

She nods and starts to walk away, pauses, twists to wave at us, and finally, leaves us alone.

Milo sighs heavily.

"That went well, huh?"

"Hmm? Oh, no. It's just, she's like a lost puppy dog. I have to be nice to her because it's the decent thing to do, but I'm rapidly losing my patience with her. How do you tell her to leave you alone when she looks like she's going to get weepy any time you turn her down?"

"Oh, believe me, I have no issues hurting her feelings." I tap my fingers on the table and huff a breath of hot air. Then the meaning behind what he said dawns on me. "You're really sweet though."

"Really?" His eyes are full of questions as they seem to search mine for an answer.

I nod. "You are kind and gentle and don't like to hurt people's feelings. That's just some of the things I adore about you."

He beams. "Just doing the right thing."

I nod. "I'll talk to Gideon about this House Leader of yours. Sounds like someone new needs to step up and take charge if the responsibilities are being delegated to students who have better things to do than perform House Leader duties."

"Nah, it's fine. I can handle it. You have enough on your plate."

I narrow my gaze on him, searching for any sign or clue that he's not letting me know the full reason behind getting involved. "You sure?"

"Yeah. I'll handle it."

I take his word for it. "Okay. If you want backup, let me know."

He chuckles. "I'll do that."

We settle back into our comfort zone, chatting about small stuff and laughing. A short while later, Milo stands from his seat and stretches. "Wanna head back to my room? I have something I want to show you."

"Look at who Jesse's rubbing off on now?" I wink.

He chuckles and runs his hand through his hair. "That's not what I meant." He stammers through his words. "I really do have something to show you."

"Okay, then show me." I stand and join him, trying not to laugh at how ridiculously adorable he's being.

CHAPTER TEN

Milo opens his door, and I'm dumbfounded.

Every inch of his walls are covered in posters of alchemy, the universe, famous alchemists, shelves hanging on the walls stacked with books, vials, and notebooks. His desk is a cluttered mess, but it's almost organized in an understandable way. His bed is disheveled with the comforter hanging half off the corner.

As I make my way through, I take it all in. I realize this is the first time I've been to Milo's room. I frown at that thought and wonder why I haven't been here before. Maybe he felt self-conscious about his stuff?

"Excuse my chaos," he says almost bashfully.

No. That couldn't be the real reason... could it?

"I love it," I say and smile at him for extra reassurance. "This is what the mind of Milo Moreau looks like?"

He shoves his hands into his pockets. "Yeah, sort of."

I nod as I continue to take in the dark greyish blue walls, the silver curtains that cover the window on the far wall overlooking the ocean crashing below. A fireplace sits in the corner, the mantel holds a few curious items and a framed picture of him and his parents.

A red, velvet satchel guards one side of the frame. It's probably filled with some sort of alchemical powder, judging by the size of it. It looks big enough to fill my palm. On the other side of the frame is a miniature brass astral globe.

Walking toward the picture for a better look, it's clear Milo favors his mother in looks but has his father's eyes. I ignore the pang of remorse at not having a family photo of my own. "You look like your mom."

"I know. Everyone tells me that." His voice follows me as I move through his room.

"It's true."

"Yeah. I guess so."

On the edge of the mantel is a pair of glasses. I feel the power oozing off them. I'm curious about them and pick them up from their resting place and slide them on just for fun. I end at his desk and turn to face him. "What did you want to show me?" I bob my eyebrows with a devious smile.

He chuckles and shakes his head. He approaches me, stopping when his toes meet mine. Never leaving my gaze, he reaches behind me and picks up something from his desk. He holds it between us. "This."

This was a bound collection of papers that we grabbed from the facility. The blueprints. "You figured out what these are?"

"Mostly. They're not complete."

I purse my eyebrows. "They're not? I wonder where the rest of them are."

He shrugs as I start to flip through the pages. "It took me most of the summer to get them put together in the most logical order I could."

"Impressive, considering you didn't have all of them."

"Wren... I think these are a design for some sort of machine."

I can't make heads or tails of the intricate designs within the pages, so I have to take his word for it. "What do you mean? It looks like a bunch of random drawings."

He points to a spot on the page. "This gear here, is

just one piece of the equipment." He flips to a later page. "See here?"

I nod.

"That's the part I just pointed out."

On the lower corner of the right-hand page, a small design glimmers in the light, almost invisible, and had it not been for a slight shimmer, it would have escaped my notice. "This image, have you seen it before?"

It somewhat resembles a transmutation circle, but lacking in some of the necessary components. A hexagon formed of six triangles fills a large circle. A smaller circle sits in the center, and at each point of the hexagon are even smaller circles. It's such a strange and confusing symbol. But it's familiar.

He takes the bound pages and walks to the bedside lamp and angles it into the light, shifting and moving it to get a better glimpse. After a few brief seconds, he shakes his head. "I don't see anything."

I hand him the glasses and he tries again. "I see it. Excellent find, Wren."

I smile a bit bashfully at his compliment. "I've seen it before. I feel it, deep in my gut. I just wish I can remember where I saw it." I shake my head and cross my arms over my chest as I lean against his desk.

"Some of my life and memories from before the trolls have been forgotten."

His gaze is filled with concern. "Well it's not uncommon when you live through a traumatic experience for your mind to experience memory distortion. Maybe that's what you're dealing with."

I swear if Milo suggests I go see a therapist or something like that, I'll give him a piece of my mind. I tilt my head slightly and focus on the shimmering image, trying to reach into my mind, asking myself why this looks so familiar. An icy chill runs down my arms when a tiny voice in my head tells me that it has something to do with Aunt Patricia.

Memory distortion, indeed.

The image bears no resemblance to the Blackwood family monogram. It doesn't bear any of our letters. So why does Aunt Patricia's name keep forcing its way into my head?

"This is going to sound weird, but I think this has to do with my family… my aunt, to be exact."

His eyes widen in response. "Are you certain? Some memories, can be a little distorted."

"My gut is telling me this comes back to my Aunt Patricia."

"Good catch by the way." Milo continues to study the image. "I hadn't noticed the design before."

"I barely caught it myself. But, even if I'm mistaken, this is worth checking out."

He brings the pages back to me. "What do you want to do?"

"Team meeting."

"I agree. I'll get Jesse and meet you there."

I nod and follow him out the door, the pages clutched in my hands. Before we split up, he kisses me one last time. It's deep, passionate, and makes me a little light-headed. He leaves me with a smile, and I watch him until he disappears before I head toward the House of Winterwolf.

CHAPTER ELEVEN

Milo and I just finished explaining the blueprints. Gideon sits at his desk, Soren stands next to it, and Jesse sits in a chair in front with his leg draped over the chair's arm, looking for all the world like what we just shared wasn't life altering in any sense of the phrase.

"There's more to it, isn't there?" Soren asks through a yawn.

"Yes." I look to Milo. "Milo found an old fable that I feel answers the reason for my power and what the Order may want with it."

Gideon's eyebrows raise on his forehead as he adjusts himself in his seat. It's late, and past time for lights out. But this is pretty important. "Well, Milo?" he asks.

Milo dips into the spiel and it feels just as true and right as the first time. My magic stirs within me and pulsates, all on its own, in a different way than when my magic reacts while in the midst of all my men.

Once Milo finishes the recap, silence settles in the air in a not-so-pleasant way.

Finally, Gideon nods.

"I knew there was something otherworldly about you," Jesse says. "Now we have proof."

"It's not proof." Soren moves to lean against the wall behind Gideon's desk. "It's only a story that vaguely connects to Wren's possible powers. No one knows for sure."

I shake my head. "No. It's true. I feel it. My magic moves with the story. It's never done that before. That alone should not only prove that a: my magic is sentient, and b: that there is more truth than your skeptical mind is going to allow."

Soren turns his exhausted amber eyes on me. His lips are pressed into a thin line, and I get the very distinct notion that he is in no mood to be challenged right now. I shrug, nonchalantly. I can't help it if he's in a mood and not willing to listen to reason.

Gideon flips through the pages of the blueprints, brow furrowed in concentration. "Where's the emblem?"

Milo beats me to it, pointing out the exact location. Gideon puts on the glasses and takes a moment to angle the page, just like Milo did back in his room. "I've never seen this image before, but you're sure you have?"

"I know I have. I'm still trying to work my way through my memories, but I believe the best clue is my aunt's estate."

"No." Soren stands from the wall, shaking his head.

"Would you hear her out, at least?" Milo says.

Soren's eyes widen at Milo's interjection. I nudge Milo and smile proudly at him. Soren's gaze switches between me and Milo. I stare him down, daring him to say something to Milo for standing up for me.

Soren pinches the bridge of his nose and starts to pace. "Unbelievable," he mutters.

"Look, if I can find out where I saw the symbol and confirm that it's connected to my aunt, then we'll know for sure she's part of the Order. It will no longer be just suspicion."

"What if you get caught?" Soren asks, anger flashing through his words.

"What if I don't?" I step forward, standing my ground. "All I need is one shot."

"One and done?" Jesse adds with a snicker.

"Is there not a moment where things aren't a joke for you?" Soren snaps.

"Hey!" I snap, pointing a finger at him. "If you have an issue with me that's one thing, but don't you dare take it out on the rest of the men. What the hell is wrong with you?"

He gapes at me a moment before snapping his mouth shut and returning to his pacing.

Gideon sighs as he leans back in his seat. "We're all tired. It's late. You want to go to your aunt's and search for the emblem?"

"And the missing pages," I say.

He nods. "I have to agree with Soren's reservation about you going. I can't get a good reading on her, and Savannah has shared with me her own concerns. Considering where the blueprints were found, it doesn't look good for your father either."

"I know. That's another reason why I *need* to go."

Jesse sits up in his seat and he runs his fingers through his hair. "As much as I hate to admit this, knowing how much I love a good sneaking around, I have to agree with Soren and Gideon."

I narrow my eyes on him. "Thanks, traitor."

I mean it lightly, but it doesn't come out that way. He looks at me with almost a questioning glance. I wink, just so he knows I'm not mad at him.

"If everyone agrees Aunt Patricia is hiding something, if she's involved with the Order, there has to be something that points in that direction at her house. It's too convenient for it all to fall on my father's shoulders. Yes, it doesn't look favorable," I hold up my hands to stop the interruptions I see filling my men's faces, "but my father was the one who was tortured for years. The blueprints were never meant to be found by us."

"Yet, that's what happened," Milo adds, who has been relatively quiet for most of this conversation.

"Exactly. Why?" I let that question hang in the air for a few moments. "If anything, it's just another piece of the puzzle to figure out and put together. Regardless, my intuition tells me it's my aunt. I don't like the idea of all of this being a member of my family, but I would believe my aunt has hidden agendas with the Order rather than my father."

"This doesn't look good for your father regardless how we spin this," Soren says. "These blueprints can just as easily indicate he's involved, especially since they were found at the facility where we know he was previously held."

"I know." I shake my head. "None of it makes sense. But I stand by what I said."

"What's your plan?" Gideon asks.

"I reach out and see if we can all go to her house one weekend. We go, and while two of you distract my aunt, me and the other two will go on the scavenger hunt. If we don't find anything, we'll all visit my father next."

"She's got a point." Jesse stands and stretches out his body. "She can at least ask her aunt for permission to stay a weekend with her, and we can all go from there."

Gideon nods. I look to Soren who is staring at the floor for a few long moments. Before long, he meets my gaze and shrugs. Nodding, I turn to Milo. He nods once, but the grim expression on his face tells me he's not completely sold.

Right now, we don't have any options.

I take a piece of paper and pen from Gideon's drawer and jot down a quick letter to my aunt. Practicing all the steps I learned with my father, I draw the symbols and focus my intention on my aunt's estate. I trust she will find it.

As soon as the last bits of burning ashes disappears, I slap my hands against my legs. "Good night."

Mumbles of the same sentiment follow me as I make my way out the door and to my room. My mind is a mix of emotions and jumbled thoughts. The blueprints are a double-edged sword, and it will either help me vindicate my father or condemn him. I know deep down my father would never betray me, but I do have to consider Soren's point. Unfortunately, it's a possibility until I can prove otherwise.

No matter how I spin the thoughts, I still can't swallow that pill. I know deep in my bones my father is innocent. I just need proof.

I crash onto my bed, knowing the truth will soon be revealed. I have to have faith in that.

CHAPTER TWELVE

Days later, I'm sitting in Gideon's office with Jesse, Soren, and Milo as we discuss my aunt's response to me staying with her for the weekend. I found the letter waiting for me on my desk after my last class. Per her words, my men aren't allowed to come, but Savannah is.

That condition of hers strikes a warning. A small red flag that waves in the back of my mind that my intuition says it is much more than for the sake of propriety that Aunt Patricia won't allow my men to go with me. I tell the men as much.

"There's more behind her not wanting any of you with me. I feel it deep in my gut." I shake my head. With my men at my side, I'm unstoppable. We make an amazing team. For me to walk into my aunt's lair without them would put me at a disadvantage, and I'm sure Aunt Patricia knows this. That woman is more cunning than I thought. "She shouldn't even know we're all more than friends."

They all seem to think about that for a moment. Gideon's and Soren's eyes switch out of focus as they seem to look deeper into their thoughts, maybe figure out a possible reason for it all.

"At the very least, allowing the headmaster to come to her home would've been seen as an honor, I think," Milo says as he reads over the words, looking for any enchantments that may have been left on it. So far, it's clear. "Even if we weren't more than friends at this point. It appears like she understands more than she sees. And if we are to do a little recon in her estate, we have to follow her rules." He holds up the letter. "I'll keep this with me for a bit if that's okay. I just want to make sure I'm not missing anything."

I nod. "No problem. I don't need to keep it."

"A visit with me accompanying a student would also seem out of the ordinary," Gideon adds, bringing the conversation back on track.

I pause to mull that over. I hadn't thought about that. Often, I forget that he's the headmaster. I always seem to think of him as just one of my men. My team. Part of my family.

"Not only that, but I've been there before on official business," Gideon continues. "I have to warn you, there are magical alarms for certain rooms. There were areas that she was particularly hesitant to let me near. Those off-limits areas were enchanted as well. Though I couldn't quite get a good idea of what those enchantments were, I sometimes felt like I was being watched." His eyes darken as he recalls the visit. "These are things I don't believe she's taken down. You must be careful when you move throughout the estate as I'm certain there will be other enchantments and wards that will guard against unwanted events."

"Savannah has quite the unassuming persona," I say, keeping in mind everything Gideon had just shared. "She's sweet, bubbly, always happy... that's what she shows everyone until she has to prove otherwise, which doesn't seem to happen often, and which could be good for us. I want to say that my aunt sees Savannah as unassuming and weaker than me or her."

"Thus, an easy target," Soren adds.

"And an obstacle that is easily overcome if there are nefarious plans in the works," Jesse adds from his normal seat.

I cross my arms over my chest and pace in front of my favorite window in Gideon's office. The horizon is colored with the darkening shades of blue as the sun continues setting on the other side of the island. If I weren't so consumed with trying to figure out a plan for this weekend, I would allow myself to become lost in the wondrous beauty this island constantly brings. But this is important, and my focus can't be divided.

"Sure, we're taking a risk. One I'm not taking lightly. Perhaps, my aunt will see Savannah's presence as unremarkable and have a lower guard with lesser defenses." I tap my finger on my chin as I mull over everything my headmaster revealed. "Either way, I appreciate knowing what she has up around her house. We at least have something to look out for. With luck, we can avoid setting off any alarms and having my aunt being none-the-wiser when it comes to searching for the blueprints."

"It sounds like she has quite the arsenal for someone who wants to come off as having nothing to hide…" Jesse's words are colored with intrigue. "Top that off with not wanting even the headmaster to join for the weekend, it all suggests that she has something to hide indeed."

"Not necessarily," Gideon adds. "It could simply be improper to her for men to join on a weekend retreat with a young, unmarried woman. Especially with how close we all are. Patricia has a strong sense of ethics and old-fashioned morals. That being said, I'm with

Wren. There's a deeper, more hidden reason." His eyes slip out of focus again.

"Regardless of the reasons she won't let you join me, I still need to find those missing pages and figure out the damn symbol. Which means tweaking our plan so that I still get the chance to find the missing parts of the blueprints and learn what type of machine they're attempting to build."

"No one is arguing that," Gideon adds. "But we need to have a solid plan so that there is an escape if Patricia makes a move against you. We also need to be especially cautious if we are sending Savannah into this as well. We have to consider her safety."

I nod. "We could use a protection charm, like we did for me."

"True," Milo says. "But it takes a considerable amount of time to prepare and perform that particular enchantment. We don't have the time to prepare or the ingredients. But there are other ways we can ensure her safety." His eyes meet mine and I'm filled with warmth at the sheer depth and adoration that fills them.

I smile and give a short nod in thanks.

"Say they have protection charms and they get there fine," Soren says. "Then what?"

I have to appreciate the angle he's coming from.

As much as he can be an asshole, at the end of the day, he doesn't want to take unnecessary risks any more than I do. Biting the corner of my lower lip, I quickly formulate a plan in my mind. "Then Savannah and I will pretend we're just there to relax and spend the weekend with her. And to show Savannah where my family is from. When the time is right, I'll do some recon, using the information Gideon shared to keep from tripping any alarms and making my agenda clear, searching for the symbol and any information on that machine, be it blueprints, plans, or anything that may describe what it's used for."

"Leave it to my devious girl to do some mischief." Jesse smiles proudly.

Warmth fills my cheeks as I return the expression. He flatters me. Honestly, I'm just trying to make a solid plan.

"What I mean is, how will we know you made it there?" Soren asks. "You should check in once you arrive and just let us know you arrived safely."

"Are you sure Savannah is even willing and able to go? She may have plans." Milo's voice floats to me from the opposite side of the room. "We could be setting this plan up for nothing if she has other plans or doesn't feel comfortable with going. She's done a lot for us without asking, but this may be too much for her."

"Excellent points." Gideon shifts in his seat. "Let's get her here and find out." He takes a blank sheet of paper and draws a symbol over the top of it in black ink. He rests his hands on it, and the glow of golden magic bleeds from under his palm.

I'm caught in the glittering light, amazed at how Gideon keeps revealing bits of his power and being held mesmerized at the fact that he's mine. I'm not surprised but impressed, nonetheless. Everything seems to come so easily to my headmaster. With each passing day, it becomes clearer how he earned his position so quickly. A megaphone appears in the air, hovering like it was just waiting for a call from its master. He removes his hand from the page, leaving nothing but a blank surface, and my mouth parts in awe. Once the paper is replaced to its original home, he settles his hands over the surface of his desk. Meanwhile, the megaphone makes its way through the door that opens on its approach. Once the door is shut, Gideon reclaims our attention.

"Shouldn't be too long now."

His eyes catch mine and a glimmer of pride shows through them as he flashes a wink. The movement was so quick that I almost didn't catch it.

"Meanwhile, we have yet to consider an exit in case things go wrong." Gideon's eyes still rest on mine, and I realize he wants me to come up with a plan.

"Portal," I say with a shrug.

"You haven't learned that yet," Soren says with a pensive expression.

"Then teach me." I stare him down, almost daring him to say no. "I can do this."

"Not only that," Gideon says, "but we have to consider keeping Patricia off our scent. If something happens, and Wren suddenly disappears from the estate, that's going to raise eyebrows."

"A contingency plan?" I ask.

He nods.

A knock on the office door interrupts our conversation. Savannah enters and her eyes are a brighter shade of purple as she bounces into the room. "You called for me, Headmaster Storm?"

Gideon chuckles. "We're past formalities by now, I think. But yes, we did. Do you have plans for the weekend?"

She shakes her head. "What can I do for you?"

"Come with me for a weekend of espionage?" I ask.

Her glittering gaze settles on me as she beams widely. "Do tell me more." She settles into the seat next to Jesse and listens as we tell her the plan. Her eyebrows knit together as her lips form a straight line as we catch her up on everything.

"Count me in," she says, eyes wide and expression full of excitement.

I knew I could count on her.

"Now for the contingency plan," Soren states. "We were just about to discuss that when you came in."

Savannah nods. "We could write a letter with a code word. That would let you know there's trouble. You," she points to Soren, "could come and get us from there. We could use some sort of excuse that would give us a logical reason for coming back and keep Aunt Patricia from suspecting anything."

"Pop quiz."

Everyone turns their attention to Milo as he looks between us. He shrugs and pushes his glasses up on his nose in that way that makes me smile at him every single time.

Gideon nods. "We do have a history of providing specific tests throughout the year that are random. It's an old practice that's not used very often, but that could work."

"Why can't we just portal out?" I ask. "You could send us a letter, and have it look formal and using the pop quiz as an excuse, and we could let Aunt Patricia know I have to come back. I'll even add something to the effect of, I'll come back next weekend to make up for the lost time."

"Devious," Jesse says. "I like it." He smiles proudly.

I shake my head. "Will that work?"

Gideon pauses a moment to think it over. "It's possible. We could have both available. Let's work on the code word."

"What if instead of a code word," Milo says, "we start with something simple and unassuming like the first letter of each word being a letter of the coded word? This way, when we get the letter, we can underline the first letter of each sentence to see the true message?" His eyebrows knit together as if in deep concentration. "That could tell us if they need us to come get them."

"Or a misspelled word?" Savannah adds with a shrug. "That would work too. Something simple, but could pass as something easily overlooked as a careless mistake?"

"Or even punctuation," I add.

"An anagram?" Jesse asks.

Gideon nods. "Those could work, but we have to remember to keep it simple. If it's *too* perfectly imperfect, Patricia may catch on."

Before long, we have a plan set. To check in, the first letter of each word will be underlined upon receipt. If Savannah and I find something, there'll be a punctuation error on the first and last lines. And if there's an emergency, a misspelled word midway in the letter.

"Now that we have that settled, who wants to teach me how to portal?" I look between Soren and Gideon.

Savannah sits forward. "We can focus on that later. I got you."

I shake my head, though I can't help but smile in gratitude at the way she is always available for me to rely on when I need her. "I appreciate that Savannah, but I need to know how to do this too. Especially if my aunt does something to make it impossible for you, at least I'd be able to step in and help. Or, if we get split up for some reason."

She pauses to mull that over for a moment and eventually nods with a smile. "I love how smart you are."

I chuckle. "I aim to please." I settle my gaze back on my headmaster before eyeing the professor of defensive magic.

They also exchange a look. Soren shrugs. It's like they're having a silent conversation and both of them know exactly what the other is thinking. Gideon casually cocks his head to the side as if he responds to something Soren somehow conveyed to him. It's fascinating to watch.

I just want to be in the loop too.

Gideon stands from his desk. "I have an idea that could involve all of us."

"Okay," I say, dragging out the word. I hope that he will continue to fill in the blanks, but instead of explaining, he continues to walk toward the hidden stairway behind the floor-to-ceiling portrait that leads to the roof of the massive castle.

Without a word, each of us follow him up. Savannah and I exchange a questioning glance as we file through the door. I shrug as I climb up the winding stairs.

CHAPTER THIRTEEN

Up here, it's cold. The chilly autumn air blows stronger at the top of the tower and I wish I had brought a coat with me. The sun has settled on the other side of the world, and the silver light of the crescent moon barely lights the world around us, leaving a breathless view of the stars and Milky Way. But this is good. It adds more of a challenge to this lesson I'm about to embark on.

The six of us stand on the flat roof above Gideon's office, huddling close together as Gideon discusses his game plan.

"I'll take Milo, Jesse, and Savannah to different points on the island. They'll send up a signal to show where they are when it's time. You," he points to me, "will then follow our instruction with the goal of landing where they are at and bringing them back here." He points to the spot where we're all standing.

"And Soren?" I ask, my teeth nearly chattering as I shiver in the cold breeze.

"I'll follow you and provide pointers, giving you aid when you need it." He answers in such a way, it's like he has a "teach mode." His no-nonsense tone is similar to the one he initially had with me when we first began our trainings and again in class.

I nod. "You're not going to follow me to Aunt Patricia's are you?"

He levels his serious gaze on me with his lips pressed in a thin line. "No."

I shrug. "Then why follow?"

"Only for the first few times," Gideon adds. "We'll practice until you have this down pat."

I nod. "Okay."

Gideon's eyes close and he takes a few deep breaths before starting to form a portal. As he clears his mind, magic glows from his left hand, growing from the ring on his pinky finger. He holds it out over the area in front of us and forms a circle. As he does, a pillar of light shoots into the sky, reaching a few feet above us. Once again, the light is a sky-blue color with specs of glittering white sparkles throughout the light, floating upward, disappearing as the light of the portal fades into the night mere feet above our heads.

Gideon beckons Savannah forward. As soon as she is in the portal, she's gone. A bright light flashes behind me, and I spin in place to see the last of the magic rolling away and disappearing into the shadows. Next is Jesse, who appears on the west side of the island, and finally, Milo who ends up on the north side.

Gideon looks to me just before the portal disappears with a snap of his fingers. Soren steps forward, taking up my full attention, and with his closeness, I appreciate the warmth he brings to my magic. The chills from the wind have lessened to the point where I'm at least not shivering. My teeth hurt a little from chattering, but with Soren's warmth, I don't have to do that anymore.

I'm simply *warm*.

Like on a summer's night, instead of one in the midst of fall.

"Intent and focus." Soren holds his hands out in front of him. "Those are the two things you really need to have down before you use a portal. Next is a clear mental picture of where you want to be."

"Thus, practicing on Blackbriar before leaving."

He nods once. "Now, hold out your hands like so."

His hands are in front of him, palms facing the ground.

I do.

"Close your eyes."

I arch an eyebrow at him.

He sighs. "Just do it."

I concede.

"Feel the breath enter and leave your lungs. Feel the muscles in your neck and shoulders relax… the wind beneath your hands."

I take a breath in. My lungs expand and though the air itself is frigid, my lungs instantly warm it with the heat of my body and magic working in tune to keep the discomfort of the cold away. As I exhale, the air is warm, and I imagine a cloud emerging from my nose.

The more breaths I take in, the more I realize that my muscles, not just in my neck and shoulders, but throughout my body relax. It's nice. And the wind blowing under my hands? It feels like silk brushing against my skin, smooth and free flowing. There's a velvety sensation as well, and that piques my curiosity.

"Good." Soren's voice comes to me almost like a whisper. A caress of words. "You can open your eyes now."

I do and notice that he's standing with his hands at his sides and a proud little smirk stretching his lips.

I smile. "That was amazing."

He nods. "It's a calming meditation that helps clear your mind."

"Awesome."

Gideon steps forward. "Look behind you."

I turn just in time to see a purple light shoot into the air like a flare. Only, instead of this light arching at its highest point before falling back toward the earth, it hovers like a bright orb in the sky.

"The signal."

"Mm-hmm." He's right behind me, and the sound rushes into my ear with his warm breath coursing down my neck. My eyes flutter shut and I almost lean into the headmaster. I catch myself before I get too carried away with lustful thoughts. I have to focus on doing this portal thing, after all.

"Now over here." Gideon turns me to the west side of the island where a green light hovers into the sky.

He turns me again. "And over here."

A red orb floats, pulsating with pink and orange. "Whoa."

"Got it?" Gideon asks.

I feel myself nod as I study the light and the way it shifts between shades and colors like fiber optics.

"Good. Now, close your eyes and take in a few deep breaths."

I do, and I instantly feel more in tune with my magic.

"Picture Savannah's light," Soren instructs. He's close to me now, hand resting gently on my right arm, and I almost open my eyes to see if these men of mine know they are tormenting me in delicious ways. I don't though. I do as I'm instructed and picture the purple light, burning like a small ball of fire. "Using this hand," he taps his fingers on my forearm, "Imagine instantly traveling there while drawing out a circle with your hand."

Magic pulses through my arm. A warmth, mixed with a powerful buzzing, seeps through my hand as I form the circle.

"Open your eyes," Gideon says, his voice full of pride.

A glowing portal of pink, blue, and purple, with silver specs of light hovers in front of me. My portal stretches about two feet higher than I am tall, and I stare at it in awe.

"I did it!" I smile, proud of myself as I'm filled with excitement.

"Now the real test," Soren says gesturing to the portal.

I settle my eyes on his. He nods once. I take a deep breath and step into the portal. The mixed sensation of sinking and floating is stronger this time than it has ever been. The force is almost strong enough to whip me around as if I were in the middle of a tornado, but I hang onto my focus and intention so that I don't lose my way. And when I leave the portal, I'm falling. I let out a loud scream as I collide with Savannah, knocking her to the ground. Somehow, I land on her, belly-to-belly. We look at each other, and no sooner than our eyes meet do we bust out laughing.

Crunching stomps approach and before I can even look, strong arms grab my own and pull me up from the ground. I'm spun, and the sensation is a bit much for me as my stomach clenches against the movement. Once the spinning in my head settles, I rest my gaze on a pair of amber eyes.

"Are you okay?"

I nod, eyebrows scrunching. "I'm fine." I look to Savannah. "Are you okay?"

She holds up her hand with a thumbs up. "Can we do that again? I think I wanna try."

I chuckle under my breath. "I could've hurt you. Or worse, killed you."

"Or yourself," Soren says in a sharp tone.

I snap my attention to him and narrow my eyes. "I'm fine."

He shakes his head. "Next time, visualize the ground, not just the light."

"Be clearer in your instructions," I snap back.

He huffs then takes a step back, turning away from me, likely pinching the bridge of his nose.

Savannah shuffles to a standing position. "Ready to head back?"

"Yes."

"Okay, this time, you have to picture both of us making it back." She slips her arm through mine and leads me a few feet away.

I repeat the process, being very explicit in the details of the portal. Once the portal opens, it's a softer shade of pink with silver specks throughout. I smile, bobbing my eyebrows at Savannah. She lets out a loud laugh and we step through, landing on the roof. I almost lose my balance. Gideon quickly grabs me and pulls me closer to him.

"Get a room," Savannah playfully chides.

He releases me, making sure I'm steady on my own feet first. "It can be a bit disorienting at first."

"No kidding." I let out a deep breath. A puff of cloud leaves my lungs.

"Ready to try again?" he asks.

I nod.

This time I focus on Jesse's light. The green one. I

know this area. It's where we first met Lady Alene. I picture that. Once my portal is formed, I smile at the others and step through. But instead of landing on the stone like I anticipated, I'm suddenly entangled in branches, directly above Jesse.

"What did the poor tree do to you?"

I shift as much as I can, struggling to pull myself up enough to get a better view at where I am. "It got in my way."

"Hmm..." he muses. "Clearly the tree sees it differently."

"Are you going to stand there and criticize me, or are you going to give me a hand?"

He starts clapping.

Jesse, adorable jokester, actually claps.

I roll my eyes as the joke dawns on me. "Asshole."

"Hey," Soren says, approaching us. "There's only room for one asshole here, and I am it."

Wonderful. Now I get ridicule from two men.

Fan-freaking-tastic.

I manage to wiggle myself free and hop to the ground, landing with a soft thud. I face the two men. "Well, now that you two have had your fun, I'm going to try again. Unless either of you have something useful to say?"

Both men act like they're considering tips as they

cup their chins, run hands through their hair, and take other pensive-like positions.

"Thanks so much for the help," I mutter and form another portal. This one I have down. Once it's formed, I pull Jesse through. We land on the roof, and this time, I don't lose my balance.

Hmm... interesting.

"Two down, one to go," Jesse says. "Don't hurt any more trees."

I glare at him. "Har har."

I quickly create another portal, focusing on the area where Milo is and jump in. This time, I land in the ocean right off the dock of the island. The splash is deafening and the water is shockingly cold. The waves slosh around me and tug gently at my body. I struggle to get my arms to move and perform quick strokes while propelling myself forward with kicks. Being in the ocean at night is creepy, especially with the types of creatures inhabiting the area. I eventually make it to the shallow part where I can climb up onto the ground.

However, lo and behold, Soren meets me there, smirking down at me with his arms crossed over his chest.

"You do know the ultimate point of landing is 'land,' right?"

I groan and splash salty water onto his fancy professor pants. "At least help me up, would you?"

"After getting me wet?" He looks into the air as if he's considering it and returns his gaze back to me. "I think you can handle it."

"Asshole."

He bows, smiling proudly.

I shake my head and though I try not to, I still chuckle.

As soon as I'm on land, he helps me stand with soaking wet clothes that added about twenty-five pounds to my weight. He walks me to Milo who, thankfully, doesn't have a snide remark about my inability to be accurate with portals.

Once back on the roof, I practice one point specifically on the island, the front doors. This way, I don't land in a tree, in water, or on another person.

Within a few more hours of diligent work, I finally manage to portal to various places on the island without incident. Of course, I still get teased each time I return to the roof, but as I land one last time, Gideon calls the training to a close.

"It's late and cold. You've done well, Wren. I'm proud of you."

I smile.

"Solid job. Well done," Soren says.

I gape at him. "Really?" It comes out more flat than it does a question, but he nods.

"Not many people can make the progress you've made tonight in just a few hours," he adds.

My eyes widen in shock as everyone takes turns congratulating me. Jesse throws his arm around me and whispers in my ear, "How about I warm you up tonight?"

"Nice try." I elbow him in the ribs.

"So, is everyone comfortable with me portalling from my aunt's house?" I ask.

"Well, portalling off the estate, maybe." Gideon nods. "Portalling straight here? Not yet. Don't worry, we'll keep practicing until you get it down enough for longer distances."

I nod and we all file behind Gideon back through the secret door into his office. Soon, I'm in the warmth of my private room and I'm peeling the still damp clothes from my body and climbing into a warm shower.

All the while, I keep my focus on what this weekend is going to bring. I know what I'm getting myself into. But I still need to be cautious and careful so my aunt isn't made aware of my true intentions. One way or another, I'm going to get answers and clear my father's name.

CHAPTER FOURTEEN

We arrive on the estate grounds shortly after the last class of the week. Savannah pauses to take in the wrought iron gate, bordered by a tall stone wall, with a giant, flourished "B" in the center of the gate.

She whistles. "They sure don't make them like this anymore, do they?"

I shake my head. "No, they don't."

There's a clear view of the English-style cottage a mile ahead, down a stone path. Its tall pointed roofs reach high into the sky, almost piercing the thick grey clouds that promise a cooling rain soon. I can almost smell the storm in the air.

Being back, my heart hammers in my chest and my intuition flares. My stomach tightens into knots. And there's a foreboding sense that overcomes me. Arriving here after so long, returning to possible danger, doesn't escape my notice. I'm going into this with my eyes wide open. But there is a sense of knowing the promised safety my aunt gave me is nothing but hot air and a pipe dream meant to mislead and get me to drop my guard.

I have a mission to complete. And nothing is going to stop me from doing just that.

We approach the gate. It responds by automatically opening. Savannah and I exchange a glance, and with a shrug, we walk through.

Among the well-manicured grass that lines the drive, large green topiaries dot the line, leading toward a large circle drive with two sets of stone stairs that curve up to the front door of the home itself. Between those sits a small rose garden.

"This place is enchanting," Savannah says.

"I guess so." The back of my neck tightens and aches. Sure, on the surface Aunt Patty's house looks amazing, but what lies beneath is a whole other story.

She settles her amethyst eyes on me. "You don't think so?"

I shrug. "I just have a heavy feeling settling in my gut."

That feeling Gideon spoke of, as if he were being

watched. It settles on my shoulders and I fight the urge to look around and see if there's anyone lurking in the woods sheltering the estate's grounds beyond the manicured lawns on either side of the drive.

"I feel it too," she says, soft as a whisper. "Try not to let it play on your mind. Remember what we're trying to accomplish here."

I nod, pressing my lips together and straightening my spine as we climb up the staircase to the left.

As we reach the double doors, Aunt Patricia is already standing in the middle of them, her scrutinizing eyes taking in each of our steps. A flowy summer dress hangs on her slender frame, making her look even more statuesque. It's the most casual thing I've seen her wear yet. Her long silver hair pours past her shoulders, the ends nearly reaching her waist.

Her lips are pressed into a thin line as we approach. "Storm is coming," she says simply, stepping out of the way as we walk in.

"Hello, Ms. Blackwood," Savannah says.

Aunt Patricia nods. "I assume you are Savannah?"

Savannah nods and smiles, holding out her hand. "It's a pleasure to meet you."

Aunt Patricia ignores Savannah's outreached hand. "A pleasure, indeed. Come, I will show you to your rooms. You may leave your things there."

Savannah casts a worried glance in my direction. I subtly shake my head and follow after my aunt who doesn't seem to have time for simple pleasantries. Always stiff and formal.

"I trust you girls had little issue arriving?" She leads us up a set of stairs directly in front of the doors on the inside, leading to the second floor.

"That's correct, Aunt Patricia."

"Very good," she says and glances over her shoulder. "I hope you will forgive me, I don't normally have visitors. I did have your rooms refreshed with new linens. Each of you have your own stocked bathroom."

She takes a right and walks to the end of the hall, where a window reveals the vast forest and mountains surrounding the estate. She pauses in front of the window and faces us. "Wren," she motions to the right. "You have your old room. I hope that is all right."

I incline my head, forcing down the lump in my throat. "It's perfect. Thanks, Aunt Patricia."

She nods with a faint smile, stretching her lips. "Savannah, dear. You will be across the hall. Please let me know if you are missing anything within your rooms. As soon as you are settled, come directly to the sitting room." She nods toward me. "You remember the way?"

"Yes, ma'am. I think so."

"Do not go anywhere else. Come straight there once you are done. I have rules I must share with you, and you will not be allowed to roam my home without first being made aware of where you can and cannot go."

"We'll be down in about five minutes, Ms. Blackwood. Thank you so much for allowing me to come, by the way. I'm very honored to be in such a magnificent home." Good old Savannah. I love how she tries to find the good in something.

"It is very old, dear. It has been in our family for many, many generations."

"I would love to hear the story sometime." Savannah smiles as she walks through her bedroom door.

I head for mine at the same time. I mutter a quick thank you and step into the room I was kidnapped from when I was fourteen. It's a foggy memory. In fact, everything to do with this house is cloudy as I try to recall the time I had spent here. I second-guess if I can make it to the sitting room or not. Now that I'm here, what I thought I remembered is completely wrong, and that unsettles me.

At least my aunt's demeanor is relatively the same. That has to say something, right?

Once I set my bag on my bed, I walk through the room and take in everything.

Lavender walls surround me, bordered with decorative wainscoting in a silver sheen on the bottom half of the walls. Lavish crown molding lines the top with the corner pieces pointing toward the floor in elegant swirls. My bed takes up the left wall, a four-poster bed with thin, sheer curtains dangling toward the floor, dusting it with their ends. A glass door opens up to a small, private patio on the far wall, and on the right is the closet and door to the bathroom.

No posters cover the walls. No pictures. No art.

I frown, trying to pull up any memory of this room, but it's useless. I'm coming up with nothing.

And with that, I leave the room, meeting Savannah in the hall as she steps with a bounce from her own room. She takes one look at my expression and whispers, "What's up?"

I shake my head. "I don't remember my room at all."

She rubs my back gently. "It will come. Remember why we're here."

I nod. "Did you send the letter to Gideon?"

"All taken care of."

"Good." I sigh and look around at my strange surroundings. "Let's find this sitting room."

"I hope we don't take a wrong turn." As she says the words, her eyes glitter with hope. It would be a good test.

I smile, loving her line of thinking. "Troublemaker."

She bows. "I try."

A giggle bubbles out of me. "Let's go see what we can find."

We make our way down the stairs. On the right is a wide, open doorway revealing a wall of windows and long table with extravagant chairs surrounding it. I point toward the area. "That must be the dining room."

"Obviously."

On the left is a burgundy wall with golden, decorative frames forming rectangles and a strip of gold in the middle. A door stands closed, which makes me wonder what's behind it. I doubt it's the sitting room, though. Light from a window shines through the hall, highlighting the specks of golden glitter inlaid into the grey marble flooring.

"Hmm… I wonder what's down there."

"Only one way to find out," Savannah says, still keeping her voice down. And that's a good thing. Even the soft patter of our feet seem louder than it should here. That's something we'll have to keep in mind when we do our first run of recon tonight.

We walk toward the hall and peek around the corner. Windows dot the hallway on the right, and the wall is a collection of portraits of people from the Blackwood family. I skim some of the names, but none of them stand out. My father's portrait doesn't even grace the walls and that bothers me. It's like he's been removed. Aunt Patricia's view of my father must be part of the reason. But he's still blood.

My face pulls down into a frown as I realize I don't recognize anyone in the portraits. I wonder just how far back my lineage goes.

Eventually, the hall opens into a room filled with a collection of expensive leather furnishings in neutral colors. On the far wall stands a large fireplace with crossing swords hanging above the mantel. Large floor-to-ceiling windows take up the rest of the wall and on the left is another doorway to a hallway. A door sits open into another room that looks more like a pantry to me, but I suspect that is where the kitchen is.

Though the place is faintly familiar to me, one thing stands out for certain… my aunt isn't here.

"Now what?" Savannah asks, brushing her fingers

along the length of the leather sofa facing the fireplace.

I shrug. "Sit and wait, I guess."

"No fun."

I level my gaze on her. "We have to get the rules first, Savannah."

She chuckles as my aunt enters the room and says, "Indeed."

Savannah jumps and uses all her strength to stifle her laugh.

"I did not mean to startle you," Aunt Patricia says.

Savannah, still chuckling despite her efforts, waves away my aunt's apology. "It's fine."

"Please, sit." She approaches a plush chair and takes a seat herself while Savannah and I take a spot on the sofa.

As soon as we are settled, my aunt sucks in a deep breath and digs into her rules. "As I have said, this place is old. Because of its age, the third floor is strictly off limits. That includes the attic, which I'm sure you find especially disheartening, Wren, as you loved to play up there as a little girl."

I catch Savannah's gaze as she looks at me with curiosity. I subtly shrug. I don't remember that, but nothing seems new there. It's an on-going theme with this place.

"Stay to your rooms after ten o'clock. You may exit them at eight in the morning. Breakfast will be served in the dining room no later than nine. Lunch is fend for yourself. Feel free to fix sandwiches or salads to your satisfaction. Dinner at six. You may roam the land but remain out of my gardens. Do not pick the flowers. And do not leave these grounds for any reason without first letting me know."

We nod. Sounds strict, but I'm not worried about that. I'm more curious than anything about the third floor and the attic.

"Now that you have been told the rules, dinner will be served in fifteen minutes. From there, I ask that you stick to your rooms as I have a business matter to contend with and I cannot keep an eye on you during those times."

With a sigh, she stands from her chair and heads through the door that leads to the kitchens. "Within the limits I have set, please make yourself at home."

As soon as she's out of range, I face Savannah with a confused expression. "Prison much?" I keep my words to a whisper.

"No kidding." She shakes her head. "I can't get a good read on her here. Especially on the place itself. It's almost like my gifts are being blocked."

I nod and chew on the corner of my lower lip. This

raises more red flags. "After dinner, when she's taking her call, we'll do what we talked about."

"Meanwhile," she stands and stretches her arms high above her head. "I'm starving."

I grin at her, knowing that with her around, there'll be no dull moments. "Let's eat then."

CHAPTER FIFTEEN

Dinner was... different.
If the tension were any thicker, I wouldn't be able to breathe. Worst of all, I can't shake the growing discomfort of being here, and I think my aunt knows it. Over our casual dinner conversation which felt more like an inquisition, my aunt seemed to study my words, narrowing her eyes ever so often as I replied to her questions. With Savannah, she seemed to barely acknowledge my friend's answers. Almost like she didn't really care to hear her replies but for the sake of appearance at least she would glance in her direction and nod once in a while at her.

If it's one thing that I know for sure, it's all of this is a huge front. A show.

My intuition has been on high alert this whole

time. From the tingling sensation of magical wards resting along areas of the home, which raises an eyebrow, to the hollow emptiness and forbidden rooms. This estate seems more like a cold vault, protecting unspoken secrets, rather than a warm family home.

It's time to carefully plan our recon. I don't know where my aunt will be during her call, which she left to prepare for just after we finished eating. I don't feel comfortable talking with Savannah about these things until we're behind closed doors. Even then, I want to keep it at a whisper.

There's something not right here, and the longer I'm within these walls, the more apparent that becomes.

Once inside my room, I change into more comfortable clothing to make it appear that Savannah and I are abiding by the rules and getting ready for bed. We have three hours before we should remain in our rooms, and not knowing how long my aunt will be on the call, it's best to assume we are short on time to find the blueprints or anything to tie my aunt to the Order and send word back.

As soon as I'm changed, I tiptoe in my socks to Savannah's room. I softly tap the back of my knuckle against the door and wait. Within seconds, the door opens with Savannah standing at the threshold. She smiles and opens it wider to let me inside her room that very much mirrors my own with a few small changes. Her room is pale blue, versus the lavender of mine. She also doesn't have a patio leading off her room, but does have large windows that reveal the forests and mountains that surrounds the entire estate. I press my finger to my lips to signal that we need to keep as quiet as possible.

She nods and follows me to the middle of the floor where I turn and face her and keep my voice as whisper soft as I can. "I still don't remember anything about this house."

She shakes her head. "I feel it too. What should we do?"

"Stick to the plan, but we have to be especially careful now. Can you feel for any traps or enchantments?"

"Sort of. I can get impressions, but that's probably not going to help us."

Shoot.

"We have to do something."

"Do you even know how to get to the third floor or attic?" Her amethyst eyes study mine as I try to pull to mind any recollection of this house. Eventually, I huff and shake my head. "I have an idea."

"Spill." I smile.

"Well she did say make ourselves at home. And we still need to figure out where her room is."

I nod. "Let's check this hall first."

"Okay."

I'm first to reach Savannah's door. Slowly twisting the knob, I pull open the door as quietly as possible and poke my head out into the hall. Coast is clear. Opening the door fully, I silently step out into the hall. Savannah follows, shutting the door quietly.

She follows me out of the room, and with the darkening shadows stretching throughout the house with the rainstorm just starting outside, it should be relatively easy to make it through the hall without much notice.

We move past the stairs, silent as ghosts, and we find three doors. Two on the right, and one on the left. The door on the left is locked. But the first of the two on the right isn't. But it's just an empty room. Nothing but sheet covered furniture and random boxes stored in the corners of the room. Barely any light fills this dismal and forgotten place. It's almost depressing to see it in this condition. Almost surprising too, considering how pristine and in order everything else is when it concerns my aunt.

"This would be the perfect place to hide blueprints," Savannah whispers over my left shoulder.

I glance at her. "You think so?"

She nods. "Think about it. It's the perfect disguise."

I have to admit, it does seem worthwhile to at least quickly go through everything. We press forward, shutting the door behind us. Savannah works through the left side of the room, while I work through the right. We both carefully pull away sheets and shield our noses from flying dust as we examine the boxes and furniture.

Nearly an hour later, and with the clock ticking, we haven't come up with anything but dust and tickles in our throats. So far it seems to be a bunch of packed up knick-knacks, old books, and photos. Furniture stacked in the one corner of the room looks in almost new condition, and it feels like this is just a multi-purpose, catchall room. I wonder if my aunt wasn't telling the truth about the attic, because most of this stuff would normally go there.

Finally, I join Savannah as she fishes through a dust-covered chest of drawers. "Find anything?" I ask, still keeping my voice low.

She shakes her head.

"All right. We've spent a long time here. I think we should hang it up for right now."

She nods and follows me back into the hall.

We check the other room to find only that. A room. Albeit lavishly decorated with the finest of items. This must be my aunt's room. Though we still don't know what is behind the locked door, it's on the list to check later. For now, we reconvene in Savannah's room.

"Why keep all that junk in that room?" She tucks her legs under her and grips her ankle with one hand while keeping herself propped up with her other.

I shrug. "I have no idea. Unless she told us the truth about the third floor and attic."

She cocks her head to the side. "It's hard to say."

"Who conducts business at this hour of night on a Friday?" I ask.

"Someone like her, apparently."

"No, there's more to it. It's too convenient." I fall into my thoughts, processing everything in the room, the lack of signs that there's anything to prove my aunt as being a part of the Order.

I can't stop thinking about that door with the lock on it until I realize, in our scoping of the second floor, we didn't find any stairs that continued up. "That's it!" I say a little louder than a whisper.

"What?" She has a puzzled expression.

"That locked door is the stairway to the third floor."

Her eyes widen as her lips stretch into a wide smile. "You're one smart cookie."

"Got any spells on hand that unlock doors?"

"Never leave home without one!" She winks.

I shake my head, laughing under my breath. "Thank the gods for you, girl."

"When do we leave?"

I think about that for a moment. We'll need to go once my aunt is asleep. We can't risk going now or she could catch us, and we can't risk going too late either, missing our window of opportunity. The fact that the door to the next floor is right across the hall from her room also creates a bit of a challenge.

"Midnight?" I ask.

"Sounds like a plan. I'll update the guys and let them know what we're up to. Should I let them know about our suspicions?"

I shake my head. "Without proof, it won't do us much good."

I don't know when the decision was made that Savannah write all the letters, but in retrospect, it's genius. She could claim to be writing her family, keeping them updated. Aunt Patricia doesn't know her well enough to know differently, and I highly doubt she would ask to read them for proof. That's just an invasion of privacy, and I won't let that fly.

Savannah sends the letter, leaving no trace of it behind. As ten o'clock draws ever closer, I make my way to my own room.

"Listen closely for my signal," I say before leaving.

"Will do." She blows me a kiss as I walk out the door.

I make it to my room and wait. I sit on the floor with the patio door open, watching as the rainstorm passes through all too quickly. The smell of ozone left behind makes me wish for the salty air of Blackbriar.

It's like being homesick. And Blackbriar is most definitely home to me. But I reassure myself that I'll be home soon. This mission of ours is for the purpose of figuring out the source of the blueprints and whether or not my aunt can truly be trusted.

I hum to myself, resting my head against the jamb, processing what it would mean to find more of the blueprints. I know the symbol within them is here. I see it in my mind and I know that deep in my bones. All this passes through my mind like a slow moving river as I sit in the room I was allegedly taken from in what seems like another life.

Really, it was. Because that life is over now. Now, I have a new life, with a new family, and a team of men that I would do anything for and protect them with my last breath.

No more trolls.

No more fighting for scraps.

No more escaping only to be dragged back.

No more ridicule.

A tapping on my door pulls me from my thoughts with a start. I quickly twist around to find my aunt standing in the doorway. She flips the light on and walks in.

"Sorry to surprise you like that. I only wanted to ensure that you were comfortable, most of all."

I shrug. "I'm comfortable enough, thanks Aunt Patricia."

She nods slightly. "If you would like, I can make you some tea. I am about to have some myself. A house this large and old tends to come to life at night."

I shake my head, instantly recalling what she told me about the night I disappeared. When the trolls took me from this very room. "No, thank you. I'll be able to sleep."

"Very well. It is almost ten. Please adhere to my rules."

I nod. "No problem, Aunt Patricia. Goodnight."

"See you in the morning, dear." She turns around, her nightgown flowing behind her as she flicks off the light. She looks at me once more then leaves the room without another word.

That was weird.

I wonder if she knows that we went through that room, but if she does, she certainly isn't giving that knowledge away. Something tells me that she was hoping to glean something from me. Some sort of information that I may not even realize I divulged to her. It's a good idea not to go drinking tea with her, now that I think about it. A tiny pang of guilt hits me at entertaining that thought toward someone from my family. Perhaps it was simply a goodnight call, as she made it seem. But this is my aunt. She's a puzzle, to say the least.

A cold breeze blows through me. I stand and shut the patio door, crossing my arms over my chest to keep the warmth within me and head for the bed, curling up in the blankets.

I'm here for a reason, and as the minutes tick by, I'm closer to finding what I need to clear my father's name.

Before long, a door whispers shut, followed by a click. That's it. My aunt has gone to bed. Now just to wait until midnight. That should give her enough time to fall asleep.

CHAPTER SIXTEEN

Midnight arrives and both Savannah and I sneak out of our rooms, silent as ghosts. We nod to each other in greeting and make our way to the other end of the hall. While Savannah fiddles with the lock, I lean close to my aunt's bedroom door, listening for any sign that she is onto us.

A soft click echoes through the dark silence. We hold our breath as we wait a few agonizing moments for motion, sound, anything.

When nothing happens, we let out our breaths and inch the door open slowly so we can explore.

I half expect the door to creak, but it moves freely on the hinges, suggesting that it's well oiled and cared for instead of remaining sealed for however long. The stairs don't so much as groan as we move up them.

And before long, we reach the landing of the third floor. A hall stretches out in front of us, and another one to the left. In the center, it looks like a giant room.

Savannah and I exchange a glance and look past the door for the large room, finding a dilapidated library, sadly disused. Milo's heart would break if he saw this room. I shake my head as we move through the rows of mostly empty bookshelves, searching for any clues. With nothing to speak of, we leave the library and make our way through the halls finding the stairs to the attic, and a number of large rooms that seem in various stages of abandonment.

Just when it seems we'll have to risk the attic after all, I find something glinting in the light in the middle of a wall. I step closer, angling myself to get a view with the most light and gasp. It's the same symbol on the blueprints. I push on the wall, but I can't get it to budge. There's a secret room behind this wall, and I want in.

"Savannah," I whisper. "I found the symbol."

She shuffles her feet toward me and looks at it a few moments before frowning. "I don't see anything."

"Stand over here." I step away and let her stand where I was.

She does, and after a few moments of studying the wall, she shakes her head. "Still nothing."

"Bend around until you get the light hitting it just right." I circle the area where it's at. "Should be right around here."

She bends and tilts until she stops and does a double-take, reaching out to touch the symbol on the wall. "You're right. This doesn't bode well."

"No. But it's a step in the right direction. Now, we just need to find a way in."

She pushes on the wall in different spots but shakes her head. "It's some sort of enchantment. It's likely unlocked with a key word or some specific spell."

I lean forward, pressing my ear against the wall, and tap the wall with my knuckles. The sound echoes outward. "There's a room behind here."

Savannah steps back and crosses her arms as she ponders how to get through. "I don't see how we're going to get in here."

Steps shuffle toward us.

We suck in our breaths as I walk to Savannah and rest my hands on her shoulders. "Play along," I whisper.

She nods.

I slide my hands long her arms to her wrists and gently start to pull on her.

"What's the meaning of this!" Aunt Patricia's voice is sharp and furious.

I jump and spin to face my aunt. "Shhh! She's sleep walking."

"Sleep walking?" she asks, but it comes out almost as though she doesn't believe the lie.

I nod, not missing a beat. "It doesn't happen all the time, but when it does, she can be difficult to find and get back to bed. Please, if you're not going to help, at least get out of the way so I can put her back to bed."

Aunt Patricia stands with her arms crossed as her eyes study both me and Savannah as though she's trying to detect any hint that we're lying. She's trying to pick a part the lie to uncover the truth.

"I state rules for a reason," she mutters. "This is not at all acceptable."

"Yes, Aunt Patricia. I know very well how this looks. If you have questions about it, contact Headmaster Storm. He'll tell you himself."

"It does not happen often, you say?" She seems like she's starting to buy it, especially since mentioning that Gideon would confirm this. But a part of me feels like this is just more digging to find a weak spot in our lie.

"Very infrequent, Aunt Patricia. One to three times a year, tops." I face Savannah again and grab her wrists.

"Why wasn't I informed of this?"

I groan inwardly and face my aunt again. "She normally has a potion she sips before bed when she feels a spell coming on, but we forgot it in our excitement to come here." I look back at Savannah. Her eyes have shifted out of focus, almost like she's looking through me and my aunt.

Savannah mumbles to herself. "Not right now."

"Hmm…" She stands there for a moment longer, silent and still as though she's a statue. Finally, she sighs. "Very well. I'll help you get her down the stairs. I can't have you injuring yourself at my home. Her especially. I'll talk to Headmaster Storm in the morning." She beckons me forward.

With a nod, I face Savannah again and pull her gently by the wrists toward the stairs. Aunt Patricia follows behind her. I take a step down and keep my voice calm. "Savannah, I need you to walk down with me."

She giggles. "Down, down, down." Her voice comes out almost sing-song like but soft and low. She lets her head bob and lull to the side.

Good girl.

She makes it downstairs with me, and as I pull her down the hall toward our rooms, I watch my aunt lock the door and use a spell to ward the lock as well. She stands in the middle of the hall until I'm at Savannah's door.

"I'm just going to sleep with her, make sure she doesn't get up again," I tell my aunt.

"Very well, Wren. Please do." She leaves through her door to her room.

I let out a breath I had been holding, still keeping up with the act until we're through the door and it's also shut.

"That was close," Savannah says, hand resting over her chest. "I've never been so frightened in my life. I saw so much darkness around her."

I nod. "I think we have enough proof to get the hell out of here. She's on to us now. I can't let you risk your own safety any longer."

"Agreed. Should we go now, or should we wait?"

"We should hold off for an hour. If we try to leave immediately, she will rain hell down on us and trap us here. Knowing her, she will check on us at least once. When she sees that we're still here and in bed, she will let her guard down. Then we can leave."

"That's comforting." It comes out sarcastic.

Still, I agree. Nothing like being watched constantly. I bite the corner of my lower lip and huff. "I just wish we could figure out what's behind that wall."

"I agree the symbol is enough. Let's get to bed, and I'll send the letter after she checks on us."

I nod. "There's no way I'm getting any sleep. I'll stand watch and you can get some rest."

"Not happening," she says, climbing under the covers. "I'm up with you. All the way."

I give her a grateful smile as I climb into the bed as well.

Like clockwork, my aunt finally arrives and opens the door to Savannah's room. But instead of staying by the door to watch our chests rise and fall with the rhythm of sleep, she walks over and shoves a finger into my side. I open my eyes and sit up. "What's wrong?"

"Nothing, child. Go back to sleep."

I nod sleepily and yawn as I lay back down and pull the covers over my shoulder. Aunt Patricia's footsteps shuffle quietly to the other side of the bed. Savannah jumps and grumbles, rolling over and snuggling into her pillow a little more.

With a heavy sigh of relief, my aunt leaves the room. I peel my eyes open enough to watch her take out a key. She closes and locks the door.

A pinch forms in the center of my forehead.

Shit.

That was *not* part of the plan.

We give it a few moments before I call the all clear. "That's it. We're leaving now."

"I agree."

I rush to the door to double-check that the door is locked. It juggles but doesn't turn.

Yup.

Locked.

Fan-freaking-tastic. This night just gets better and better.

"We have to portal out of here now."

"I'm trying." Even whispering, her words come out strained.

"What's wrong?" I approach her and try to add in my own energy to pull up the portal. It's like trying to move cement. "What the hell?"

"She must have wards blocking travel." Savannah sighs and takes a seat on the foot of the bed.

"What's the likelihood of her blocking letters?" I ask.

She shrugs. "I'll try that."

Within moments, the letter is written and burns away into nothing. If there is a ward preventing letters, it's not apparent on our end. All we can do now is sit back and wait.

Gods, I hope that letter burns to life on Gideon's desk. Otherwise, we may have to explain ourselves in a way that no lies are going to cover up.

The next morning, a click in the handle lets us know we're able to leave the room. We give it about twenty additional minutes and then I run to my room to change. I pack my bag, hoping beyond all hope that my men received the letter.

No sooner than I leave the room, joining Savannah in the hallway, a chime sounds through the house. My heart lurches in my chest. We cannot leave this place fast enough.

Savannah and I try our best to play cool until we're downstairs and see my aunt talking with Soren outside the door. We step outside.

"Hi, Professor McCallister." I interrupt the conversation. "Is everything okay?"

He nods. "In fact, Miss Blackwood, I have just informed your aunt that you were called to a skills check."

"What's that?" I ask shaking my head, keeping up with the ruse.

Savannah nudges me. "It's like a pop quiz. The school selects students at random for it. It's the council's way of grading the academy based on the performance of its students."

"It's not like the trials, is it?" I ask with a ghastly expression that I hope clearly signifies how unpleasant this idea is to me. To keep up the pretense of this being a surprise and all.

"Nothing of the sort," Soren says. He shifts his attention to my aunt. "Well, Ms. Blackwood, it is a pleasure. Hope to see you back at the academy soon."

She nods, plastic smile and all. "Surely we could reschedule just this once? Perhaps Savannah could take Wren's place?"

Oh hell no.

That right there tells me everything I need to know. Aunt Patricia is up to something, and it's nothing good.

"I'm sorry, Ms. Blackwood," Soren says. "My hands are tied on the matter. You know as well as I do, we can't reassign the skill checks."

"Very well." She faces me. "I understand you have to leave. Perhaps we can pick up another weekend?"

I nod. "I would like that." I even add a fake smile of my own.

Take that!

"Go get your things." She waves us off.

Savannah and I spin on our heels and calmly make

it up the stairs. Once we're out of sight, we dash through the doorways and into our rooms, quickly grabbing our bags and rushing back out toward the front door again. We continue in keeping our cool as soon as we round the edge of the wall before the stairs.

Once we're out the front door, Aunt Patricia's goodbye sounds pleasant, but her body language suggests she's close to murder. "Until next time, Wren."

I nod. "Goodbye, Aunt Patricia."

"Thanks for letting me stay again." Savannah smiles and waves.

Aunt Patricia lifts her nose in the air. "My pleasure."

Without another word, we make our way down the drive to the gate. We don't talk with Soren or even with ourselves. The weight of being watched rests heavily on my shoulders, and I let my eyes drift over every shadow to my left. Savannah seems to occupy herself with the area to the right, and Soren keeps his attention forward.

As soon as we are past the gate, we portal back to the island.

And I have never been so happy to be back as I am now.

Soren faces us, a serious glower in his eyes that

makes me want to gulp. "Get your stuff to your rooms then get to Gideon's office."

We nod.

With that, he turns and storms off.

I catch Savannah's gaze and we share in a laugh.

"So serious," Savannah says.

"I believe the name you gave him was Mr. Hottie McMoody."

She shakes her head wistfully. "So fitting. See you in a minute."

I wave. "See you."

CHAPTER SEVENTEEN

We sit in Gideon's office as a long uncomfortable silence settles in the air. Savannah and I had just finished recapping how we found the same symbol that was on the blueprints during our visit.

The looks on the men's faces could force the strongest man to shudder. Especially Gideon's and Soren's. They're angry. Rightly so. Things had quickly gotten out of hand and being locked in a room really set Soren's teeth on edge.

"Can you explain why I received a letter asking me to confirm Savannah's affliction with sleep walking?" Gideon asks.

"That's Wren's incredible idea," Savannah says. "Quick thinking and a little improvisation."

I blush a little.

He nods. "I sent a response confirming that. And I'm glad I did. Is that when you found the symbol?"

"Yes. Though we didn't find anything obvious, that symbol is more than coincidence." I shake my head and shift in my seat. "That, and the way I don't remember anything about that house. Why can't I remember that place?"

"Gideon, she can't go back there." Soren faces his best friend. His body stiffens as he tries to restrain his anger, and he starts to glow with his fire magic. His lips are pressed into a firm line. "Regardless of not having proof, you know that woman will make a point of getting her back there."

My headmaster nods as he processes everything. He doesn't say a word as he just sits at his desk trying to piece everything together.

"You know I'm right." Soren huffs.

"I agree," Milo says from his perch. "There's too much coincidence for it to all add up to nothing. It was too much of a risk before."

"Should she go back," Jesse says, "we might as well include the silver platter."

My heart warms at how protective my men are. Even with Savannah. With that being said, however, I don't like where this is heading. I can almost hear the alarms going off in my men's minds.

Wren is in danger! Must protect! Must lock her away! Alert! Alert!

"If the words *escort*, or *no alone time*, exit anyone's lips, I'll blast you all with a fire ball."

Gideon's eyes meet mine and his lips quirk at the corners. It's a faint movement that he allows only me to see. I nod at him, a small smile tugging at my own lips.

"I think avoiding interactions alone with your aunt should suffice." He cracks his knuckles and stretches out his neck. "I can help with that."

"Thank you," I say. "Do we need to reach out to my father now? Maybe he has some ideas?"

Soren starts to shake his head and pace the room. He's obviously not thrilled with the idea of simply avoiding my aunt, but what he seems to constantly forget is, I'm no damsel. I have proven myself time and time again that I can protect and take care of myself. It's a nice gesture though, his incessant need to protect me and shield me from harm.

A little misguided, but nice.

"I've reached out to your father," Gideon says, pulling my attention to him. "Regarding your aunt. I've shared my suspicions with him."

"Even though he could be working for them?" Soren asks, his voice shaking with fury.

Gideon holds up a hand to Soren so he can finish. "They haven't been close for a very long time. Since before Wren was born, there seems to have been a distance between them. Their relationship was apparently estranged."

He stands and walks to the front of his desk and leans against it. He crosses his arms over his chest as his eyes slip out of focus. His eyelids look darker at the corners, almost bruised. I know better to think someone dared laid a hand on my headmaster. No, those are the marks of lack of sleep. His long sleeve, button up shirt is freshly pressed though. Even his black slacks are free from wrinkles. He still looks the part of headmaster. Finally, he sucks in a deep breath. "I still have yet to see anything questionable come from him. His soul remains free of darkness. He was a prisoner of the Order. His intentions are pure even though we haven't found anything to clear his name. As far as I am concerned, he's safe. Patricia, however, is the nefarious one in this."

"Too many unknowns." Soren paces as he mutters under his breath.

I blow out a raspberry.

"Still, Aunt Patricia's motives are unclear. I'll be extra cautious when it comes to her."

Gideon nods. "Don't share sensitive information with her. She's already suspicious as it is now. However, she's well-known and respected in the community and can create problems for us and the school out of spite."

"Never mind neither you nor I can get a clear reading on her," Savannah adds from her corner.

"I've continued to try as well." He shakes his head as he stares at a spot on the floor. "Numerous times."

"Every time I've looked, the experience wasn't great." Savannah moves to stand behind my chair. She rests an arm over the back and leans her weight against it. "I think she is aware of someone looking deeper into her. The last time I tried to look into her, it was painful." Savannah shudders and I wonder what had happened.

I frown.

If anyone harms my friend, they will regret the day, because I will come for them, and they won't like it.

"We also experienced a feeling of being watched." I recall the memory and force back a shudder. "Things just didn't add up. She told me I was in the same room from when the trolls kidnapped me. The energy felt wrong the whole time. And though my aunt may seem a bit eccentric with her ways, she was particularly stand-offish. Not overwhelming but reserved and more quiet than usual." I shrug. "It's been like that each time I've been around her since she first came here." I settle my eyes on Gideon.

"We've established she's bad news, Wren," Jesse says. "Family or no, avoid her."

"Duh." I sit farther back into the chair. "I just wish I had gotten proof."

"I'm afraid all we can do from here is wait for her to make the next move." Gideon shrugs and weaves his fingers together in front of him. "But there is another topic I wish to touch base on." He sets his eyes on Savannah.

She stands straighter. "What did you find out?"

Apparently, while I was busy with training and spending time with Milo, Savannah had spoken to Gideon regarding the flu pandemic she overheard her father and brothers talking about.

"My sources tell me it doesn't look good. They can't get a clear motive, but they know the Order is behind it based on the unusual presentation of the illness and the sudden appearance. The council and magusari have been made aware and are taking care of everything as we speak."

Savannah sighs, tension leaving her shoulders as they slump forward a little. "Thank you so much."

Gideon nods. "Based on what they found with how the disease is being delivered and contracted, the magusari dispatched special healers to combat the progression, hopefully stopping anyone else from falling under the effects. But who, specifically within the Order is directing all of this, remains unclear.

"What about my father and my brothers? Are they—"

"They're safe and getting extra protection."

She nods and pulls out a letter from her sweater pocket. "My father sent me this, this morning. It's information he wanted me to pass on to you about a man in one of the infected towns that avoided him and refused to be examined. He had signs of the disease." She hands the letter to him. As his eyes rush over the words within the letter, Savannah continues, "It struck him as extremely odd since, naturally, everyone clamors to be treated. He believes it's magical in nature, designed to mimic a virus, intentionally introduced into poorer communities by agents of the Order."

Gideon nods as he folds the letter and sets it on the top of his desk behind him. "I'll make sure to report this.

"What in the world would the Order hope to accomplish infecting innocent humans?" I ask.

Milo clears his throat and steps forward. "Infecting humans and their sympathizers is just a test run. Those people are their guinea pigs."

Everyone turns their attention to Milo, who runs his hand through his hair and shoves both into his pants pockets.

"Continue," Gideon says with a nod.

"Think about it. Many wars throughout history started out with smaller populations. Small fights here, small fights there. Even disease and famine. It strikes the smaller, poorer communities because they are the easier targets, with less access to medicine, and less money to pay for it."

"The ultimate target being whom?" Jesse asks.

Soren's face becomes a mask of calm as he simply states, "Any mage who stands against them. If no one is willing to stand in the Order's way, that places them a step closer to ultimate power and ruling as they see fit. They'll finally emerge from the shadows to take what they believe is theirs."

The more I hear about this collective, the more I really dislike them.

"So, they are itching for a new world order, where they rank supreme and they are two steps ahead in that plan, which is to take out all their opposition before making themselves known?" A pinch forms in my forehead and I rub at the spot to ease the throb.

"Gideon..." Soren says. "You know what has to be done."

He shakes his head, lips pressed into a firm line. "I'll take care of it. Meanwhile, I think this meeting is over. Let your father know that it's going to be handled. I'll ask for extra protection details as well. We'll do whatever we can to make sure as few innocent lives are lost as possible."

Savannah throws her arms around Gideon. "Thank you so much for this."

At first, Gideon seems shocked. Eventually, he hugs her back, a gentle one. Nothing like what he gives me. He pats her on the back, mutters a quick "welcome," and pulls her arms from around his shoulders.

Savannah doesn't seem to mind. She steps back and says, "I've got someone waiting on me." She spins and winks at me, and I know exactly who she's talking about. A hot date with her mentor from the trials.

I chuckle under my breath and wave goodbye to her.

"Speaking of hot dates," Jesse says as though he just read my mind. He settles his intense, steel blue eyes on me. "Don't we have some sparring to do?"

"I believe we do." I rise from my seat and walk past him. When I don't hear footsteps following me, I turn at the waist. "You coming, or not?"

"Aye, Captain." He peels himself from his seat and joins me.

"See you guys later," I wave at Gideon, Milo, and Soren. All of them watching with varying degrees of jealousy. What can I say? It's Jesse's turn to have time with me. But their looks do cause me to laugh again.

CHAPTER EIGHTEEN

My back hits the ground *hard*.

The breath leaves my lungs and I cough through the dust cloud that encircles me. For Jesse's playful demeanor, he knows how to deliver a hit. The toes of his shoes stop just an inch before my shoulders and he leans over me, waving at the air to clear away the dust.

With a smile, he clicks his tongue at me. "You do realize the point is for you to stay on your feet, right?"

I wink. "I just felt like the ground needed a hug."

He quirks an eyebrow. "Slamming against the dirt doesn't equal hugging. Are you sure you didn't hit your head?"

"I don't know," I say, milking this for all it's worth. "Why don't you check and see."

He smiles knowingly. "Nice try, darlin'. But that trick is one of my faves."

"Can't blame a girl for trying." I kick my feet in the air and tighten my stomach muscles as I land on my feet. My latest trick I've learned, thanks to Jesse. But instead of standing, I kick out my leg behind me and land a blow to his shin. His foot slides back and he lands on his other knee while I follow through, spinning to face him and standing straight, taking a step back out of range of his grasping hand trying to grip my thigh to sweep my feet from underneath me again.

"Nice try, love." I snicker, waiting for him to climb back to his feet.

Instead, he looks up at me, a daring glare in his eyes and I realize what he's trying to do.

"Cheater."

He smiles deviously as he appears to be standing still.

Adorable asshole move, but it's working.

The illusion of him still crouched on the ground is set, and I have to clear my mind and breathe slowly to listen for the slightest move that he's about to take me out for the fifteenth time. Unfortunately, I become aware of the first fourteen as my back stings and burns. I'm probably going to be bruised, but a potion should fix the pain part.

A click echoes from my right, it's faint, but it's there. Another soft crunch comes from behind me, muted and almost detectable, but one of the benefits of Jesse sparring with me is also learning how to fight through an illusion.

A whisper of a breeze floats to me from my left, and it's the tell-tale sign of an incoming attack. I quickly block it and parry with a front kick. It lands with a grunt and the illusion fades away, revealing my illusionist doubled over, clutching his gut.

"I'm learning to regret teaching you my secrets, woman."

I fake a pouty face. "Poor baby."

He chuckles and winces. "I may have to take a potion this round. Impressive."

I blush. "I have an amazing teacher."

He stands straighter. "Better than Soren?"

"Don't go there." I chide him playfully. "You all have a special, irreplaceable place in my heart."

He shrugs. "Have to know where I measure up. It's a guy thing. Besides, sharing you is hard enough." He pauses to think about that more. "If I had it my way, you'd never leave my bed."

"Thank the gods *that's* not the case."

"Any better ideas to keep you from getting into mischief without me?" His face becomes serious as he stands straighter and settles his intense gaze on me. His sweaty hair dangles in ringlets.

I cock my head to the side. "It's amazing you and Soren don't get along better. You actually have a lot more in common than you think."

"Never tell him that." He smirks.

Instantly, I detect the tell of another illusion being set.

"Nice try. I got you had on this one."

His image in front of me chuckles. "Do you now?"

I suck in a breath of surprise. His voice comes from everywhere around me, like there are speakers amplifying his voice in every direction.

"How did you do that?" I spin around, searching for any flaw in the details that surround me.

"You have to catch me to find out." His voice comes out the same.

I spin in circles searching for him, but I can't see him anywhere. There's no hint to his presence and it's almost as if he disappeared out of thin air.

"Challenge accepted."

His laughs bubbles through the air. "I'm rubbing off on you."

"Keep that between us," I add. "Can't let the world know you're corrupting me."

"Am I?" He asks.

I still can't see him. Though I'm still trying to figure out where he is. "Maybe."

"Tease."

"You love it."

"Indeed, I do." His voice seems proud. Lighthearted. I wonder what the tell could be in a scenario like this. I narrow my eyes on my surroundings, nitpicking each detail for the tiniest hint of a flaw that would indicate where he is.

Better than just a simple training session, I'm having fun.

He makes it easy for me to see the lighter side of things, and I adore that about him. My magic—rather, my meteorite—may have chosen him, but I'm grateful to have him in my life. I wouldn't want it any other way.

"Think fast," he says and tackles me to the ground from my right.

He softens the crash to the ground with one arm around my back and a hand cradling my head.

The world blurs in the seconds that I'm falling to the ground. In the process, I twist to face him, landing on my back within a soft patch of grass. He settles on top of me and we lock eyes for a moment.

"Good thing grass is forgiving, or I wouldn't have any skin left." He searches my eyes for something.

"Couldn't have that now, could we?" I wink and he chuckles, stomach vibrating against mine as I'm sandwiched between him and the grass.

"No, the horror of a scar. Can you imagine, this perfect complexion marred by a scar?"

"Ghastly."

He brushes my copper-red hair from my face and trails his fingers along my cheek to my neck. Within a blink, his mouth crashes into mine, parting my lips and sliding his tongue along mine, sending delicious waves of heat down my spine. Warmth settles between my thighs and I clench his shirt in my fists as I drown in the passion of his kiss.

"I think I have a much more comfortable spot where we can finish this game of ours," Jesse says. In a flash, he portals us to his room and pushes me against the bed where he showers me with kisses and lovely, delightful touches that sends my nerves into an erratic mess.

This man of mine. He knows how to make me laugh and let go of all the seriousness life has to offer. I'd be lost without him.

CHAPTER NINETEEN

Despite the cooling temps of fall, the sun provides unseasonable warmth, soaking into my skin. It's a welcome sensation.

Jesse and Milo are having a light-hearted debate about whether or not history is a necessary component in a solid, well-rounded education for a mage while Savannah and I enjoy the sun that breaks through the canopy of trees. I've tuned my men out for the moment. Their conversation become hard to follow at times.

We sit in an orchard, waiting for Lady Alene to begin class.

Jesse bumps against me.

I narrow my gaze on his handsome face, his steel blue eyes ensnaring me. "Can I help you?"

"What do you think?" he asks.

I shrug. "I stopped paying attention to your debate a while ago."

"We're past that. What I wanted to know is if you thought it was weird the patron mage of our school is teaching a class."

"What's so weird about it?" Savannah asks.

"She's probably bored and enjoys helping," I say. "Why shouldn't she be allowed to teach a class?"

Milo leans forward, catching my attention. "I think it's because she's lived what we are learning now. She has first-hand experience."

"Right," Savannah adds. "She's been there, done that. Why can't she share that knowledge with us?"

"Exactly." I nod in Savannah's direction. I breathe in deep the intoxicating smell of drying leaves and the ripening fruit from the trees that blends with the scent of salt from the ocean that is close by. We're away from the castle, and part of me wonders if these are the trees from the trials I had gone through.

"Patron Mage, and my general displeasure with the subject aside," Jesse says, "I think it's weird. We're learning from a statue."

"You'll get over it." I bump him with my elbow.

As the last of our classmates arrive, Lady Alene moves to the center of the small circle of benches in the middle of the orchard. "Good afternoon, class. We have a lot to cover today. Let us begin."

She centers herself within the circle of students and waves her hand in a wide arc. Instantly, a white light fills the area. Just like before, it feels like I'm surrounded by clouds. Images begin to take shape, first in the forms of shadows, then becoming clearer, and filling in with color and light.

"Long ago," Lady Alene says, voice as soft as a whisper, coming from all around us, "mages worked alongside humanity."

Images of mages dressed in robes, almost like monks, walk in groups within crowds of others. The clothing is old, reminding me of a time before time, where magic was more commonplace and known. Women wear long dresses with bell sleeves and belts made of silver, rope, or golden cloth around their waists. Most keep their hair tied back in a braid decorated with flowers or gem-adorned chains. The men don thick vests made of cloth or leather. Most have a dagger, sword, or bow with them. Some have a combination of the three.

In the pictures that flash around me, the roads aren't paved but made of dirt. Horses were the main vehicle of travel, and carts full of goods sat in front of doors to shops, while children played and danced as their mothers worked on their daily chores.

It reminds me of simplicity, harmony, and general basic living. Growing up, I often wondered what it would be like to live in this era. Now, I'm getting a very close idea.

I smile, loving it all.

"Things were much simpler in this time." Lady Alene's voice breaks through, narrating the images. It's almost like watching a life-like movie. Or living a dream. "How do I know?"

The image shifts to a woman in white robes, adorned in silver armor, with long blond hair braided, flowing down her back like a waterfall. The image pans to face her, and the woman is gorgeous! Blue eyes as deep as the ocean glitter with light and love. She smiles at a small child pulling on her hands, and it's like staring into the sun with all its dazzling brilliance.

"Because I lived it."

She follows the child through a plank door, disappearing into a tavern.

"That woman is me."

A series of oohs and ahs echo from far away as the images change, focusing on life all around the world. Each still image flashes for only a second before changing again.

"Despite the differences between all these places, there were many things we all had in common. To list a few, food was grown and consumed locally, work was local as well, though we mages tended to travel to wherever we were needed."

I watch as Lady Alene works to bandage a leg, give potions to the sick, aid in developing tools to make life easier. All these things she has done, and more. The life she had lived seems rich and full. I wonder if that's why she became a Patron Mage.

As time progresses within the scenes that continuously flash before my eyes, I notice things like technological advances becoming more prominent. Things that started as much more rudimentary forms of communication morphed into cell phones. Horses and wagons and carts turned into trucks, vans, and trailers.

"Yes, magic is the basis of all scientific and technological advances that we know and love today. Things you all take for granted were once luxuries. Even computers…"

The images that she shows next flash through books, blending together into a machine meant to advance life and progress human evolution. Wires emerge as the books seem to fold into themselves, collapsing and becoming flat before shifting into metal, with wires and chips, until a computer stands in its place.

"In my time, we didn't have to hide who we were. We were accepted as wise men and women who guided communities, and as doctors, healing diseases."

The images change to show a collection of potions and bandages.

"We were accepted as soldiers."

Once again, the images change, showing mages defending villages, kingdoms, and protecting travelers from predators.

"But as we helped to progress humanity as a whole, the need for us became less and less, forcing us to blend in and take on the professions our talents were best suited for."

The images fade to black, turning into blurring shadows before blending into a white cloud-like light that surrounds Lady Alene. The light dims, bringing our world back into focus.

Lady Alene's arms come to rest at her sides as her stony features take in the faces of all the students surrounding her. "Any questions?"

A student from the House of Winterwolf raises his hand. She calls on him.

"How did you become a Patron Mage?" His voice is

annoying. It's like nails on a chalk board, and I wince as he speaks.

She smiles as she answers him. "That is a tragic tale. One that I may share with a select few of you. But that is not covered in this course."

The kid actually pouts. I quirk an eyebrow and shake my head. "Grow up."

Jesse snickers next to me.

I set my glaring gaze on my adorable joker. He pretends that he doesn't notice, but he does. I know he does.

"Any other questions?" Lady Alene asks.

No hands raise into the air, and part of me is grateful for that. Sure, I have questions. But none of which I'm willing to ask in front of a crowd of students. If I ever get the chance to just hang out with Lady Alene, maybe I'll ask them then.

"Very well. Our next topic is Blackbriar and when she became an academy."

Interesting. This is not the first time I've heard of Blackbriar being referred to as a girl. Strangely, it fits.

And the more I think about it, the more I like it. This island is more than just a home to me. She's like a world all her own. The island provides shelter, food, freedoms most only dream of. She protects us. And that resonates within me on a level that stirs my soul.

Lady Alene walks around the wide circle as she speaks. And by walking, I mean gliding weightlessly over the ground as she never seems to leave a trace of where her stone feet have been. No track in the dirt left by the edges of the skirt that's part of her permanent form.

"Blackbriar Castle was once home to a very prominent and famous mage of the time, Lord Cormac." There is a hitch to her voice. It was heart breaking to hear it. I frown as I stare at the back of Lady Alene's head.

Savannah leans closer and whispers. "I heard Lord Cormac was her husband."

"That explains the pain in her voice," I whisper back.

She nods. "They were a power couple."

I wonder what that would look like. But if it's true, or if another student heard the emotion in her voice, no one shows it. And Lady Alene doesn't confirm that fact. Instead, she continues on.

"The castle itself was built in the year five-hundred fifty-six. Upon Lord Cormac's passing in the year six-hundred-six, he established his once vast and beautiful home as the academy we now know and love today. As of now, Blackbriar Academy is one of seven academies across the world considered to be the most prestigious. You are among the precious few who are qualified to attend."

Her voice floats over the air as she speaks with such love for the island. It's magical and uplifting. It's easy to see that this place is her home.

"In human terms, this is considered an ivy-league school. The best of the best. So do not take your education here for granted. Have pride in Blackbriar, and wear your colors well."

CHAPTER TWENTY

"Another place of historical value is Crimson Isles."

Lady Alene continues to move within the circle of students as she lets that next bit of information settle between us.

"I know this place!" Savannah says. "The string of islands got their name because of the way the sands glow red during sunrise and sunset."

"There's my little informant." I smile. "I've missed you."

She chuckles to herself. "Well, I can't just give you all the information, now can I? You have to figure some stuff out for yourself."

"I appreciate that."

"I thought you would." She winks.

Jesse leans in to whisper in my ear. "I can take you to some of the lesser-known places. Ones that will require you to be in the most tantalizing positions."

I playfully roll my eyes and shake my head. "Of course, you can."

Milo looks up from his note taking. "I call dibs on showing her the library."

"It's a date." I smile at him. It's fitting that he would want to show me the library, and I can't wait for that to happen. His eyes widen with excitement at the mention of a date with me. He grins from ear to ear, and that expression makes my heart flutter.

"Everyone has already been to Crimson Isles, I take it?"

My group nods.

"You haven't?" Jesse asks.

I shake my head. "Is that a bad thing?"

He smiles mischievously. "You're in for a real treat then."

Lady Alene's voice reclaims my attention. "In December, we will visit Crimson Isles for the Mage Championships."

A rush of excitement takes over and Lady Alene smiles. "Yes, it is very exciting, however, none of you will be allowed to participate as students."

A series of disappointed sounds works its way through the class.

"Is that new?" I ask Savannah. "The rule about students participating."

She shrugs. "They have contests where students are allowed to participate, but they are normally competitions that are just for fun. The championships are dangerous. There are just too many liabilities."

"How dangerous?" I ask.

"Very." Her amethyst eyes are serious. "I've seen some pretty devastating injuries come from them."

"Our attendance," Lady Alene adds, "is in support of one of our own professors."

She casts a glance toward me, and Jesse jabs me with his elbow again.

"Professor McCallister will represent not only our academy, but our country as well," Lady Alene continues.

I suck in a breath. "Why is he keeping all this stuff from me?"

Savannah shakes her head, crossing her legs and weaving her fingers over her knee. "Men. That's what they do."

I press my lips into a hard line. "Well that's not going to fly."

She bumps me with her shoulder. "Relax, he probably has it wrapped in a surprise, complete with a nice little bow."

"I don't like surprises." I cross my arms over my chest and huff.

She laughs under her breath. "I'm sure he has a perfectly good reason."

"He had better."

"She's right," Jesse says, and the fact he's sticking up for Soren is a shock in and of itself.

"You're kidding me." It is very much a statement, not a question. Still, he seems to feel the need to respond.

"Take it easy on him, he's not able to spend as much time with you now, and he's trying to do nice things for you."

"Killing himself is not a great start," I mutter.

"If anyone could come through the Championships, it's Soren." Milo gives an affirmative nod.

"Not you too." Can't a girl just be angry with one of her men anymore? At the same time, it's nice to see them sticking together.

"As our instruction time draws to an end," Lady Alene announces, "I want to talk about the harvest festival. To end the class, we will pick apples for our enchanted cider."

"Oh! I love the harvest festival!" Savannah practically dances in her seat. "So much fun!"

"Okay…" I say, dragging out the word.

She shakes her head. "You'll find out soon enough."

Lady Alene steps closer to me as she explains the festival. "This is the celebration of a cycle drawing to a close. It is a celebration of abundance and prosperity as well. This is the chance to reflect and prepare for new and exciting things to come. It is an important celebration full of rituals and coming together as a community to uplift each other and celebrate the bounty of the year."

I smile as she sets her stony gaze on me. Her expression is light and full of hope and wonder.

"Now for the apple-picking!" she claps her hands and a flash of blue light with silver specs of glitter fills the space between them. "Baskets are located at the bases of the trees. As you pick your fruit, keep in mind all that you are grateful for. That helps to make the cider especially sweet."

She gestures toward the trees surrounding us with a nod, signaling that it's time to start.

"You three have fun with your apples. I'm on another mission." Jesse smirks to himself.

"What mischief are you planning on getting yourself into?" I ask, narrowing my eyes on him.

"Herbs, my dear. Herbs. Can't have cider without them."

I quirk an eyebrow. "If you're thinking about spiking the punch and getting everyone on the island on some sort of psychedelic trip, you are wrong."

"Who said anything about psychedelic trips or everyone? Even though I like your thinking, I sometimes wonder if you know me at all." He shakes his head playfully. After a few seconds, he shrugs. "Part of the fun will be finding a cozy, secluded spot after a few cups of my special cider."

With that he disappears through the trees. I stare after him, gawking. "He's going to be the death of me."

"He better not be." Savannah and Milo speak at the same time, look at each other and start laughing.

"Whoa. What have you two been doing?" I ask jokingly.

They each take one of my arms and pull me toward the trees.

I smile. This is the life.

While picking apples, I think about the Crimson Isles. I've never been, but I want to know more about the place before going and having to watch Soren battle it out with other mages.

"What are the Crimson Isles anyway?" I ask.

Savannah chuckles. "Only the greatest place in the world."

"It's a string of islands," Milo adds, "that gets its name because the dirt and sand surrounding the islands turn red during sunrise and sunset."

I lean in closer as he helps me reach an apple just out of reach of the tips of my fingers. "That sounds amazing."

"It's also the home of the magusari," Savannah adds. "Which is where the championships are being held."

"Don't remind me," I mutter. I'm going to give Soren hell for this. I smirk as a plan forms in the back of my mind. We're supposed to meet up later for a date. And I have just the idea to make him squirm.

"It's not really that bad. Mages are tough and fast healers." Savannah nods to me. I get it. I've healed rather quickly from some of my more brutal encounters, thanks to potions and quick thinking from her.

"True," I admit. "What else can you tell me about the Isles."

"They're older than even Blackbriar." Jesse pokes his head from around a tree. "Riddled with enchantments and lore and mystery." He bobs his eyebrows as he talks in a low voice, hamming up the mystery with just his words.

I laugh. "Awesome."

"It's home to unicorns," Savannah adds. "The only known place where they can be supported and protected from humans."

"Protected from humans?" I ask.

Milo lifts me up to help me reach another apple. "There are wards and enchantments keeping the place hidden. It's more protection for them and from them."

"Oh."

"But the night life." Jesse kisses the tips of his fingers. "Exquisite."

"It's like a world of its own," Savannah adds. "You'll love it. Trust me."

I smile as I think of the wonder and enchantment the place must have for everyone to be so excited to go. "I already do."

CHAPTER TWENTY-ONE

I peek around the doorway, finding Soren sitting at his desk grading papers.

Smiling to myself, I formulate a plan in my head. We're supposed to spend some time together, but he seems so focused on whatever is on his desk that he doesn't even notice me standing in the door now.

Silent as a ghost, I move quietly through the room, careful not to make a sound with my steps. I make it to the white board and let out a breath, slowly.

Without looking up from his papers, he says, "You'll have to do a better job than that to sneak up on me."

I stop mid-step and pout. "You're no fun."

"I'm plenty fun." He grins, still focused on his papers.

"Yeah. I see that." I cross my arms and refuse to move until he looks up at me.

He huffs as he angrily marks a page with furious strokes of his pen. "You know what I mean."

I nod, even though he doesn't see it, and I spin on my heels to lean against the white board. "Do I? I think your fun button broke. Along with your watch." I add that last part to drive home my point.

He finally looks up at me, and his brow furrows with confusion before checking the watch on his wrist. "Shit. I'm sorry."

"Is this going to be a normal thing now?" In my best "professor" tone, I add, "Tardiness is unacceptable, Professor McCallister."

He groans. "Damn it, woman. It's a job. One I took to stay close to you. Now, come here."

I bite the corner of my lower lip and fight against the smile trying to break free. I don't want to let him off that easy. He's going to have to really work at it. I shake my head, staying put. "Nope. I rather like this spot. I'm starting to see what you love so much about it."

Out of the corner of my eye, I see him pinch the bridge of his nose. "I deal with obstinance all day long. Bring it here, woman."

I tap my chin. "Hmm… No, I think I'll just stand here and wait for my *date*."

He chuckles under his breath. It's sarcastic more than humorous, but that's the point. He's in hot water with me, and he damn well knows it. "Come here, *now*."

I quirk an eyebrow and turn my head to look at him, glaring. "Or what?"

"If I have to come and get you, I'm bending you over this desk and spanking you."

I chuckle. "Oh, really? Should I go and pick out my own paddle as well?"

His face contorts into an expression of disgust. "No. I wouldn't be that rough with you."

I shrug. "Suit yourself. I was up for a little role-playing."

"That's taking things a bit far, Wren."

"It's better than being stood up," I say, letting a little more of my "fake-ish" frustration through.

He sighs and stands from his chair, pointing to the ground at his feet. I pull away from the white board, keeping my arms crossed over my chest, facing him with my chin raised. Groaning, he storms forward.

In a few quick seconds, he's in front of me. Without missing a beat, he bends me over, pressing his shoulder against my tummy and grips the back of my legs, lifting me into the air. I'm hanging over his shoulder, laughing as he spins with me and carries me back toward his desk. I'm still laughing as my butt rests firmly on the top of the hardwood desk.

"You were saying?" He asks, catching my gaze and keeping me pulled into his amber eyes.

"I believe it's you who was saying something." I talk between laughs. "What? No spankings?"

"You ruined that one with your paddle comment." His voice is low and dangerous.

I love it.

Playing with fire.

"First of all..." My voice comes out even, finally sobered from my bout of belly laughs. "That was a question. Secondly, you're late for our date. I reserve the right to give you endless hell for that."

He lowers his head with a sigh. Both hands are propped up on the desk on either side of me, and his face is within inches of my own. I wait for him to look at me. The moment he does, I kiss him.

"Does this mean you forgive me?" He asks between our kisses.

"On that part at least," I say as he pulls away.

"What else are you not happy with me about?" His gaze is serious and it's hard not to get pulled into them. To fall into his amber eyes and just be in the moment. But I can't let this go.

"Oh, you know, having to find out through Lady Alene, Savannah, and Jesse that you're participating in the Mage Championships, which is apparently deadly. And it's not so much that you are doing that, but the fact that I had to find out through them."

"You know about that?" He groans. "Damn it."

I don't back off. "We even picked apples for the cider for the harvest festival. Were you planning on telling me then? Or was it going to be after Jesse spikes my drink with aphrodisiacs? Are you two in on something I should be aware of?"

He rests his forehead on mine again. "Can't a man keep a surprise for once?"

I quirk an eyebrow. "What, exactly, is the surprise? You die?"

"No!" He pulls back sharply, eyebrows knitted together as he glares at me. "It's your first trip to Crimson Isles. I had a special room set up for us to share and I had planned a dinner and tour as well. The Championship is just that. It's not as dangerous as you were told it is. Believe me."

I shrug. "Don't like teaching so much you have to go risk life and limb to show off a little? Is it really that boring?"

"I love teaching. I'm thinking about doing it for as long as I can." His gaze drops to my thighs as he lets out a heavy sigh. "I love teaching *you*."

I let out a sarcastic snicker. "Nice try. Spill."

He pulls away from the desk and runs his hands over his face. "I'm gonna kill Jesse."

"No, you won't." I lean back on his desk. "He stood up for you. Mentioned it being a surprise." I roll my eyes. "I dislike those, by the way."

He gawks at me like I've grown another head.

I chuckle. "I know, I am just as shocked as you."

"I had planned on telling you about the Championships before now. I forgot about that being covered in class today." He squeezes his eyes shut and turns his face to the ceiling. "I've been training every weekend you're at your dad's. Even some evenings."

I nod. "Fair enough."

He closes the space between us, spreading my legs as he nestles between them. "I will work on keeping you more in the loop."

I smile. "You better."

He laughs under his breath as his hands cup my ass and forcefully pull me into his growing erection that presses ever so gently against my opening. He nibbles on my chin, moving to my neck, tantalizing the sensitive spot just below my ear, sending waves of warmth through me, settling between my thighs.

His hands move. One supports my back while the other grips the back of my head, fingers weaving through my red hair as his mouth collides with mine. I melt into him, giving in to the growing need building inside me.

He buries his face into my neck and hair as he breaths in deep and lets out a groan. "I wish you could stay with me tonight."

"Who says I can't?" I ask.

He pulls back with a serious look. "Students aren't allowed in the faculty wing."

"Without special permission," I add.

A flash of confusion crosses his eyes. It's there and then gone just as quickly. "I like your thinking."

I snicker as he pulls me even closer to him, continuing where he left off as though we never stopped.

His hand travels down my back to my thigh, inching closer to the hem of my skirt. Sliding his fingers underneath the fabric, his fingers flick at the elastic of my underwear and find their way to the sensitive flesh swollen with desire.

I moan as he works me into a growing orgasm. He sighs deliciously in response and plunges into me, curling and arching his fingers in delicious strokes that edge me ever so closer to release.

My climax nears its peak when a knock sounds on the door.

All at once, everything disappears and I suck in a deep breath that flushes through my system, further sobering me from the heated sexual tension.

Soren groans with aggravation as he pulls away. Helping me off the desk, he pulls me into him in a tight hug. "To be continued."

I smile and pull away. "It's a date. And you'd better not be late this time." I shove a finger into his chest.

He grunts, rubbing the spot. "Wouldn't dream of it." His lips quirk as his amber eyes take in my mouth.

I kiss him quickly, one last time before I walk away. I'm going to really make him work for the next one. All the ways I want to tease and pleasure him fills my thoughts as I walk out of the classroom.

CHAPTER TWENTY-TWO

This week has flown by, and now I'm at Gideon's estate, sitting in the kitchen with my dad while he makes goulash. The aroma of the spices fills the air, and it reminds me of a time before the trolls.

More and more, the effects of my time in captivity fades away into just a mere ghost of a memory. It's a true testament to how far I have come. My past is imperfect, messy, and painful... but it won't control my future. I've learned from it and will continue growing stronger. Though I know I have a great deal more to conquer, I'm grateful to have made it this far.

Most especially, having my father back.

"We picked apples for the harvest festival." I take the spoon next to the pot and dip it inside, pulling up a spoonful of the delicious mixture.

My father taps me gently on the arm. "Don't spoil it."

I chuckle at his soft way of telling me to wait. It's been so long since I've heard that. I set the spoon back down next to the pot and go take a seat at the table.

"How did you like the apple picking?"

"It was fun. Blackbriar sure has a lot of traditions they love to keep up with."

He chuckles as he stirs the pot. His head bobs up and down as he taps the spoon against the side of the large pot before setting it on the holder resting on the counter. With a stretch and yawn, he joins me at the table.

"They do, indeed. But our traditions are rooted in where we came from and who we are."

I nod. "True. I love it, even though I don't understand a lot of it."

He hums pensively. "That's my fault."

My eyebrows knit together. "No, it's not."

He stares at me for a few moments. Worry and hurt shine through his brown eyes, and it's almost as if he's searching mine for reassurance. I reach across the table and cover his hand with mine. "I don't blame you at all. I'm learning about it now, and that's what's important here. You are not at fault."

His brown eyes crinkle at the corners with his faint

smile. It's so different than with Aunt Patricia. He opens his mouth to say something but seems to think better of it and pauses. It takes him a few seconds to change gears. "What else is new?"

I shrug. "Nothing, really. Just more of the same stuff on different days."

I don't know if I want to share about the visit with my aunt just yet. He has enough to worry about, and I can't do anything about it unless Aunt Patricia makes her next move. Nothing adds up as seamlessly as I really want it to. There are still so many missing pieces to the puzzle that I wonder if we will ever know for sure. And just when it seems my father is on the verge of sharing something, he gets nervous and shuts down.

What does he want to tell me?

Beyond that, I'm not sure what to say. I don't think conversations are my strong suit with my father. What do I say? What am I supposed to do? What's okay and what's not?

My mind spins with numerous questions rushing through my head. The only thing I have to go off of is how things were when I was younger. The only memories that remain are from a time where things were so much simpler, and a mysterious order of mages wasn't after me or my family.

"What's the same then?" He gets it, I think. Always knowing what to ask to keep a conversation going.

Hell, for all I know, this is just as awkward for him, and he needs just as much time getting used to all of this.

He has been through his own share of nightmares. Things he has to come to terms with as well.

So, maybe that's part of how alike we are. But it still doesn't quell my suspicion that he's holding back.

"Classes, training, hanging out with my friends. Things like that." I take in a breath of the aroma from dinner through my nose. "What about you? Are you bored yet?"

"I have plenty around here to keep me busy."

"Like what?" I stand to grab bowls and spoons. As I near the oven, the smell of the garlic bread mixes in with the goulash and it's a heavenly, mouthwatering scent.

He chuckles. "Isn't it my job to interrogate you?"

I look over my shoulder and smirk. "Oh, is that what this is? An interrogation? You do know that most parents don't use that term with their kids."

And just like that, we're laughing and poking fun at each other. Though I'm still slowly adjusting to being a daughter again, I have to admit that this feels *good*.

Albeit, things are still a little different after having lived so long without him. But the more time I spend with him, the more things just click and become easier. I hope we stay on this path. Maybe then he'll feel comfortable enough to share more about his time with the Order.

There's still a part of me that is worried I'll push too hard and end up losing him again. Worried he will disappear once more and never be found. It's an unsettling thought that makes tears bite at my eyes, a lump form in my throat, and an iron weight fill my stomach.

I clear my throat and push that fear back. My focus is on making the time I do get with my father the best it can be.

"What about your men?" he asks with a knowing smile. Even though I don't physically see it, I hear it in his voice.

Heat fills my cheeks and I'm glad that I have my back to him.

"Soren is competing in the Mage Championships this year. Blackbriar is going to show him support." I set the bowls down next to the pot and pick up the spoon to stir the contents, releasing more of the savory scent into the air.

"You'll love Crimson Isles. I had hoped to take you there when you were much younger." His voice trails off as though he's slipping into his own thoughts, recalling memories of things that hold some level of regret within them. He sighs. "Just never worked out for us."

"None of us had a real choice in the things that happened, Dad. I get it. All we can do is make the best of the time we're given, right?" I replace the spoon and rejoin him at the table.

"Right." He narrows his eyes on me, hanging on to his smile. "When did you get so wise?"

"I have a few great teachers. And it's one of the many things I got from you."

"Indeed." The timer over the stove goes off and my father leaves the table to fill our bowls with the wonderful smelling goulash. "What about Gideon, Jesse, and Milo?" He asks while taking the garlic bread out of the oven.

"What about them?"

He looks over his shoulder at me. "How are they doing? What's new with them?"

The first thing I have to do once I clear my father's name is have him get out more so that his sole source of news isn't the goings-on of me and my men. But still, I'm glad that he cares enough to ask.

"Gideon? We haven't had much time together. He's been busy doing headmaster things. Jesse is Jesse."

He laughs. It's such a deep, gut laugh. I enjoy the sound of it. "When you can use his own name as a description, that says a lot."

"You have no idea." I leave it at that. I'm not sure delving into the details of Jesse is what my father is bargaining for. I believe he knows enough about him as it is to have a generalized idea.

Two steaming bowls of goulash are sat on the table, and my father places the garlic bread pan on a potholder on the table in between us. Once he's settled back in, he picks up his spoon. "And Milo?"

"Milo is good. Never ceases to amaze me with his cleverness."

"Oh? How so?"

I shrug and dig into my goulash. The flavors dance along my tongue and I'm in heaven. "This is delicious."

"I'm glad you like it, but you're not answering my question."

I meet my father's serious gaze.

I suppose I can't put it off any longer.

Here goes nothing.

I set my spoon down and take a deep breath. On the exhale, I dig into the story. "When we raided the Arizona facility, thinking you were there, we found a collection of papers that looked like some sort of blueprints."

My father's eyes darken, and his lips pull down at the corners.

"He grabbed all the ones he could find and put them together. It's some sort of machine, but they're incomplete."

"How so?"

"Missing pages. Some of them seem intentional according to the order of the pages."

He nods.

"When he showed them to me, I was wearing a set of enchanted glasses and saw that there was an emblem on one of the pages. I recognized it as something I had seen before at Aunt Patricia's house."

"You did?" he asks, almost shocked, but impressed at the same time.

"You already know this don't you?" I shared. Now, it's his turn.

Honestly, I'm not sure I want to know the answer. This could go one of two ways. He knows of the machine, what it does, what its purpose is, and that's because he works for the Order too. *Or*, his role in all of this is exactly what it has appeared to be this entire time. I'm hoping for the latter. My father *can't* be mixed up with the Order like my aunt.

Either way, I have to face the fact that the truth is going to be revealed. And I'm not sure I'm ready.

My father places his spoon next to his bowl and pushes it away. So far, this isn't looking good. He takes a few deep breaths to clear his thoughts and I prepare for the worst possible news I could ever hear.

"Milo is indeed smart. Almost too smart for his own good."

What?

My heart skips a beat, and I instinctively push myself a little farther away from my own father, giving myself enough of a gap to get the hell away from him once this goes south.

"Why do you say that?" I ask.

"That is the symbol of the Order. They put it on everything they do. It's always hidden. Mostly, it's revealed through a code word. However, I placed that symbol there, enchanting it so that only a person with a pure heart and intention is allowed to see it. Milo unlocked them."

"I don't…"

"Let me finish." He holds up a hand and his voice is soft and patient.

I don't like where this is going. At. All.

"I made the machine based on a design that was given to me with very little information on what its purpose was. However, in creating the blueprints, I figured everything out." He bows his head as his brow furrows in frustration. His hands form fists on top of the table.

It's hard to tell what his next reaction will be, and I don't like it. I quickly look for my path of escape.

He sets his gaze on mine in a silent plea for me to remain seated. "It's designed to pull the meteorite out of your body. It was designed for you. Because my skill specializes in unique powers and not only where, but how to find them. I tried to sabotage the project by leaving out pages from the blueprints so that its completion could be delayed."

He lets that settle between us for a moment, so that I can connect the dots. But I don't need time to connect. They are laid out for me. My father's specialty is finding powers like mine. The Order enslaved my father, forcing him to work on finding the meteorite that I have inside me. It appears they were pulling out all the stops for that. He was in a tough position and did what he could with what little resources he had.

"So, you purposefully left directions and designs out so that they couldn't complete it?"

He nods. "Because the machine won't just extract the shard out of you, Wren. It will kill you."

I frown. "Why didn't you tell anyone about this? Why didn't you tell *me*?"

"Because of the way you're looking at me now." His voice is soft, full of pain. His eyes take on a glossy sheen and I realize he's on the verge of tears.

"You could have destroyed them." I pull my gaze away and stare at a spot on the table. "You could've burned them."

He shakes his head. "They watched me too closely. The only reason I was able to get away with what I did was because, at first, they didn't know there was anything missing. I withheld strategic parts whose absence would take time to be noticed. That room you walked into was what was left after they confronted me about the missing pages. They caught onto what I was doing and demanded that I finish the plans, or they were going to deliver you to me piece by piece. I had no choice."

"And the missing pages?" I ask.

He points to his temple.

"That's why they kept you alive? Because you have the only way to fix the machine?"

"They knew if they killed me, their chance at a completed machine would die with me. It gave me leverage to ensure that they wouldn't cross the line and go after you."

Well I'll be damned. That's where I get my cleverness from. My father was the key to the blueprints this entire time, staring me in the face and asking about school.

And I didn't even see it until now.

CHAPTER TWENTY-THREE

I blow out a raspberry and lean back into the chair.

There's so much to process here. I know he was doing his best with what he was given, trying to hang on until he could find a way to escape the Order. I just wish that he had revealed this sooner instead of being afraid I'd shun him.

Shaking my head, I try to make sense of it all.

"I had hoped you wouldn't find the pages. I didn't have time to collect them before I ran. I know how this looks, and I won't blame you if you want to go back to Blackbriar. But please know that I'd do anything to protect you and I'll be damned if they ever complete that machine."

I turn my attention to him. I see the sadness and regret in his eyes. He's nothing like my aunt. "I believe you. You were forced by the Order, unlike Aunt Patricia. But, my men need to know about this."

"Of course. I wouldn't have it any other way." He pauses to mull over that for a moment. "They are very protective of you. I'm happy you have them."

My lips stretch into a grin at the thought of them. "Yeah. Me too."

"I'm truly sorry, Wren. I didn't want you to hate me for this and part of me felt like I was protecting you by not revealing this sooner."

My gaze softens as it settles on him. "We're a family. No more secrets. We can't protect each other if we can't be open with each other. I'll be right back."

Before he can say anything else, I leave the table and head to the room I've stayed in each time I've come to visit. It's a basic room, with all the necessary furnishings. Its simplicity is appealing, yet it doesn't detract from the rest of the house's grandeur.

I sit on the side of my bed and pull out a piece of paper and pen from the drawer of the nightstand. With quick strokes, I write, *Need you here, pronto.*

Within moments, the letter dissolves in fire, disappearing into the air with just a hint of ashes collecting on the surface of the nightstand.

Standing from the bed, I heave a heavy sigh.

Now, we wait.

Within hours, my men arrive in the backyard of Gideon's estate. They enter through the back door that leads to the eat-in kitchen and gather around with wide eyes and concerned expressions.

Gideon approaches the table, letting out a deep breath from his lungs. His shoulders relax a bit and he leans over the table, eyeing my father and me with urgency. "What's the problem?"

I almost become lost in his blue-green eyes. Lost in the depths of them, in their concern. But I prevent that for the most part. I clear my throat. "I know what the blueprints are."

Gideon's eyebrows knit together as his lips pull into a taught frown. "And that is?"

"A machine designed to forcefully remove the meteorite from Wren," my father answers. He rolls his tongue in his mouth as if reacting to a bitter taste.

The other three of my men instantly surround me, ready for battle. Ready to whisk me away at a moment's notice because, like me, they automatically assume my father is responsible. The only one that doesn't move is Gideon.

"Explain." That one word leaves no room for questioning.

My father nods and digs into his story, recounting everything he's told me.

"How did you learn of the symbol?" Milo asks.

"They use it for everything. To mark their locations, themselves, and how they communicate with each other." My father sits back in the chair and hangs an arm over the back of his seat. "They weren't planning on keeping me alive—or escaping, for that matter."

"That's it," Gideon says. "That's why we can't uncover any charges. They know all they have to do is sow seeds of doubt around you, make it difficult for you to show your face in public."

He nods. "My sister is also involved within the group, not just loosely connected. Based on what Wren told me, there's no doubt in my mind about that now."

"That has been my suspicion." I look to each of my men. "The only question that remains is why? What does she hope to gain in all of this? What's more important to her than her family?"

"Regardless," Soren says, "we stick to the plan. Stay away from her."

My father stands from the table and checks his watch. "It's late. You all should stay here for the night. Head back tomorrow." He pointedly looks at each of the men, skipping over me. There's a hidden message in that look, and I quirk an eyebrow because I know very well what that message is.

Stay here and help protect Wren.

He can't leave Gideon's estate, so he wants me here under his watchful eye.

I huff and cross my arms over my chest. "Not you too."

My father settles his gaze on me. "I'm still your father."

"No one is arguing that." I bury my face in my hands. Frustration doesn't even come close to what is going on in my body right now. "I don't need a protection detail."

"He's right," Gideon adds. "It's late. And, it's my house. We'll stay for the night."

I look from over the tips of my fingers, narrowing my eyes at him, hoping my glare says just exactly how little I care about this being his house or not. I'm not a freaking damsel. A fact I feel I have proven time and time again. Why is he even siding with my father and wanting to stay here tonight?

"Here we go again," Soren mutters. His footsteps lead away from me as he walks out of the dining room. "Dibs on Wren's room."

I roll my eyes and groan. "You're never going to give that up, are you?"

Milo places a hand on my shoulder. "Remember what we talked about in the library?"

Yes. He's referring to the meteorite and feeling the same thing I feel when they're near. But with an added dose of the need to protect mixed in there.

Frowning, I nod.

"It's in our blood." He gestures to his chest. "The need to protect you. That is never going to go away."

"I know. I'm not asking it to." I rise from my chair and face my men. "I just want you all to understand I don't need to be held under lock and key or escorted everywhere. I want you to understand and recognize I am able to protect myself. Stop assuming I'm delicate and fragile."

"As long as we're coming clean and sharing the whole truth, it's probably useful for you to know that they can also use the symbol to track." My father's voice comes out soft and hesitant. "I don't think they've branded me, but I have seen them imprint the Order's symbol on others."

"How do you not know whether or not you've been branded?" Soren asks as he walks back into the kitchen.

"It's not as painful as you would think. There's been a number of times where I've been knocked out and moved. They could've done it any of those times."

"We should check." Gideon moves toward my father.

"And you wouldn't find anything." He faces Gideon, a reserved expression on his face. "It's extremely difficult to find. Besides, I've looked."

"If they had branded him, wouldn't they have claimed him by now?" Jesse asks. "Naughty prisoner escaping, and all."

My father shakes his head. "Gideon's wards are very thorough."

Gideon nods. "I'm alerted any time anyone tries to come across my wards. It hasn't happened yet, but that doesn't mean they aren't looking at ways to break through them. That's why I have friends here."

"Gryffons." Jesse smirks. "Clever little creatures."

"That's right," Gideon says, crossing his arms over his chest. "If the Order gets past my wards, the gryffons are there to help. They'll at least provide me enough time to make it here."

"So, we may need to move him again?" I ask.

"No," my father says. "This is the safest place for me. We may need to break up the routine of you coming, however. They could be gauging your pattern as we speak."

"Excellent idea," Soren says, leaning against the entry frame separating the kitchen from the living room. "And by staying overnight, we'll be able to know for sure if Michael is being tracked. Better to find out now than later."

"And what if they do break in and take him?" I ask, narrowing my eyes on each of my men. "What then?"

"That is a risk I'm taking. But I'd rather help Gideon fight them here, where we have an advantage, than while being on the run and separated from you." My father runs a hand through his hair and forces back a yawn. "Again, it's getting late. We should all get some sleep. Especially you," he says to me. "We have training planned for tomorrow. Because if they do trespass this estate, they'll regret it."

I nod. "Fine. For the record, I'm sleeping alone."

I move past the men and head directly for my bed, smirking to myself. They want to be buttheads about this whole protection thing, then I can be a butthead about who gets to sleep with me.

CHAPTER TWENTY-FOUR

The transformations this island goes through never ceases to amaze and enchant me.

As I make my way toward the gardens where the harvest festival is being hosted, I pass by torches that line the path, setting a warm glow to everything the light touches. The moon is full and hangs low in the sky, making it seem impossibly larger than it normally is. Festive music fills the air.

My hands brush against my jeans as I walk. I love the feel of the fabric, and a smile pulls on my lips. I got myself ready for this evening. Makeup and all. Savannah would be proud of me. Though I went with a more casual style, with a cami, sweater duster, and my comfy tennis shoes, I still clipped the top half of my hair back, allowing my red hair to fall over my shoulders and along my back.

Despite the fact that we are knee deep in chilly temps, the warmth that surrounds me is almost otherworldly, and I wonder if an enchantment was placed on the torches to provide extra warmth.

This is an outdoor festival after all.

As I arrive at the gardens, I see the entry is guarded by two large stag statues. A long table takes up one of the open spaces and is full of fruits, squashes, roasted meats, and other types of festive, fall foods.

All around the garden are other statues of centaurs, faeries, chimeras, hydras, and firebirds. Gnomes gather around some of the statues, bouncing up and down, playing with each other. I catch sight of some of them doing what I can only guess is dancing. I stifle a laugh and love those creatures even more.

I find Jesse and Savannah hanging out in a corner. As I approach, Soren joins my side. I smile at him as he wraps an arm around my shoulders.

"Hey, you." He gently squeezes me into him.

"Hey." I breathe in deep the scent of his cologne and I fight against the urge to curl my toes. He just smells so damn good.

Jesse catches my gaze, pausing in whatever he and Savannah were talking about, to give me that come-hither stare of his. I bite the corner of my lower lip, ensnared in his eyes. That one look tells me all I need to know.

"Bout time you showed up." Savannah pulls me into a hug and then holds me back at arm's length, taking stock of my appearance. She nods approvingly. "You did well. I'm proud of you."

I chuckle. "Thanks. I had a pretty amazing teacher."

She leans in, beaming. "That's what friends are for."

"Slumming it with the lowly types tonight, eh, Professor McCallister?" Jesse asks Soren.

Soren huffs and shakes his head.

I give Jesse a pointed look. "Give him a break for one night, at least."

"Where's the fun in that?" Jesse asks.

"I think you'll find a way to manage." I move between my men in an effort to keep the proverbial peace and set my gaze over the crowd of people filling the gardens. Gideon casually talks with Lady Alene on the opposite side of the drink table, helping students fill their cups with the special enchanted cider we helped pick apples for. My mouth waters for a taste. "I'm going to get some cider."

Without waiting for a response, I make my way to Gideon, who looks at me as I arrive and pick up a cup.

He ladles some of the spice-filled liquid into my cup and smiles. "Enjoying yourself?"

I shrug. "For the most part."

"You'd better relax and have a good time." He winks.

"You should come join us later."

"I may have to. Just to make sure you are actually enjoying yourself."

I laugh under my breath and wave at Lady Alene before turning around and walking back to the group.

Milo isn't there yet, and I wonder what's taking him so long to join us.

"Have you guys seen Milo?"

Savannah shrugs. Jesse and Soren shake their heads.

"Are you sure he's coming?" Savannah asks.

"Yeah." I look over the crowd. "I thought he would be here by now."

I catch sight of him, he's walking toward us, but his attention seems to be constantly pulled to his right. His lips move like he's saying something, but he doesn't look thrilled about whatever it is he's saying.

And then I see her.

Agatha Collins.

As soon as Milo takes a step toward us, she grabs him by the arm and pulls him right back to her. Poor

Milo. I can see his patience is growing thin, but he's too gentlemanly to knock a girl off her pedestal.

I, however, don't give a damn about her feelings.

"Hold this." I hand Jesse my cup.

"Where are you running off to?" he asks.

"To prove a point."

"Don't do anything that would get you into trouble." Soren's voice calls after me.

I don't respond. Instead, I keep my sights zeroed in on Agatha and her little manicured claws constantly pulling Milo back to her. Each time I see her do it, I get a little angrier. I'm done playing games.

I stop in front of them as I overhear Milo tell Agatha, "Okay, I really need to go now."

"Just one more minute, please! I promise it will be worth it!"

I step into view. "What the hell do you think you are doing?"

Agatha does a double-take, and though there is a flash of fear initially, she beams at me. "Oh, nothing. Just hanging out with a couple of friends. Isn't that right, Milo?"

She cups the top of Milo's arm. My eyes zero in on the fact her hand is touching my man. I meet Milo's gaze, and it's filled with a silent plea. He's tried to break away from her enough times that he's seeking assistance.

And I'm going to *deliver*.

"First of all, Milo isn't your friend. Second of all, hanging out doesn't involve preventing him from leaving when he wants or needs to."

She laughs. "Honestly, Wren. I'm not keeping him here against his will."

I roll my eyes. "'Just one more minute, please! I promise it will be worth it!'" I embellish the tone and movements, including her smile while hanging onto Milo. "Does that sound familiar?"

She has a wounded expression, but I don't care, the girl has pushed my patience too far. "That's not how I sound."

"Isn't it?" I ask.

"Honestly, Wren. I have no idea what the problem is."

"He is *my* boyfriend. If you so much as lay another finger on him, I'll break your hands." I step closer, pointing a finger at her and jabbing it into her chest. "If you are even so much as within the *vicinity* of him, I'll rain hell down on you quicker than you can bat those pretty blue eyes of yours." I lean in extra close and lower my voice to a deadly tone. "Are we clear?" I don't break away from her gaze. To do so would give her the wrong impression.

She barely nods.

I back away. "Good." I switch my gaze to Milo. "Are you okay?"

He nods. "I have told her repeatedly that I'm not interested. But she doesn't seem to take no for an answer. She pretends like it's an invitation for more." He shoves his glasses up his nose and I fight the urge to smile. "Didn't know what else to do. I'm glad you showed up though." He leans in and kisses me on the cheek.

I smile at him and turn my deadly glare back on Agatha. "Back off."

"I swear it's not like that," she croons, playing innocent. "I really only want to be friends with him. Can't we be friends?"

"Back off or deal with me. Got it? You can act sweet and innocent all you want, but that shit's not flying with me."

Agatha glares at me and I stand there waiting for her to try something. Lucky for her, she makes the smart decision by storming off with a huff.

Good girl.

"Ready?" I ask Milo once she's finally out of sight.

He smiles and offers me his arm. I take it with

flourish, playing up the action, and we make our way back to our group.

I meet Soren's gaze as we approach. He nods in her direction. "Problem?"

"Handled. For now," I say through a sigh.

"What was that about anyway?" He crosses his arms over his chest.

Milo digs into the story, catching him up on everything. Soren nods. "I'll keep an eye on her and keep her busy."

I snicker. "Gods help the poor girl."

"Sounds to me like she brought it upon herself," Savannah adds.

"Wren, our knight in shining armor." Jesse smirks. "That'll teach her to mess with our girl and her men." He hands me back my drink.

I hold up the cup. "Damn straight."

"Looks like I missed out on some fun tonight." Gideon appears at my side and looks at me from the corner of his eyes.

"It's been handled. Believe me." I take a sip of cider.

He nods. "Her soul seems to be rather neutral. She could go either way, so I suggest you use caution. A guiding hand should do the trick to make sure she doesn't go in the wrong direction."

Interesting. She's neither inclined for light or dark.

Instead, she rests smack dab in the middle. "I'll take that under advisement."

"He has a point," Savannah adds. "It wouldn't take but a tiny shift for her to sway toward one side or the other. Very few mages throughout history have managed to maintain the balance between the two sides. She strikes me as exceptionally vulnerable and needy."

"So that doesn't happen often then?" I ask.

"In fact, it's rare. Especially for the academy." Gideon gently rests his hand on the small of my back. Our eyes meet with a smile, and he excuses himself, walking off to mingle with other students.

While the others continue talking about the girl needing strict boundaries and how to help instill them in her, I withdraw into my own thoughts about what it could mean if a student were to go dark on the island. What would happen? How devastating could that end up being?

Either way, I know I'm going to have to be extremely careful around her. She pushes all the wrong buttons, and I don't want to be the one held responsible for her going off the deep end.

Before long, the evening grows late, and Milo faces me. "I'm going to head back in."

"Getting cold?" I ask, poking him in the side.

He chuckles. "A little. I'm getting tired."

"Want company?"

He smiles. "Absolutely."

After a quick goodbye to the rest of the group, I take Milo's arm and we head back inside.

CHAPTER TWENTY-FIVE

On the way to Milo's room, we talk about his run-ins with Agatha.

"What do you want to do?" I ask.

He shrugs. "If what Gideon said is true, then I will need to be as gentle as possible."

I snort. "Yeah, like that method has worked so far."

"What do you mean?"

I gesture behind us. "That whole incident. Plus, I know you. You are kind and way too polite to be anything but gentle."

He levels his gaze on me. "You have seen me fight, right?"

"Duh." I nudge him playfully. "I'm talking in reference to your interaction with women. You're very much a gentleman. It's part of what I love about you." I snuggle his arm a little. "Chivalry is very much alive with you."

He laughs under his breath a little and looks away from me. His bashfulness gets the better of me every time too. But I don't want to share that with him just yet. "My parents raised me right, I guess. But going back to what we were talking about, you should probably be a little more patient with her. She's new and has a way of getting what she wants."

"What do you mean?" I pull away from him a little. "Do I need to worry?"

"No." His voice comes out appalled as we reach the door to the House of Drakon. He opens the door, and thankfully, the commons is empty. We continue through until we reach his door. "I'm not going anywhere. I assure you."

I smile. "You better not."

He escorts me into his room and shucks off his jacket while I slip out of my sweater duster. He takes it from me and hangs it on the hook next to his, just inside the door. With a gesture, we move deeper into his room and take in what I can only consider to be organized chaos covering his desk.

"Research for a new project?" I finger a page on the desk and turn to face him.

He's standing toe-to-toe with me, eyes dark and lustful. I drop my gaze to his lips as his hands slide over the sides of my waist. He forcefully pulls me into him. I wrap my arms around his shoulders as I fall into his brown eyes.

"I could never do anything to hurt you. Never." His voice is almost a whisper, low and deep. He spins me and walks me back into a wall, sandwiching me between it and him. His hard abs press against mine and I can feel every breath he takes.

"I am free to be who I am with you. You never force me to live up to the expectations of others. You're so receptive of all my interests. It's nice to have someone to share my knowledge with so openly."

I watch the words leave his lips and I take in the stubble growing along his jawline. My body is on *fire* while my blood is flushed with ice, the side-effect of my magic when I'm around him. The sensation is dizzying in the most delightful way.

"Not many people have stood up for me. I'm flattered you took a stand like that. I will forever be grateful for everything you do, Wren." He slips a hand to the back of my head, sliding across my cheek, weaving his fingers through my hair and brushing against the clip pinning my hair back.

The things I want to say, I can't because his mouth

brushes against mine, and my breaths still. I savor the way his lips move along mine, soft and gentle. The tip of his tongue barely enters my mouth and I become putty in his hands.

My sexy nerd sure can kiss.

The words that fall silent at my lips ring true regardless. I would never allow anyone to take advantage of him. He's sweet and kind. There's something about Agatha that I don't like. It makes me fiercely protective and possessive over him.

Milo deepens the kiss and my mind loses all sense of thoughts beyond the sensations erupting through my core with the way his mouth presses against mine. He presses against me, pushing me farther against the wall.

A moan filters between our kiss, and his growing erection presses against the crotch of my jeans making me weak in the knees.

He does the last thing I'd ever expect him to. He lifts me up, gripping my legs and wrapping them around his waist as he pulls me away from the wall and carries me to the bed. Gentle as ever, and not breaking from our kissing, he sits me down on the edge of the bed.

I break from the kiss and scoot toward the center of the bed as he pulls off his shirt and I'm stunned.

This man is *built*.

Muscles ripple from his shoulders to his waistline, with defined dips and valleys. I bite the corner of my lower lip and drink in the amazing beauty standing before me.

"Gorgeous," I mutter.

He climbs over me. "Not nearly as beautiful as you."

My heart flutters in my chest as he kisses me. His hands rove over my body as he expertly removes every article of clothing from our bodies. Now there is nothing between us. Nothing to stop us from fulfilling our deepest desires. But instead of jumping into the act, he grabs a pillow and lifts me up, setting it behind my head. Next, he pulls on the throw at the foot of the bed, shakes it out, and pulls it over him before finally laying over me and kissing me with such tenderness and passion.

My breaths leave me once more.

The tip of his rock-hard cock presses against my entrance and teases inside ever so slowly. I arch my back, hungry for more of him, wanting him to fill me completely and satiate my need.

He grins devilishly as he pulls away and peppers kisses along my body, down to my thighs. He pays special attention to each one of my breasts, teasing my nipples with flicks of his tongue and sucking and massaging.

Heat flushes through me and pools between my thighs, and to my surprise, I nearly orgasm as he worships me with his mouth. He has yet to actually enter me or touch me. It's so gentle, and sweet. *Beautiful.*

True to Milo's fashion. This experience is full of emotion, and I feel every sensation with such intensity that it's almost overwhelming.

But that's the thing with Milo.

I can feel. I don't need to shield him from my emotions, and he opens me up in ways I never thought I could be, touches me in ways I never thought I could be touched. With Milo, I'm *free*.

Best of all, I know this is only a precursor to what's in store for me.

He returns to my mouth, cock pressing against my entrance as it slides up and down along my sensitive folds, deliciously rubbing against my clit. My climax builds, and I buck into him, wanting him to slide into me already, to fill me with what is sure to be an amazing ride.

He pushes against my hips, smiling at me, desire alight in his eyes as he continues to tease me with his sheer length. And this man is hung.

I moan with need, overcome with the sensation and reaching my peak of resistance. Just before my body convulses with the wave of pleasure that builds in my core, he slowly, tantalizingly enters me. Inch by glorious inch he fills me.

A sigh escapes my lips, and he chuckles under his breath, surely pleased with the reactions he's coaxing out of me, and I have to smile in response. This is all him. He deserves the credit.

He grinds against me, instantly pushing my climax over the edge. I bury my face into his neck, clinging to him as he rides me through this wave of what seems like an endless rush of pleasure. And when it ends, he doesn't stop. I wrap my legs around him, widening my hips to allow him full access to all I have to offer.

Soon, another climax builds, and as it does, his grinding becomes smoother, tenderly easing me into my next release.

I surrender completely to him, giving him the reins to send me through wave after wave of pleasure. It ends only when he decides, and as he releases his warmth inside me, he buries his face into my neck.

He falls to my side with a heavy and contended sigh. I curl into him, knowing that I belong to him, and he belongs to me. Nothing can ever take him away from me, and I'm forever changed in this sweet and endearing moment.

CHAPTER TWENTY-SIX

As the weeks pass, the day we leave for Crimson Isles draws closer, along with the excitement of the trip. The entire academy is buzzing with anticipation since one of our very own professors will be participating in the Mage Championships. I've already had to step over glitter and glue in the hallway as some students decided to make their own posters showing support for Soren. I've also had my share of eye-rolling as a few giggling girls talked about how handsome he is.

Despite all that, I'm happy for Soren. He's going to kick ass, and my team and I will be rooting for him.

"I can't wait!" Savannah excitedly bounces up and down as we stand in the halls following lunch.

"I'm excited too." It doesn't come out very convincing.

"You should be, it'll be a weekend you won't forget." Jesse leans in closer to whisper, "Especially when I get through with you."

I shake my head. "You think so, huh?" Leave it to Jesse to provide the distractions from the rising worries within me.

"Is that a challenge?" His steel blue eyes darken a shade.

"Maybe." I play coy, which only eggs him on.

"Challenge accepted." He smiles mischievously, and I have to wonder if I created a monster.

"I've been needing to restock on some of the herbs that are getting low, for my research. I may also pick up a book or two while there."

Oh, Milo. Never change.

"That sounds like fun. We're still going to the library though, right?" I ask.

"Of course." He smiles.

There's been a shift between us. A good one.

No, scratch that.

A *great* one.

Images of being wrapped in each other between his sheets fills my mind, and heat rushes between my thighs.

"This trip is a big deal," Savannah continues. "Blackbriar hasn't been represented in the Mage Championships for quite a few years. I've heard there are some pots going for bets on Soren."

"Oh, gods no. Don't let him know that." My heart skips a few beats as I'm reminded not only of how big of a deal Soren's participation is, but just how dangerous the championships are.

"It's not exactly a secret." Her amethyst eyes take in mine. "Besides, it's friendly competition, which is completely healthy."

I cross my arms over my chest and lean back against the wall.

"I'm in." Jesse shoves his hand into his pockets. "What's the going rate?"

I smack him on his arm. "You better not bet on Soren."

"Of course not," he says handing over a wad of wrinkled cash to Savannah. "I'm betting against him."

"Even better," I mutter.

Milo shakes his head.

"Relax. It's only a problem if he finds out." Jesse leans against the wall.

"You know he's going to find out." I level my gaze on him.

"That is the beauty of my plan. I hope he does. I may even tell him myself."

"You have a death wish."

"He has to catch me first." He winks. "Besides, he'll be too busy with the championships or the magusari to be bothered with me."

"If you say so."

"Mmm…" Savannah closes her eyes wistfully. "Hot, yummy men in uniform."

I laugh.

"There you go." She smiles. "Come on, there's a rally to get to."

I nod and peel myself from the wall as Jesse and Milo lead the way through the busy halls littered with glittering posters with Soren's name on them. Banners in Blackbriar's colors fill the halls with streamers to top the celebratory morale.

I frown again. I don't like the idea of one of my men doing something reckless like the dangers involved in the championships. I know Soren can handle himself, and probably come out on top as champion, but I don't like the risks.

"What's the matter?" Savannah asks, weaving her arm through mine. I relax my arms and let her.

A sigh escapes my lips as I try to nail down my thoughts. "I can see why everyone's excited for our school to be represented, but don't you think some of them are going overboard?"

"Why?"

I shrug.

She gently, playfully shakes me. "Relax would you! Soren is very capable of defeating any foe who stands in his way. It's an honor for this school, and the championships are like the Superbowl for the human world."

I stop mid-step as the connection suddenly makes perfect sense. Except for one question that remains unanswered. "But why?"

"Why have the championships?" Savannah tugs on my arm and we continue down the hall toward the arena.

"Yes."

"For the same reason humans have the Olympics. It's a demonstration of strength, mental and physical—you know what? Think of it like a trial the mages put themselves through to demonstrate who is top dog. Similar to what we had to do to be accepted here but focuses more on endurance and ability." She snaps her fingers and points at me. "Actually, think of it like a constant test that repeats every four years."

As we step through the doors of the arena, I'm instantly pulled to a giant banner with Soren's picture sitting in the center. House of Phoenix's banner stands guard on either side, and the crest of Blackbriar sits beneath his image.

Soren stands below all of that as students surround him, holding up posters and plastic pom-poms. He smiles and waves at the students before him. Shaking my head with a smile on my face, I lean against the nearest wall so I can take in everything, especially, my handsome asshole.

I don't pretend to understand mages or their need to demonstrate who's more macho. This world is still quite new to me, after all. But what I do understand is how happy this whole thing is making him. And that settles my fraying nerves more than any explanation could.

Soren's got this.

I know he does.

CHAPTER TWENTY-SEVEN

Inside the arena, we are separated into groups by house as we prepare to leave for Crimson Isles. This is the first time in the arena since I first arrived where it appears to be a simple room with high, arching, cathedral-like windows lining the top of the external-facing wall. Large wooden beams crisscross at the top, supporting the large pointed ceilings. Muted light filters in through the windows, casting dust-filled beams of white at an angle toward the floor, which is nothing but dirt and bits of hay.

It smells aged with must and earthy undertones.

I stand with my house, tuning out the talks of how they are still collecting bets on Soren, because that's the last thing I need to help with my anxieties.

Once I absorb everything I can about the room

we're all standing in, I search for Milo, Jesse, and Savannah.

Milo is standing off to the side, leaning against a wall with a notebook and pencil in hand, scribbling along the pages. I wonder what he's so focused on. His jaws clench a little, and a pinch forms in my forehead. Something is bothering him. I want to find out what, but we are supposed to stay with our houses.

Stupid rules.

Jesse jokes with some of his comrades from his house, wrestling and playing around, with a dazzling smile stretching his lips. I chuckle under my breath as he's in his normal mood.

Savannah is off to the right of me somewhere. I find her only by the purple streaks in her hair. Her back remains to me.

I sigh. Waiting is so much fun.

Soon, Gideon walks in and calls everyone's attention to him, as he stands in the center of the four houses.

"Who's ready to leave?" His voice booms throughout the room, replaced only by the sheer volume of cheers that echoes through the entire massive room. As soon as the cheers die down, he laughs. "I thought so."

He conjures a portal.

It's tall and wide, glowing with a vibrancy befitting Gideon's depth of power. I have never seen a portal so large, but considering the number of people he's letting through at once, it makes sense.

Still, his power never ceases to amaze me.

I'm so proud to call him mine.

House by house, in groups of five, everyone steps through. Once it comes to my turn, I smile at Gideon and step through the portal, feet planting firmly on cobble stone that forms the narrow streets, damp from the morning's condensation.

The buildings around me are like stepping into the past. Everything is stone. The old doors are made of planks with iron handles. It's hard to tell where one building ends and the other begins as they all seem to have been purposefully built in sections. Alleys are the only breaks between clusters, and people move all around me, completely unaffected by the sudden appearance of an entire academy's worth of students in their streets. They smile and wave, and I even spot children chasing each other and laughing as they run.

Savannah runs up to me, beaming. "Yay! You're finally here!"

I laugh. "It's so freaking beautiful!" I look up at the sky and suck in a breath. "Look at how blue it is!"

Not a cloud is in sight among the backdrop of the purest sky blue I've ever seen.

Everything here has an air of enchantment. It's not surprising for a magical island. Although I was expecting something more along the lines of Blackbriar, the beauty here is mesmerizing in its own way.

Gideon calls our attention. "Who would like to go on the tour of the isles?"

Savannah pulls on me. We grab Jesse and Milo on the way and meet up with Gideon with excited smiles.

"I figured you would want to go." He nods toward an opulent horse drawn carriage and we all gather around it as we wait for anyone else who wants to go. Sitting in the front seat, holding the reins, is a human-ish figure with wood-like skin, mossy green hair, and crystal blue eyes.

As we approach, he gives us a nod. "Good day. I'm Rowan."

"Nice to meet you, Rowan," I say.

Savannah smiles. "Sidhe?"

He nods. "How did you know?"

She shrugs, smirking proudly.

I chuckle and say, "Trust me. She knows a lot of things."

Savannah and I laugh together as we climb into the carriage and settle in.

Before long, Gideon joins us.

"You're coming too?" I ask.

"I wouldn't miss this for the world." He winks.

Heat fills my neck, burning its way toward my cheeks. I take a steady breath as pressure builds between my thighs.

All this with just one look.

I silently chide myself to get a grip.

These men of mine sure know how to get me hot and bothered in the most delightful ways.

"Who's keeping an eye on the other students?" I crane my neck to get a view of the house leaders and several of the faculty wrangling excited students into smaller groups. "Never mind."

"When is Soren joining us?" Jesse asks. "I do want to give him hell before he starts the championships."

"He'll be along later on. Right now, he's training." Gideon stares out the side of the covered carriage. "There's a great tavern right there."

I poke my head out. "The Siren's Call?"

"Original," Jesse mocks.

I poke him in the ribs. "Like you would do better."

"I could." He shrugs. "I'll save my top five for when we're alone."

"Of course," I mutter.

The streets are not built in straight lines, but with

curves and angles, all filled with similarly clustered buildings and alleys. It's like walking through a story book.

A light breeze wafts toward me, and the air is full of the scents of the ocean and something sweet I can't quite place my finger on.

We pull up in front of a castle-like structure. It's reminiscent of a medieval fortress, built with stone, and a few colored crystals mixed in that hum with magic. Towers guard each of the four corners, with a navy-blue flag with a gold symbol in the center of it. From where I sit, it appears to be almost a dreamcatcher in essence, but none of the lines touch or cross. It's beautiful and the sight of it instills a bit of hope and justice. But, perhaps, that's the point.

"This is the citadel." Gideon speaks wistfully. "It's the home of the magusari, and where we will be coming to watch the championships." He points to one of the flags. "See that flag up there?"

I nod.

"That's the symbol for all magusari. It represents all that we stand for."

I can't help but notice all of the differences. The Order's symbol is the opposite of the magusari's. They take magic that should be a gift, squandering it in selfish pursuits of power and their twisted sense of justice. Looking at the symbol of the magusari instills a level of hope within me. Whereas the Order's symbol is twisted and sucks all the hope away.

"You miss it?" Savannah asks. Only our inner circle knows Gideon is magusari.

"Sometimes." He leans back in his seat. "We'll be back here soon enough. I just wanted to stop by here so Wren can see it." He taps on the roof of carriage and we're off to our next stop.

He smiles at me. "You're really going to love this."

I smile and lean forward, looking out each of the windows as I try to guess where we are going next. "I already do."

The carriage veers to the right. I watch with a sense of awe as the large buildings shrink into cottages and more land is freed from the towering structures, revealing unicorns prancing in the fields. The carriage pulls to a stop on the side of a dirt road next to the field, and I lean out of the window for a better look. Black as night, the unicorns collect in small groups or prance alone waving their smoky black tails through the air. Silver horns protrude from their heads like swords, and if that's not enough of a reason to keep a distance from these creatures, their glowing red eyes is enough warning.

But there's still a power in these creatures that

makes me want to draw closer. Even knowing they can be man-eaters from time to time.

"This is the only known island in the world that is able to support these creatures." Gideon's voice is closer to me, and I look over my shoulder to find him closer to me. I smile at him.

"They're magnificent." I breathe the words.

"And dangerous too," Jesse adds. "They are not the sparkly creatures humans tell their children about."

"I know." I sigh as I retake my seat. "Shame." Still, even knowing the danger, I want to reach out and touch one.

"Well, I mean, I can think of other ways to die a horrible, gruesome death, but if that's your wish…" Jesse gestures to the unicorns.

I quirk an eyebrow. "That's dark. Even for you."

"You haven't seen anything yet." He smirks.

"They have a special handler that takes care of their needs. The same family has protected and guarded them for many generations," Savannah adds as she leans into her corner.

Milo sketches an image of a unicorn into his book, adding all the gritty details. I shudder.

"Their caretakers have been the only ones not attacked by them," Milo adds. "Something to do with an enchantment. The story changes depending on who's telling it."

"Interesting. I would like to hear that story on our date." I grin at Milo. He nudges his glasses up his nose as he smiles almost bashfully. He gets what I'm hinting at. If not, I have no issues demonstrating exactly what I mean.

The carriage jerks forward as we make our way back toward the citadel. I take in the view of everything around me, everything magical, everything wonderful and vibrant and mesmerizing.

"Where are we off to now?" I ask, eager to see more.

Gideon smirks proudly. "Oh, you'll see."

Even after elbowing my way past a few bumbling students who had one too many drinks at the tavern, my excitement over watching the championships unfold has my spirits soaring. As we're escorted to our seats in the stands where we could see all of the action, I finally get the chance to take in everything around me.

The cheers from the crowd could rival the roar of

the ocean. They drown out my own thoughts as the enthusiasm in the air seems to fuel the electric energy surrounding me. Patrons from all walks of life fill the stadium seats, holding up colored banners of their champion of choice. The stadium fills the right side of the court. The left side is occupied by small hut-like shelters where the champions themselves observe their comrades and opponents battle it out for the world to see. Gideon is sitting at the back of the area. He's with the other judges, and I wonder how it must feel to watch his best friend battle for the title of Mage Champion.

Loud horns trumpet into the air. I crane my neck to find out where they are coming from, but the crowd stands up and cheers even louder.

"This is it!" Savannah nearly squeals. "This is the start!"

"Oh!" I stand up and watch as competing mages flow into the arena and face the crowd.

Soren stands in front of me, waving at the crowd. He catches my eye and I smile at him. I mouth *good luck*. He nods.

A voice booms over the cheers through a loudspeaker somewhere near the judges' seating.

"Ladies and gentleman, it is my honor to host this year's championships. I am High Councilman Brock DuBois."

His name is chanted as people sing, literally, his praises.

"I don't get it," I mumble.

Savannah leans in closer. "He's virtually the mayor of Crimson Isles and has done some pretty fantastic things for the people. He's very loved and popular here."

"Ah. Makes more sense now."

"Don't worry, we'll get you all caught up."

"It's much more fun to keep her in the dark," Jesse says.

"It really is," Milo and Savannah agree as they speak simultaneously.

I look between the two of them. "Traitors."

They laugh and I join in with them. Because it's fun to learn things, and I'm sure they find my reactions fascinating. They certainly seem to enjoy teaching me things most mages know by now.

"Soren McCallister," the High Councilman says, pulling my attention to Soren as he steps forward. I realize I've missed over half the introductions of the competitors.

He winks at me as he steps back into his line. I smile at him and shake my head. He better not get himself hurt. I have plans of my own in store for him, and it won't help if he's injured.

Once the High Councilman introduces all the champions, those who brought favors are asked to hold them out for their champion.

Savannah nudges me with a bright red scarf in her hand. The fabric is sheer, and I stare at it in confusion.

"For Soren."

I meet her gaze as it dawns on me. Heat burns through my cheeks as I take the scarf and hold it out over the edge of the wall for my champion. He jogs toward me, stopping a step or two away from me before bowing gratefully. He closes the gap, eyes holding mine as he holds up his arm.

I quickly look over at the other champions getting their favors tied around their upper arm. Slipping the fabric around his bicep, I tie it with a bow. I'm honestly not sure if I did that right. He leans forward, pointing to his cheek.

I laugh under my breath and lean over, pressing my lips to his cheek for good luck.

"See you soon," he says as he jogs back to the line.

"All champions having received their favors, must now prepare," High Councilman DuBois says.

"What's happening now?" I ask as the champions break from the line and partner up throughout the open dirt.

"Duels." Jesse leans on the railing with the bottom of his forearms.

"This is a brutal match," Milo adds.

"Why?" I ask.

Savannah shakes her head, beaming from ear to ear. "Because they have to fight until their partner surrenders."

"Soren said it wasn't as bad as it sounded." I narrow my eyes on him. "Why do I get the feeling he was just trying to comfort me?"

"You'll soon find out," Jesse adds.

A horn blares through the air. Instantly, the mages begin fighting each other. I keep my eyes on Soren as he dukes it out with his partner. He's swift, tactful, and with every parry, he adds a blast of magic that hits the ground of his opponent's feet.

It's almost hilarious to watch the other guy hopping back and to the sides to avoid getting burned.

But Soren doesn't let up.

He's pushing his opponent farther back, toward the entrance of the stadium. Once his opponent is virtually cornered, he lets out a blast of magic at Soren.

I try not to blink now. Because it looks like the opponent is now pushing Soren back with endless blasts of magic. Soren flips backward, dodging from side to side as he makes his way back. Not once does he turn his back, but Soren's opponent isn't letting him get a shot in of his own. I stand up from my seat and lean forward.

I desperately want to jump in and help out.

"Easy tiger," Jesse says. "It's all part of the show."

I snap my attention to him. "So, it isn't as dangerous as you made it sound."

He smirks. "Did I?"

I plop back into my seat and cross my arms over my chest as I return my attention to the fight.

Gods, I love watching him fight. He moves with such grace and precision. Everything he does is thought out, and though he was giving his opponent a lead, I know he's about to turn the tide to his own favor and take the win.

Sure enough, he stops moving back at the same time the opponent lets up with his nearly constant assault. His chest heaves up and down with panting, and a slight stumble along the dirt signals his growing exhaustion.

And there it is.

Soren knew his opponent would lash out as soon as he was backed into a corner, tire himself out with the offense. Now that Soren has him right where he wants him, he can end the fight.

Soren closes the gap between the two of them and

it catches the opponent off guard, judging by the wide-eyed expression on his face.

But the poor guy is just too tired to move forward.

Soren swipes the guy's feet out from under him, spins back up to his feet, and ends up holding his hand out, full of powerful fire magic.

The other guy lays his head on the ground and pants a few breaths before lifting his hand high and releasing a blast of white light into the air.

Jesse, Milo, and Savannah stand up and cheer.

I smile, rising to my feet, applauding my professor for a job well done. Though the fight seemed easy for him, I'm sure that's how it only appeared.

But one thing is for certain.

I'm proud he is all mine.

Soren holds up his arm with the scarf tied around it as a higher-pitched horn blazes through the air. He helps his opponent up from the ground and they both move back toward the shelters across from me.

Me and my group reclaim our seats.

"That was only the first round," Milo says. "There are strict rules to follow for the initial cuts. No face shots, only ground assault with magic. End the fight as quick as possible."

I nod. "That really wasn't so bad."

Jesse snorts. "You have only seen the first round, my dear."

"Stop it." I glare at him.

"Well, we can check the championships off our list," Savannah says. "Once you turn twenty-one, we can hit up the night life. That's another thing on the bucket list." She points a finger at me.

I shake my head. "I'm already twenty-one. In fact, I'm about to turn twenty-two."

"When?" Her eyes are wide with surprise.

"December ninth." I wonder what's so special about this. I haven't celebrated a birthday in so long, it's just another day to me.

"That's next week!" She grabs my arm and leans forward. "Guys! We have to do something."

I hold up my hand. "No. You don't."

Her gaze settles on me. "Why not?"

I shrug. "I haven't celebrated my birthday since I was fourteen."

"Nope!" She shakes her head once. "We're doing it."

"Um. Okay," I mumble, feeling a bit awkward.

"In fact," she says. "We're doing it tonight. Meet me at the Siren's Call. It's a rite of passage. You have to start celebrating you."

"If you say so." I smile a little.

"I do, thank you very much."

I laugh.

Milo and Jesse talk about something between the two of them. Once they finish, Milo leans forward. "I'll meet you at the tavern too. We can discuss this more then."

Savannah nods and looks to me. "I knew he would see it my way. We're changing that no-celebrating thing. Why did you stop?"

"Trolls."

That one word should explain it all well enough. And for the most part, judging by everyone's expressions, it does. It does strike me as odd at how often it seems everyone forgets that part of my life.

"Well, no more, my friend! You're celebrating last year's birthday tonight!"

I lift my hands in surrender as I laugh. "Okay, okay!"

CHAPTER TWENTY-EIGHT

I put on my jacket for my little birthday outing with Savannah. I'm beside myself. No one has ever really made my birthday a big deal in so long, I almost forgot what it was like to have someone excited about me getting older.

Living with the trolls, I was never celebrated. Unless you consider being the pun of all their jokes and treated like a slave as celebration. Who knows, they probably think I was well cared for. Their pathetic little plaything.

Squeezing my eyes shut, I force the idea of the trolls away. I want to bury the very memory of them so far in the back of my mind that they can't ever create a dark spot on something good happening in my life ever again.

Because they don't hold power over me anymore.

They don't get to control how I live my life now.

I'm the one who's in charge here.

I look around the room, smiling to myself as I try to commit everything to memory. I replace the darker nightmares with the amazing experiences I'm receiving now. I nod to myself and walk out the door.

It's like being in another time, in another world here, and as I walk into the crisp evening air, I breathe in deep the lingering perfume in the air. I shove my hands into my pockets and walk down the street, toward the tavern I'm meeting Savannah at.

A strange vehicle pulls up to the street, with its wheels screeching to a halt. A familiar figure exits the car, and I quickly duck behind the fender of a vehicle to avoid being seen. The figure looks in my direction with a frown pulling down at her lips, and it's then I realize who the person is.

And seeing her here isn't a good sign at all.

Aunt Patricia adjusts the scarf over her head and quickly makes her way through the door of the building directly across from the tavern.

If she's here, there's a reason, and it can't be good.

She and I have been practically in radio silence since Savannah and I spent the night at her estate. One night was all it took to know whatever Aunt

Patricia had up her sleeve, it was directly related to the Order.

So, naturally, seeing my aunt rush into a shop that has long been closed for the day piques my curiosity probably more than it should. The fact that she's rushing and trying to keep herself covered and unseen only adds to my list of suspicions when it comes to her.

Something isn't right, and I need to figure out what.

It's far more than just coincidence that she's here at the very moment I am. I know better than that.

As soon as my aunt is inside the building, and I'm hoping far away from the windows, I stand from my hiding spot. I have to know what my aunt is up to. But first, I have to find Savannah. Keeping to the shadows, ducking in and out of them as often as possible, I head for the tavern across the street.

I stop next to a giant SUV and spot Savannah standing outside the building, waiting for me. As soon as she sees me, I wave her over. Calmly, she makes her way toward me.

"What are you doing?" she asks. Curiosity lights up her amethyst eyes.

"I just saw my aunt go into that building over there." I point through the tinted windows.

Savannah knits her eyebrows together and carefully pokes her head around the windshield of the SUV to see. She returns her gaze. "That's an expensive magical supply shop. It's been closed since like three this afternoon. What business does she have going in there?"

"My question, exactly."

She sighs as she shakes her head. "This isn't good, Wren."

"No. It isn't. I need to figure out what she's up to. Raincheck on the drink?"

"To come with you and do some sneaking around?"

I nod, lips pressed into a grim line.

"What are we waiting for?" She gestures for me to lead the way.

"We'll need to be as quiet as possible if we're going to figure out what she's up to."

"Already ahead of you." She pulls out a couple of chunks of crystals and hands me one.

"What are these?" I ask, looking at her.

"They're enchanted to keep our steps soft and our presence unknown. This coupled with your enchanted necklace should do the trick to keep us undetected."

I lean against the car and look at the sky as a smile pulls at my lips. "You had another vision."

"Yup. Let's go."

I shove the crystal into my pocket and take the lead, heading back down the street and crossing the road a short distance from where the car dropped my aunt off at. Coming from this direction feels safer than crossing directly in front of the building. I don't know if anyone is keeping an eye out on the storefront or not. So, coming from this angle makes more sense.

"There's an alley, right here." Savannah points it out. "There's a back door to the shop and a delivery door as well."

I nod. "Good idea." This makes it even easier.

We turn down the alley, effectively erasing the chance of being watched from the front.

Our steps whisper across the brick stone that makes up three sides of the alley. It's narrow and barely large enough for a delivery truck unless they are super skilled at driving through tight spaces. The back of the building is within a small alcove where, sure enough, there's a delivery door as well as a backdoor at the top of a small set of iron stairs. We climb them carefully and kneel in front of the door.

"What now?" I ask.

She smiles, pulling out a piece of chalk from another pocket and draws a transmutation circle, complete with a diamond, runes, and smaller circles. She replaces the chalk, then places both of her hands on either side of the circle, thumbs touching the outer line.

A soft blue glow rises from the circle, burning a hole into the room on the other side. It's an office of sorts. It reminds me of the interrogation rooms mobsters used in the old movies my father and I used to watch. My aunt sits facing me, rubbing her temples with her manicured fingers. Two men stand off to the side, backs facing me, but from the looks of it, my aunt is in hot water.

I press my lips together as I strain to hear what's being said.

As if she read my mind, Savannah bleeds a little green light into the circle, and I can suddenly hear everything as if we're standing in the room with them.

"I have it all under control," Aunt Patricia says.

"You have nothing under control," one man says. His voice is deep, callous, and he sounds like he's in charge. "You failed."

"It was a simple set back." Aunt Patricia slams her hands on the surface of the table she's sitting at. "I refuse to be spoken to like this. I outrank you."

"For now." This time it's the other man in the room. His voice is softer, but not by much. "Not for long."

Aunt Patricia glares at the man that spoke. "They wouldn't dare—"

"They would," the leader says. "And they will."

Aunt Patricia stands, leaning over the table, propping herself up with her arms as she levels her gaze on each of the men. "Watch the tone. I will not warn you again."

"The others are tired of waiting," the leader says. "We were sent here as your final warning."

"Your opportunity is now," the second man says. "No excuses. No more stalling. No more mistakes."

Aunt Patricia stands straighter as the other two men rise from their seats. "I'll get her. The next time we meet, it will be me delivering the threats to you."

"We'll see," the leader says. "She's escaped you twice now."

"The first time was different." She waves a dismissive hand in the air. "I didn't know she had it. I just wanted to be done with her." Aunt Patricia seems livid.

I suck in a breath. She's talking about me. I know it in my bones.

And she is after me.

First, I'm filled with shock. Then realization hits me as flashes of my memories come flooding back to me. Of that night so long ago now, it seems. Where I was being bounced on something hard. I remember feeling like my stomach muscles were getting bruised. I recall the sensation of being carried, but the feeling is diluted either from drugs or concussion. The smell was wretched, but I couldn't stop it from entering my nose. The world was too dark, and too blurry, to make out anything. Within seconds, I was out again.

This can only mean one thing. Aunt Patricia is the reason why I was kidnapped by the trolls.

Anger boils through me with that thought.

But the information we're getting here is pretty solid. Savannah and I exchange a look. Hers is begging me not to react and give away our location. Mine is one of murder and wrath. She barely shakes her head. I nod, agreeing with her. We may now know what my aunt has been up to, but there is more to hear.

"Don't think about pulling what your second did. They will find out." The second one speaks as he moves closer to my aunt. I can't get a good look at him, though. He's wearing the hood from his jacket pulled low over his head. What I can see is blurred. I suspect he has an enchantment on him that keeps him from being fully seen.

"That idiot got what he deserved." Aunt Patricia lifts her chin.

"You'll lose more than just your seat." The leader's

voice is thick with warning, and that tells me all I need to know.

Not only is my aunt a part of the Order, she's one of their heads.

"You'll wish your death is as swift if you even think about pulling a stunt like that." The second one continues on as if my aunt hadn't spoken.

"He was too close to the girl. I am not." Aunt Patricia faces the second man and stares him down. "Blood or no."

"Power like hers is corruptive."

"I am not like Deacon. I am not power hungry, and I have a brain. She will be ours. I will not fail." My aunt is livid. She spits out her words as though they are acid. "I will get the girl. You get the damn machine up and working."

I pull away from the image. The pain of betrayal has a particular sting that is almost crippling. Though, at first, I was hurt. Now I'm pissed.

What Savannah and I heard was enough to prove my aunt's involvement with much more than just the Order. She was directly responsible for my kidnaping.

Savannah's hand rests on my shoulder. I snap my attention to her. Her eyes are full of empathy.

"All this time she was after me. She was behind everything."

Savannah nods. "I know. We can still stop her though."

"How? She's part of the Order. You heard them, she's also one of their leaders." I pace the alley.

Something catches Savannah's attention as she faces the door again. "We have to go."

I nod. "We can't get out of here soon enough."

We start walking out of the alley and I notice Milo across the street. We quickly rush across the cobblestone street toward him. He turns his attention to us as we arrive. His expression is a mix of surprise and confusion.

"What's going on?" He asks.

"It's Patricia," Savannah says.

"Go find the others and bring them back quickly. We'll stay and keep an eye on my aunt so that we don't lose her."

Milo's eyes widen. With a nod, he turns and runs toward the hotel we're staying at, while Savannah and I return to the alley and find a hiding spot. As soon as we are inside the shadows of the building, the door to the shop opens.

I poke my head around the corner of the brick building to find my aunt standing in the middle of the sidewalk, pulling on her gloves and adjusting the scarf over her head as she waits for the car to come back for her.

Just as she looks in my direction, I duck back behind the building.

"Shit."

"What?" Savannah asks.

"I think she—"

Something invisible grabs ahold of me and pulls me into the air. I look over to find Savannah floating in the air next to me. Her eyes are wide with alarm, but she quickly composes herself and looks for a way out.

"Well, well. If it is not my niece and her little friend." She pauses, seeming to quickly think of her next words carefully. "What are you doing in the alley?"

"Let us go." I'm seething and spitting out my words as fire courses along my skin.

She laughs. For the first freaking time ever, my aunt actually laughs. It's not a pleasant sound, and it hints at danger lurking just around the corner. "No. I think not." She takes a few steps closer. "How much of that," she nods toward the shop, "did you hear?"

"Enough to know you're a liar and you betrayed your own family."

"No," she says, calmly. "I simply traded you in for my true one."

"My father's suspicions were right. How could you do this to him? To us?" I wiggle in the invisible grasp that tightens ever so slightly.

"How could your father leave me and our family legacy for a human who neither cared nor respected what the Blackwood name stands for?" My aunt's words remain calm, like every word she speaks is calculated and purposeful.

Steps in the alley echo toward me and Savannah as we both follow the direction of the sound. The two men that were in the room rush toward us. Dark miasmic purple and black smoke like magic surrounds them. They glare at me and I return the favor with a sarcastic smirk.

Oh good. We have friends.

CHAPTER TWENTY-NINE

My skin ignites with my magic.

"Let us go. Now." Despite the growing anger within me, my voice comes out calm and thick with the promise I'm going to deliver if she doesn't stop.

The leader of the two men steps forward, chuckling darkly. "I don't think so."

"Do it now," the second man says.

My aunt stares him down. "I decide how to accomplish my task. Not you. Get the car. This will not take long."

Aunt Patricia settles her dark gaze on me, and I am ready to face off with her. I press my lips together and let my magic flow through me, burning along my skin in dancing blue flames.

"Let Savannah go." I struggle harder against the invisible restraints that keep us floating in the air.

"She has seen too much. I am afraid she has to be dealt with as well." The same smoky black cloud surrounding my aunt begins to pool around her feet, growing along the ground like fast moving fog.

Whatever that stuff is, I know it's not good. I have to figure a way out of this and get Savannah to safety. Though I know I can handle my aunt just fine, the two goons with her will make for a tense fight. They stand with their biceps bulging and dark magic swirling at their fingertips. I have to hold off as long as I can. My men should be here soon. But with no idea how long that is going to take, I prepare for the worst-case scenario.

I look at Savannah as she shifts her glare between the two men and my aunt. She seems to be calculating something. Good. She's probably figuring out the same thing I am. Find a way out of whatever is keeping us up here, and get away from those two men, all before we get touched by whatever that magic is.

"You really don't want to hurt her." My warning goes unheard.

I dig deep into my magic. The air grows thick and my skin radiates heat like a flame. My power burns hotter and becomes a deeper blue than I've ever seen it burn before. My aunt shifts slightly. It's barely noticeable, but the movement catches my attention. I settle my gaze on my aunt to find she is concerned. Her attention falters as she pauses to mull over something in her mind.

That's all the time I need. I release my magic toward her. She ducks out of the way, and Savannah and I start to fall.

"Get them!" the leader of the men shouts as Savannah and I descend through the air, toward the stone walk.

The two men rush for us as we land and roll to our feet. But I'm prepared. I blast a wall of fire toward them. The crackling flames fly toward them as they grunt and duck out of the way. I release my magic to quickly check on Savannah. She's holding her left arm to her chest and her right knee is a little banged up.

"I'm fine," she says, keeping her gaze on the two men who have now recovered from the torrent of magic I rained down upon them.

But if they're still hungry for more, I am more than happy to oblige.

This time, Savannah joins in. She jumps between the two men and my aunt who seems to have recovered from whatever it was that initially caused her to break her concentration.

Meanwhile, we are getting pushed into the street, and that unsettles me. Sure, it would be easier to fight them off with more room to move, but it would also be easier for them to gain the upper hand on us. They could surround us, use the vehicles to their advantage by making them a blockade, keeping us trapped and close to them.

"No, you fools!" Aunt Patricia's voice echoes through the night air. "Back this way!"

Her tone allowed for no arguments or negotiation. The men pause and exchange a glance, probably not thrilled at further angering my aunt. They quickly whisk themselves beneath a blanket of dark fog, turning their bodies into smoke. They bleed into the shadows and move like snakes until they are behind us.

"Wren, watch out!" Savannah's voice hits me too late.

Something catches my hair and I'm jerked backward and fall to the ground. The world blurs through my eyes as I reach up and try to free my tresses from the deathlike grip. But it's no use. I hit the stone street hard. Pain radiates through my back as black dots fill my vision and my lungs struggle to take in air.

I'm pulled across the street and into the alley way as I catch a glimpse of Savannah holding her own against the two men. She casts a blinding ball of light and it swells, swallowing everything. I squeeze my eyes shut as I continue to try and free myself from my aunt's tight grip on my hair.

As soon as she has me where she wants me, she starts to form a portal.

I take advantage of the small window of time given to me and shuffle myself back to my feet. I face her and let out a string of lightning that hits the ground at her feet.

Her concentration breaks as she settles her eyes on me. "Give up, girl. There is no use in you fighting us anymore."

"Us?" I ask, looking around, pretending to not know she's referencing the Order.

"You are smarter than this. The more you struggle against the inevitable, the worse things will get for you. You know this."

"Do I?"

I'm keeping up my façade, buying time. Time I am quickly running out of.

She narrows her eyes at me, as though she's seeing through my lie and she presses her lips together. "That power does not belong to you."

"Yet, I have it."

She groans as her hands glow with fire. I quickly

form a shield and conjure up my own magic. Stalling has never been my strong suit, but in this case, I need to play on it as much as possible. It can't be much longer until my men arrive.

"Precisely the problem." She throws a river of fire at me. It strikes my shield with such force that I strain against it. My feet slide along the stone, and I nearly stumble on the jagged edges. "You should not have that power."

"Let me guess..." I grunt against the force of the ongoing attack and reach around to fire a blast of magic. It hits to her left, searing the stone of the building next to the magical supply shop.

Something hits me on my back. My skin burns like acid and I stumble forward.

Shit.

I struggle to get back to my feet. It takes a couple more attempts before I'm finally standing again. But no sooner than I'm upright, someone restrains my arms. I look to either side of me, finding my aunt's two goons clamping down on my biceps with their calloused hands. Even this close to them, their faces are still just blurs.

This is not good.

Aunt Patricia smirks as though she has won. She

steps in front of me. "It seems we need to teach you a lesson the hard way."

The two men chuckle as my aunt rams impossibly hard fists into my stomach like a battering ram. The air is forced from my lungs as my stomach muscles give in to each blow with searing pain. I catch sight of her fist as she chambers for another hit and I realize she's blending in magic with those hits straight to my gut.

A dark rim lines my vision, and I know I can't take much more of this before I lose consciousness completely.

And if I pass out, they really will win. They'll hurt me and those I care about.

Summoning all my strength, dipping into the deepest reserves of my magic available, I suck in a deep breath, pull my knees up to my chest, and plant them square into my aunt's chest. She flies backward. I don't watch her land. Instead, I bring my knees back up to my chest and separate my feet as I push them down onto the feet of the men holding me.

A resounding, sickening crack echoes through the air as I feel the crunch of their bones giving in from the force of my hit. They yell out in pain and force themselves to stay standing on their broken feet.

Lucky for me, they both let go of me and I stumble

forward again. I barely manage to keep myself on my feet as I spin and face the two of them head on.

I ram my fist into the cheek of the leader and side kick his partner. As they recover, I quickly check for Savannah, finding her lying in the street, unconscious.

Something is wrong. My men should be here by now.

I plant a hard knee in the leader's gut and his partner gets a sharp front kick to his knee. I glance behind me as my aunt is just now climbing to her feet. I'm not going wherever she's planning on taking me, and I need to find help. I can't beat the three of them on my own.

I blast my aunt back to her ass with a ball of magic light and take the opportunity of planting a few more hits on the men before dashing through the alley and into the street. I'm ripped into the air just before I reach Savannah's still form.

A scream leaves my lips.

No. I won't let them take me.

Without warning, I fall.

I squeeze my eyes shut, preparing for the harsh collision with the ground when I feel strong arms catch me. I open my eyes, finding amber eyes staring back at me, burning with rage.

"Are you okay?" Soren asks.

"I am now." I smile as he sets me down. "We need to handle this quickly and check on Savannah."

Gideon and Milo flank my left as Soren and Jesse take up my right. We face the three in front of us, each ready to continue this battle and end it once and for all. Aunt Patricia and the two goons with her can't blast their way through us. For now, Savannah is protected, shielded by me and my men.

"Enough!" Gideon's voice echoes through the streets.

Aunt Patricia and her two men join us in the center of the street. "Give us the girl and we will leave peacefully. Refuse, and we will have to take her by force."

"Over my dead body," Gideon growls.

The leader of the two men cracks his knuckles. "That can be arranged."

Aunt Patricia straightens her back, nose lifted in the air. "Is that so?" She smirks. "Do you do this sort of behavior for all of your students, Headmaster Storm, or is she just special?"

I suck in a breath of air as dread fills the pit of my stomach. If she caught on to Gideon and I being more than platonic within the perimeters of student and headmaster, she could create more trouble for us than we bargained for.

Gideon summons his magical staff and spins it in

front of him in such expert flourish, I'm momentarily mesmerized. He doesn't seem to give my aunt the time of day on her comment, instead, he means business. He ends his move with his staff angled behind him. "Bring it."

The two men charge, and the fight is back on.

Aunt Patricia focuses on me and I feel a tug at the center of my navel. She's trying that levitation trick again. Her face blurs, which raises the question of why, but I don't pursue the thought. Pressing my lips firmly together, I shake my head slightly, dip into my fighting stance, and conjure my magic. It flows through me, easily, and it almost surprises me how quickly it responds. But I don't spend time processing through that, I only know that if I don't do something, I will likely never see my men again.

That's just not a reality I'm willing to face.

Without much thought, I blast fire, lightning, and light at my aunt. I give her everything I have, but nothing seems to phase her. She manages to block and counteract each of my attacks.

She's done playing. And so am I.

This ends tonight.

Jesse jumps in front of me while Milo pulls at my waist. "Stop."

"Why?" I ask.

He squeezes my right wrist and I realize I lost my wrist cuff at some point during the fight. This isn't good. That's my conduit. I had been using magic without it. I didn't even realize I had lost it in the fight.

"Shit."

He nods, a solemn expression on his face. His attention flicks to the crowd gathering around us and I realize with heavy dread, not only did I fight without my conduit, but people saw me do it.

We take a step back and go help Savannah. She stirs as we approach and a groggy groan rumbles from her throat. I help her to her feet. "Are you okay?"

"I feel like I was bucked off a unicorn," she mumbles but manages to stay on her feet. She holds her head and squeezes her eyes shut for a moment as she takes in a slow inhale, letting it out in a sigh.

Horns blare across the island, filling the air with an added dose of dread. The magusari will swoop in on us. I have to find my conduit.

The sound seems to alert my aunt to call off the fight.

"Milo, check the alley for my conduit."

He nods.

"No need," Jesse says and pats the pocket of his leather jacket.

I let out a sigh. "Thank the gods. Help me?" I gesture to the crowd.

He joins me and smirks. "Now."

From the outside looking in, all anyone would see is me hugging Jesse. But on the inside, where the illusion doesn't reach, I dip into his pocket, pulling out my conduit and slipping it on.

"Thank you." I kiss him on his cheek.

"I'll seek payment later." He winks.

I return my attention as my aunt and headmaster are in the middle of a heated exchange. I see the faint tells of Jesse's illusion still going strong. Most of the growing crowd leaves even though the alarming horns still blare through the night air. My aunt also keeps her face blurred. She probably doesn't realize that Jesse has an illusion surrounding and shielding us from prying eyes.

"She's not an object for you to own and take whenever you feel like it." Gideon is furious. I've never seen him so angry.

My aunt stands there with her magic swirling around her, pushing toward Gideon. But his magic pushes back, meeting in the middle. It seems, they are equally matched. Part of me wonders if Gideon isn't stalling for the magusari to arrive. He may just let them handle her, proving not only to the world that the Order exists, but to also hold her accountable for her actions. Maybe my father's name will finally be cleared.

"What she has, she cannot keep. We will have it, one way or the other. You cannot stand in our way." Aunt Patricia stands her ground, seemingly unaffected by the sheer wrath that's building inside Gideon.

"Try, and you will lose more than just the power Wren has." He points a finger at her chest but doesn't jab her with it. He's showing significant control considering how furious he is.

The two men who fought alongside my aunt seem to have recovered and realized what the blaring horns are for. "We need to go," the leader of the two men demands.

My aunt balls her fists at her sides as her jaws clench tightly. She points a finger at Gideon. "This is not over."

"Looking forward to the next time we meet," Gideon says.

My aunt walks off, joining the two men as they blend into the shadows and disappear into the alley. I balk at the back of Gideon's head.

"What? You're letting her leave?" I approach Gideon but Soren stops me.

His eyes hold mine as he takes in a calm breath.

"There are rules, Wren. Ones we cannot go against no matter what. We will file a report which will go directly to the council. Then we follow the proper channels to get this handled."

"What? Why?"

"Because this happened on Crimson Isles. This land is protected. They will get theirs, believe me."

I snap my mouth shut even though there are numerous questions I need answered.

Meanwhile, my attention is caught by my aunt's final words. "This is not over."

The magasuri charge into the streets, ready to handle the issue they were called out for. Their boots clap against the stone in their thundering approach. Each of them have serious expressions, ready for battle. The crowd that had gathered disperses, returning to whatever they were doing before getting pulled into the fight. Once the report is given, including my redacted account of finding my aunt, leaving Savannah and the act of spying out of it, we're clear to return to our hotel rooms for the night.

Gideon is still furious as he talks to, who I assume is a captain of the magusari. "We need to organize now, damn it."

"Sir, I understand where you are coming from. But we have a process. You know this better than most of us." The captain stands in front of Gideon, but doesn't seem to show fear. It's more reverence, respect.

He's out for blood, but he's told to be patient and let the laws run their course. Even he has limitations he has to live by. It's a sobering thought, one that makes me realize there's so much more at stake here than just my life.

It's my men's lives. Savannah's life. And everyone else's lives that are at stake here.

The Order is up to no good, and I'll be damned if they use me or my meteorite to do it.

CHAPTER THIRTY

As we regroup, we silently make our way back to the hotel and to our rooms. Gideon is unusually silent and the rigidness of his body leaves all of my words falling silent.

"Go get bandaged up," Soren says to me. "I'll take care of Gideon."

"No. I need to do it."

He stops me in the middle of the hall as the others return to their rooms. "I know how to calm him down. Trust me, you don't want to see that."

"I'm doing it for my own peace of mind. Let me handle this. Please?"

He presses his lips firmly together and sighs.

"I'll catch up with everyone later." I leave Soren standing in the hall and rush after Gideon who disappeared into his room. As I arrive, I don't bother knocking. I walk in and shut the door behind me.

To say Gideon is pissed off is an understatement. He is beyond livid.

I calmly stand in the middle of his lavish suite while he paces in front of the king size bed. His body shimmers with magic, rising and falling in a rhythmic way that reveals his emotional state. It seems every time he calms down a little, the shimmer lessens, but then he gets angry again and it spikes. I've never seen him so upset. He just may spontaneously combust if I don't do something—anything—to calm him down.

"Gideon." I take a deep breath as the very sound of my voice feels intrusive to the tension-filled air.

He stops pacing and settles his gorgeous blue-green eyes on me. Something flashes through them. Within seconds, he rushes to me and pulls me into him, hugging me tightly to his chest.

"I'll kill them. I'll kill every last one of them," he mutters against my hair.

I can barely breathe with the way he's holding me so tightly against him. But I don't complain. He needs to feel me close to him, and that's what he's going to get.

"I won't let them get close to touching you again."

"I know," I whisper.

Maybe all he needs is time to process things. He's clearly protective over me. That fight was *close*.

He pulls away from me. "The magusari will take too long. Too much red tape to work through. Your aunt and her goons will get away. By the time the council clears an investigation and secures warrants to bring them in, they'll be long gone."

"It's not ideal," I agree. "But what choice do we have?"

"There's always a choice. How did you even know she was here?"

"I saw her on my way to meet Savannah for a drink. We spied on her. She was responsible for the trolls kidnapping me, but she didn't know I had the meteorite then. I don't know when she found out, but I believe it was Deacon Lawrence who told her. Based on what we overheard, my aunt is in hot water with the Order. I think she's high up. And my slipping through her fingers repeatedly has made her desperate."

He nods.

"Gideon," I pull back to face him. "I think she's one of the heads."

"What do you mean?" His brow furrows with confusion.

"The way the two men were speaking with her and

what she was saying, it just makes sense. She feels like they are her family, that my father somehow betrayed her by marrying my mother. Apparently, I'm unworthy of my powers."

He kisses my forehead and rests his cheek on my head as he holds me close to him. I melt a little more the longer he embraces me. But his body isn't shaking now. I feel like I'm making progress with him.

"She's up to no good," he mutters, squeezing me to him. "No doubt."

"We still don't have proof to bring to the magusari she's with the order. Everything we have on her is circumstantial at best. Without that proof, no action can be taken."

"Doesn't matter. I'm going to make them pay for hurting you."

"I'm not hurt." I pull away from him to take in his handsome face. "I'm fine."

He takes me to a full-length mirror, keeping my back to it. "Look at that and tell me how fine you are."

I look over my shoulder and gasp. A huge hole in the back of my jacket and shirt exposes my bare, charred back. "That's…"

"You're in shock." He starts to pace again. "I'm going to fucking kill them!"

"Gideon. Calm down. I'm fine. I don't feel the pain anymore. Look…"

He settles his gaze on me, and I peel back the layers of cloth from my body until I'm standing with the top half of me naked. I turn my back to him. "See?"

His footsteps shuffle slowly toward me. I feel the magic within me pulse and buzz. A few seconds later, his fingers gently touch my back. "No pain?"

I shake my head. "None."

He slides his hands to my front and pulls me into him as his mouth kisses along my shoulder to the base of my neck. "What about here?"

I bite the corner of my lower lip as pressure pools between my legs and my knees feel weak. "Nope."

He breathes in deep as his lips hungrily nibble on my ear lobe. "Here?"

I lean into him, delighting in the delicious way he makes me feel. "Nuh-uh."

He stops nibbling to whisper, "I'll be right back."

He leaves me, taking the warmth with him as he grabs a towel from the bathroom and runs water over it. After wringing it out in the sink, he approaches me, holding out the towel. "Hang on to this for me."

"Okay." I take the towel. It smells like lavender and rosemary.

Gideon digs through his bags and pulls out a long

t-shirt, tossing it over his shoulder before returning to me and holding out his hand for the towel. I hand him the towel with a smile, and he gently starts running the cloth over my back, clearing the soot and debris from my skin.

"Does this hurt at all?"

I laugh under my breath as I have to yet again reassure my protective headmaster that I'm fine. "No."

"Good." His voice sounds huskier, and I smile to myself as I lean into him, feeling his erection press against the fabric of my pants. He chuckles. "You're going to be the death of me, woman."

"That sounds so horrible."

I watch him through the mirror as he focuses on long, careful strokes of the towel. The warm wetness leaves a trail of cold, and the sensations seep into the center of my hips. He meets my gaze in the reflection of us standing here and smiles in that way he does when he knows damn well what he's doing to me.

"We should come up with a plan," I say. "When you're ready."

"I agree. What ideas do you have?"

I smile. "Just one."

I spin around, throw my arms around his neck, and plant my lips on his. He groans against my lips and that just makes me want him more. He lifts me up and carries me to the bed, laying me down, not once breaking from our kissing. I spread my legs as he settles between my hips, his erection pressing against my pants while his mouth devours mine.

Things are getting pretty heated between us, and though I would be totally okay with us continuing, Gideon pulls away. "I can't…" His voice is soft and full of regret.

"Okay." I'm disappointed.

Truth be told, I'm a lot disappointed. My face falls as a frown tugs on my lips.

"I'm sorry." He looks me in my eyes, ensnaring me with his blue-greens. "You are still one of my students."

"I know." I smile and lift up to kiss him one last time. I take the shirt that's still over his shoulder and slip it on as he sits up. "Do you think my aunt knows about us?"

"I don't know." He runs a hand through his hair. "I need a cold shower. So I can think."

I chuckle. "Well, at least you no longer want to go on a murdering spree in my honor."

"No, I still want that. But I'm a bit more concerned about taking care of you."

I shrug. "You should first take that shower."

He smiles at me. "It is a bit uncomfortable."

"I'm sorry." I cross my legs on the edge of his mattress. "I don't want to push our luck any more than you do."

He rests a hand on my leg. "Don't be. I'm quite happy with that." He nods toward my borrowed shirt.

"I may never give this back, you know."

"I'd be okay with that." He stands from the bed and makes his way to the shower. "I shouldn't be long."

"I'll go get the others and come back. Ten minutes?"

"Perfect."

He shuts the door to the bathroom and within seconds, the shower is turned on. I take my leave and head for Soren's room first.

CHAPTER THIRTY-ONE

Ten minutes later, we're all gathered in Gideon's room. I sit on his bed with my back against the headboard, legs crossed out in front of me. Gideon stands near the window that overlooks the street where our little showdown happened. Savannah is sitting in a chair at a small writing desk, facing the rest of the room. Jesse and Milo take the sofa that sits in front of the TV. And Soren sits at the foot of the bed, angled toward the middle of the room, knee propped up on the mattress.

Savannah and I had taken turns filling in the men on what really happened versus what they heard me tell the magusari.

"Why didn't you tell them the truth?" Soren asked.

I shrugged. "I was trying to protect Savannah and

myself because apparently the magusari would frown on our little investigation. Besides, without any proof, accusing my aunt of being a high-ranking member of the Order would make things even more messy. That would bring on more questions, which would lead them even closer to figuring out what I have. We already established the less people that know, the better."

Soren thinks about that for a moment then nods. "Fair point."

"I'm impressed," Jesse says. "But next time you want to get into mischief, let me come. I hate missing out on all the fun."

"There shouldn't be a next time," Milo says. "I agree, we need a plan. But what are we going to do to make sure Savannah and Wren are safe?"

"First," I say. "We need to warn my father."

"She's right," Gideon says as he continues to look out the window. "Michael needs to know. We need to consider every angle in which things could head for the worse."

"I'll write him a letter right now." I say. "Paper and pen?"

Gideon nods toward the desk. "Make sure to tell him to expect more of a protection detail to show up. It will be a few others of my most trusted friends, including us. Tightening down on the security will also ensure his safety." He pauses to think for a moment. "Anyone not on the list of individuals, including those of us here, will not be allowed on the premises."

Savannah jumps up and digs into the drawers. She pulls out a couple sheets of paper and a pen. She brings them to me.

"Thanks."

She winks and returns to her seat.

I use the nightstand to write out the message. Once it's done, I pass it to Soren for his vote. His eyes scan it once and he hands it back with a nod of approval.

I perform all the necessary steps, sending it off in a burst of flame and ash. Though, barely any ash remains.

"Next item on the agenda is Wren and Savannah's safety." Jesse stands and stretches his arms over his head. "How are we going to keep them safe without removing their freedom and autonomy?"

"I'll block Patricia's access to Blackbriar." Gideon faces us and leans against the window. "She and anyone else not directly involved with the academy will not be allowed on the island."

"I'll work on the detail for Michael," Soren says. "And escort Wren on her trips to see him. It'll help ward against anything happening. She could be intercepted, and we wouldn't know."

He looks to me for argument. I nod. He does the same. Good. We have an accord.

"Milo," Gideon says. "You and Jesse will go back to Blackbriar with Wren immediately. Soren will be there shortly."

"Wait, what?" I say, glaring at my handsome headmaster.

He sighs. "You were already attacked once here. Do you want to risk another chance?"

"I think she will be too busy licking her wounds, actually."

Soren twists to face me. "I know you love this place. It won't be the last time you visit."

I frown. "It doesn't seem fair."

"You're right," Gideon says. "It's not. But this is what we have to work with. Your safety is my top priority. You'll be safe back at Blackbriar."

"What about the Mage Championships?" I ask Soren. "Are you just going to quit them?"

He pinches the bridge of his nose and huffs. "When will you learn that you are the most important thing to me? Not the stupid championships."

"So, you're giving them up for me?" I lean back

against the headboard and cross my arms. "That's pretty shitty."

"It's my choice. If I have to choose between you and a flashy contest, it's always going to be you."

"You're not going to win this, love," Jesse says.

I take a moment to meet the gaze of all of my men. Each of them sticking to their guns, as usual. I groan. "Fine."

"What can I do?" Savannah asks.

"Go back with Wren and keep your eyes and ears open. I'll draw up my list of people on the island I can't fully read. See what you can find out about them."

She nods. "On it."

"Meanwhile," Gideon says through a sigh, "we need to be prepared for Patricia to make good on her promise to take Wren by force."

My attention piques at that. I really hope he's not going to suggest a constant escort.

"It's time to up the level of our trainings. No more breaks. Every evening, we meet in my office. To give Wren the best odds of surviving and avoiding capture, she needs to learn how to fight like them." He nods to me. "Any questions?"

I shake my head.

"Good."

Everyone stands and makes their way to leave. I

stay behind and wait until Savannah closes the door. Gideon stares at me curiously. I grin at him.

"Thank you."

"For what?" he asks.

"For not suggesting I be babysat. For being willing to give me the tools I need to fight against the Order. For being you." I want to say so much more, but I refrain. For now, what has been said will suffice.

Short. Sweet. To the point.

He nods as he slips his hands into the pockets of his jeans. "I would do anything for you, Wren. We all would."

"I know." My lips remain pulled into a soft smirk as I walk out the door and head for my room. I need to gather my things before we head back.

CHAPTER THIRTY-TWO

The House of Drakon's common room is dark.

Not in the horror sense, but in the sense that everything is in earth tones. Two large black leather sectionals take up the center of the room. A stone coffee table sits in between them, and an earthy brown-colored rug beneath that. The whole arrangement faces a large stone fireplace. The warmth from the fire bleeds into the room as Milo and I sit at one corner of one of the sectionals.

He's jotting down something in his notebook as we carry on casual conversation. He's unusually pensive and quiet today. I wonder what's going on, but every time I ask, he shakes his head and insists nothing is up.

"What are you working on?" I ask.

He shrugs as he continues to scribble. "Nothing

much. Just ideas on compositions and transmutation circles."

"Well, you seem very... I don't know... frustrated. What's bothering you?"

He glances at me briefly, pushes his glasses up his nose and sniffs. "Nothing, really."

I frown and set my gaze on the swirls within the design of the stone of the coffee table as I puzzle over what is going on with my men.

All my men are kind of acting strange. It's confusing the hell out of me.

It has been a little over two weeks since Crimson Isles and that fun brush with my aunt and her goons. As soon as we got back, one by one, my men started hanging out with each other more and more. And whenever I would join them, it seemed like they changed the topic. They are up to something. I'm sure of it.

Honestly, it's starting to drive me crazy. Each of them insists nothing is going on.

But *something* is.

Especially with the sly grin Milo flashes each time I ask him what's up.

Finally, he slaps his book closed and sets it and his pencil on the coffee table. Leaning back, he rests his head against the back of the sofa, and I lay down on his lap. He absently runs his fingers through my hair that spills over his lap, and I close my eyes against the ceiling enchanted to mimic the night sky. Every once in a while, a dragon flies through the dark expanse that's dotted with the soft glow of stars.

"Tired?" Milo asks.

"No," I mumble sleepily. I'm fighting against the urge to slip into my dreams. His petting me is relaxing.

He chuckles. "It's okay if you want to take a nap."

"And miss out on your beautiful face?" I peel my eyes open to look at him. "Not a chance."

"You could always dream of me."

"Not the same." I stare at the ceiling as wisps of clouds float along the midnight blue sky peppered with diamonds. A full moon sets near the far-right corner of the room, and I wonder how late it is. A wonderful thought enters my mind and I smile. "We could still go to your room, though. Maybe have a workout?"

He blushes a little as he takes in a deep breath. "Is that what you would like to do?"

I shake my head, laughing under my breath as I pull myself up from the couch. "Why don't you follow me and find out?"

He hops up and follows me as I disappear down the hall that leads to his room.

Once we are through the door, Milo catches my hand and pulls me back to him. He runs a hand through my hair and cups my cheek. I bite the corner of my lower lip. He kisses my forehead, the tip of my nose, and then my lips.

I laugh as I cling to him, enjoying not only his special way of showing his affection for me but the way my magic rushes through me. He leads me to the bed, and we fall onto the mattress together.

We make out until it feels like my face is raw from the stubble growing along his jawline. I tease him about that.

"Sandpaper face." I gently scratch my fingers along his jaw.

He checks his non-existent watch on his wrist and cocks his head to the side. "It's not five o'clock yet. What is going on?"

I snicker. "You're spending too much time with Jesse if you can pull off a retort like that." I snap my fingers.

"Perhaps. Or, we could blame you." He taps me on my nose.

I squeeze him to me. "I'm gonna miss you so much over break. My sexy nerd."

Everyone is leaving for the winter holiday break in the morning. Even me. For once. I'm going to spend time with my father. I'm looking forward to it.

Milo smiles, but there's something in his eyes that flashes through. It's gone as soon as it appears, and I wonder what he's thinking of.

"What sort of concoction are you brewing up there?" I tap his temple.

"Nothing." He looks down at my mouth before meeting my gaze again.

I quirk an eyebrow. "I have a sneaking suspicion you're hiding something."

"And if I am?" He levels his deep brown eyes on me, darkened with desire, and I feel compelled to pull him to me and let him have his wicked way with me.

It's a hard thing to fight, but I do for the sake of figuring out what's going on. "That's not a denial."

"Nor is it a confession. More a curious inquiry."

I snort. "You're such a nerd."

"Hey, I wear that badge of honor proudly, I'll have you know."

"Good." I breathe him in. "You should."

"You didn't answer my question," he says as he runs his hands up my side, hiking up my shirt as he moves teasingly slow to my breasts.

"Then we're even."

Man, I love spending time with him. He always gives me a logical way to look at all the hiccups in our plans, which makes me appreciate how smart he is. He helps me to see the light at the end of the tunnel. And, he manages to keep me on edge, in a good way, with whatever he's hiding from me.

Strangely, I actually don't mind.

I don't have to worry with him, and I adore him for all he is and so much more.

He kisses me and I melt into the bed.

I adore him. I love him for not only who he is, but how he makes me simply feel. I know things will work out because of him.

Not just him.

But him, Jesse, Soren, and Gideon.

My men. My team. My *family*.

Just to show my appreciation of all that he does, I flip him to his back and smile naughtily.

CHAPTER THIRTY-THREE

The next afternoon, after showering and getting ready, I meet Soren in our secret training spot. It's cold, and the trees are mostly barren, but the view is still just as beautiful.

Crunching footsteps echo toward me, and as they approach, my magic burns through me. I smile to myself as I keep my back to Soren. As he stops just behind me, I can almost feel his warm breath brush against my hair.

"Ready?"

"Just a moment. I'm enjoying the view."

He's been sticking to his word to escort me to my father's house ever since our talk following the fight with my aunt. Since taking his position as professor here at Blackbriar Academy, we haven't had much time together. So I figured, despite the annoyance, I will go with the flow, especially since he's worth the company.

"It is a very beautiful view," he agrees.

I breathe in deep the smell of the ocean and winter on the island before facing him. "Now, we can go."

He grins, taking my hand and leading me away from the cliff. He forms a portal, glittering from the ground up in a pillar of light. I smile at him as I step through and onto the estate grounds my father is temporarily stationed at until we can clear his name.

I hope it's soon.

My father didn't take the news of the attack on me and Savannah well, and he's been overly cautious since then.

As Soren steps out of the portal, I busy myself with the beauty of what Maryland looks like in winter. Several inches of snow covers the ground, coating the tree branches. It glitters in the late afternoon sunlight, and the whole scene is breathtaking. We arrived nearly at the back door of Gideon's home, which leaves the vast land around it free from indentation. Everything is so smooth and crisp.

I simply love it.

Soren grabs my hand and leads me inside the kitchen. I head for the living room, slipping off my coat as I move, stopping at the coat closet. Once my coat is on the hanger, safe and sound, I walk through the house in search of my dad.

I hear muttering behind me and look over my shoulder to see what Soren is going on about. He's tucked into the kitchen. Whatever it is, I'm sure he's figuring it out.

"Wren," Soren calls.

I stop about halfway through the main hall, almost to the stairs that face the front door. "Yeah?"

"Can you come here?"

My heart leaps into my throat. Confusion pinches my forehead as I turn around and head back toward the kitchen. I don't know what to expect or why Soren would feel the need to call me back to him instead of just coming to get me himself, but I'm about to find out.

As the kitchen comes into view, I see streamers in various colors, that I'm very certain weren't there before. Drawing even closer, the smell of cake hits my nose and whispers filter through the air.

"What is going on?" I ask as I continue to move, albeit slowly.

"You'll see."

And I do.

Rounding the wall leading to the kitchen, I'm faced

with streamers, balloons, and all of my men, including my father, standing around the table.

"Surprise!" they call out.

"Uh… that's one word for it." I narrow my eyes on each of them.

Have I mentioned I don't like surprises?

No?

Okay, then.

"How did you…" I narrow my eyes on Jesse who stands proudly. As much as I want to playfully scorn him, I can't. I beam. He pulled off an illusion to hide everyone. "Asshole."

"You're welcome." He plays up a flourishing bow.

I laugh. "I wasn't even looking for an illusion. Well played."

He winks. "Naturally."

"Is this what you four have been hiding from me?" I ask, shifting my gaze over all of the men in the room.

"It was Savannah's idea," Gideon says.

I look around. "Where is she?"

"She'll be here soon. She had to take care of a few things before coming."

I nod and move through the room, exchanging hugs and saying thanks to each happy birthday. "You guys realize my birthday was over a week ago, right?"

"Of course," my father says. "But after how things

went with your aunt and how long it's been since your day has been celebrated, we wanted to do something extra nice and special."

"I appreciate the gesture. But please, no more surprises." I add a smile, so not to look ungrateful. I really am. Truly.

When I get to Milo, I playfully glare at him. "Liar, liar…"

He chuckles. "No one has ever accused me of being unable to keep a secret. I'm not going to start now."

I hug him. "Fair enough."

My dad breaks out the Polaroid camera and has my men gather around me. After the loud *cheese* and bright flash, I start to relax from the initial panic. The film spits out white. My father pulls it out of the camera and sets it and the camera on the table before moving to a cabinet.

"I know this whole birthday thing is different for you," my father says as he sets a cake on the table, covered with colorful ribbons of frosting and long candles, "but none of us could resist the idea when it was brought up."

I smile, flattered. "I really appreciate it. It makes me feel special."

"You should. You are special." Jesse leans against

the counter with his arms crossed over his chest and a smirk stretching his lips.

"In a way," Soren adds, "we all hope this helps to make up not only for what happened with your aunt, but also all the years that you missed out on being celebrated."

Wow.

Soren just got all feely on me.

I smile. "When did you become so mushy?"

"Don't be a brat and open your gifts."

The men move out of the way to reveal a counter with a pile of gifts on it.

"Wow."

I feel a bit beside myself with the display. The most I was given while with the trolls were scraps of food and tattered clothing they stole from camps around the village. There was the dress my aunt bought for me, but that doesn't count. Not from her. It was a lame attempt to earn my good graces so she could backstab me. The clothing given to me when I first arrived at Blackbriar were a gift from the school, which I attribute to Gideon and Lady Alene, and solely because I couldn't roam the halls covered in stained, torn rags.

Those were a necessity.

But these?

These are gestures of love. Love I thought I would never feel again.

My heart swells as each of my men picks up their gifts.

Jesse hands me an envelope. I take it from him, sliding my finger under the seal and ripping the top open. As I peek into the opening, I notice two small strips of paper. Pulling them out, I see they're concert tickets to an opera being held over the summer.

"Get ready to dress up," Jesse says, pulling my attention to him.

"I've never been to an opera before." I hug him. "Thank you."

"There's a first time for everything, love." He winks.

I place the tickets back into the envelope and set them on the table and face Milo.

He hands me his gift. It's a box, neatly wrapped with white paper and tied with a shimmery pink ribbon. I set the box on the table and pull at the ribbon before ripping into the paper, revealing a white box. I lift the top of it to find nestled in pink tissue paper is a leather-bound journal with my initials etched into the cover. Along the spine is a set of runes, and I can practically feel the enchantments pouring off of it.

I run my fingers along the cover and smile. Now I

have a book that's just like the ones he's constantly carrying around.

"It's beautiful, Milo." I face him and give him a hug and a kiss on the cheek.

"You're welcome. I'll tell you more about the enchantment on it later."

"I look forward to it."

"Don't forget mine!" A familiar voice speaks.

I face Savannah as she stands in the kitchen with two bottles of birthday cake flavored vodka and sets them on the counter. "No, these aren't it."

She walks to the counter and picks up a basket that is full of lotions, bath salts, and soaps. Inside it is also a gift card to the spa we had gone to after our trials. "You deserve to pamper yourself."

I take the basket and thumb through everything. "It looks amazing and sounds blissful."

After I give her a hug, she holds me at arm's length. "Happy birthday, girl."

"Thank you."

Gideon steps forward. "Mine will have to wait… since they are sleeping."

I look at him confused.

He chuckles. "It's a ride on one of the gryffons."

My eyes widen. "I can't wait!"

Soren walks up from behind me. "Don't get too excited, there's still more in store for you."

I look over my shoulder into his amber eyes. "Oh really?"

He nods and holds out a black rectangular box about eight inches long.

"What's this?"

"Open it and find out." Soren's voice rushes over my ear, sending delightful tingles through me.

I grip the lid of the box and pull it open to show a dagger with a black handle. Rivers of silver wrap around the hilt with green stones surrounding its base. "It's beautiful."

There's an enchantment on it. I can feel its power pulsing through the blade. I just don't know what.

"It's an enchanted dagger of energy. Whatever you use it for, it takes less effort."

"Oh, that's intriguing!" I beam at him and lean back. "Thank you."

"Last but not least," my father says as he holds out a large photo album wrapped in pink and white lace.

My heart skips a beat. I recognize that book from my childhood. My mouth parts but no words escape as I reach a shaking hand over the table to take the baby book. "How did you…" I can't finish the sentence.

"I had a little help." He nods toward my men.

I shake my head in awe as I rake my gaze over each of them and focus on the book in my hands.

In the center of it is a shadow image of a bird, surrounded in white, with a smattering of pink glitter.

"You may want to look at that later. At least, read the notes from your mother later." I meet my father's gaze. He nods once. "It was difficult for me."

I sigh as I run my fingers along the ribbons of lace. "Thank you." It comes out as a whisper.

I start to flip through the pages that show pictures of my mother, who I am a spitting image of, holding her belly with a wide smile. Some have my father standing behind her. They were so young, and so happy looking.

"Your mother wrote a letter for you when you were born, and for each year after that until you were five."

"What made her stop?" I ask, setting my gaze on my father.

"She was busy with you." He grins, but it's sad and I can tell he misses her dearly.

So do I, Dad. So do I.

After spending what seems like hours listening to my men ooh and aww over me as a baby and little girl, we share in cake, birthday cake flavored vodka shots, and loud music well into the early hours.

By the time the sky starts to lighten with the new

day, we all make our way to bed. I'm dizzy, and a little woozy, but the smile on my face seems semi-permanent. Savannah stumbles into my room and falls onto the foot of my bed, making the sensation of being on an ocean a brief and wild experience.

"What did you think of your first birthday party in forever?" she asks, slurring her words a little.

"Amazing!" I say. My eyelids become too heavy to keep open. I vaguely hear Savannah saying something and then laughing, but I'm too tired. My body wants sleep, and I give in to that need.

CHAPTER THIRTY-FOUR

In the private training room within Gideon's office, I pant for breath.

My men are using their strengths against me in an effort to challenge me, because when it comes to the Order, fighting fair isn't part of the deal. Though they are taking things hard on me, I appreciate it. Every day since the beginning of the second semester, I have been training in the evenings.

An illusion is being set again.

Break time is over.

Soren unleashes a torrent of fire, spiraling like a flaming whip around him. He snaps it at me, and I dodge the blow just one precious second before it hits. Gideon takes his magical staff and swings it at my head. I bend backward to avoid it as a rush of air whizzes over my head, just centimeters from my nose. Milo uses wind to kick up the dirt and create tunnels that swerve around me.

If I didn't know any better, I'd say they were out for blood.

Good thing I know better.

I use my physical strength to avoid the torrents of wind and my magic to parry each attack. My favorite go-to is a fireball, but I'm practicing my lightning magic as well. I'm focused, and though it's difficult with so much going on around me, I maintain awareness of my surroundings.

The room is set up like a woodland similar to that on this island. The weather changes every fifteen minutes, with unpredictable patterns. What started off as a nighttime session, turned to daytime with dark storms brewing all around us.

I dodge another whirlwind of dirt as I hurl a ball of energy toward Gideon who tried to hit me in the side with it.

"Good." He spins his staff expertly and steps back.

I pant. "Sure."

But I want to be better than good. I want to be *deadly*.

A face off with the Order and my aunt is inevitable.

I need to be better than them, faster than them, smarter than them.

As the attacks keep coming, the image of Savannah lying on the street stays at the forefront of my mind. It makes me angry and soon, I'm punching harder, kicking harder, throwing my magic quicker.

I become lost in the thought of what I would do had Savannah been severely or fatally injured that I forget to pay attention to my surroundings.

My feet are kicked out from underneath me. As I watch the room spin in my view, I realize that Jesse stepped up his game and added his own little twist on our training lessons. With so much going on, I forgot to pay attention to what he was doing.

My back slams against the dirt, but it hurts less than it used to, which is new. And welcome.

"You're supposed to pay attention to me, remember?" Jesse's head pokes into my view of the ceiling that is turning into night again.

"Oh, I know, let's switch places and see how well you can keep up."

He holds his hand out to me with a smile, getting the rise out of me that he was seeking. I take his hand and he pulls me to my feet easily. That's another new thing that's happened over the last few months. Everything seems easier.

Except this training, of course.

"We just want to make sure you are prepared," Gideon adds.

"I know." I groan. "We've been through this over and over again."

"And you're improving," Soren says.

"You are quite a bit faster now." Milo joins the circle forming around me.

"It's been quiet for too long." I shake my head. "She's up to something. I know it."

Gideon nods. "Thus, why we are training like this. You've gotten a lot better over the past three months. That's a very short span of time. With you going to your father's house, it's important that we know you can handle anything they throw at you…"

He stops, almost as though he doesn't want to say the words I already know.

In case they can't get to me in time.

My last run-in with my aunt was too close for comfort. Soren still escorts me to see my father every other weekend. But with my improvements, he's willing to let me do this next run on my own. Though I had to fight for that chance.

In fact, I leave tomorrow.

It will be different going back to my father for a

whole week. I've gotten comfortable with my new routine.

As soon as I catch my breath, Gideon snaps his fingers. "Again."

The room changes to snow, and an icy wind blows against me. As Jesse disappears, I know the illusion is set. Milo blows gales of ice toward me, and I dodge them while charging Soren before he can get his fiery whips out.

I throw an upper cut and roll to the side as Soren flips backward, avoiding the attack from Milo. Gideon charges forward, and I fight off both him and Soren, blocking and attacking with punches and kicks of my own.

My intuition flares within me and I duck to avoid Jesse's attack. He shows himself, smirking proudly. "That's my girl."

I grin and attack with a ball of light at his feet. "Don't drop your guard," I mock.

He snickers. "Touché."

Soren sneaks up behind me and wraps his arms around my waist. "Never turn your back on the enemy."

Oops.

He pulls me back toward the simulated trees. I fight against him, even though I love this.

"You'll have to do much better than that," he croons in my ear, dark and dangerous. His breath sends warm tingles down my spine.

I sarcastically chuckle. "You did that on purpose, you bastard."

"Stop complaining and let me have my fun."

I grunt as I struggle to get out of his tightening grasp. "I didn't know that word existed in your vocabulary."

Jesse appears in front of us. "Hands off my woman!" He tugs on my arms.

I burst out in uncontrollable laughter. I can't help it.

What is supposed to be a serious training session has turned out to be a game of Capture the Wren.

I fucking *love* it.

Though this isn't the first time our training has taken a hilarious turn, it is the last for at least a week. Gideon and Milo join in, Gideon taking Soren's side, and Milo taking Jesse's.

"Boys! Share!" I push the words out between bouts of laughter.

It's a tug-of-war with me being the rope.

It's so easy to let my guard down and have fun with my men. Especially in times like this, where I won't see them for a while.

I'm even having fun with Savannah. She and I have grown closer over the last few months.

I've also become very fond of sleepovers. Not necessarily all that girlie stuff, but having my nails done is nice.

"So help me if you ruin my manicure, I'm burning you all to a crisp."

They stop tugging long enough to exchange glances and shrug only to start playfully tugging on me again.

"There is enough of me to go around. Knock it off!" It's very difficult to be convincing while laughing.

Soren and Gideon win out as Jesse and Milo lose their grips on my feet.

Soren lets out a victory yell and tosses me over his shoulder.

"Soren, put me down!"

"Nope. I won. Fair and square."

"So, help me..." He doesn't listen. I warned him. "Professor McCallister!"

He smacks my ass.

Hard.

It's a love pat at most, but the stinging that tingles throughout my backside only adds to the smile on my face.

"Gideon!"

"Nope. He won."

"You won too! Where's the love? Help me!"

Jesse, Gideon, and Milo laugh at me while Soren walks me out of the training room and into Gideon's office. He sits me down on the chair and winks as he stands up straighter.

"Was that so bad?" He asks, a mocking edge to his tone.

I stick out my tongue.

He shakes his head, grinning. "Real mature."

"So is carrying me around caveman style."

He pauses to think that through and eventually shrugs as my other three men walk into the room.

"All right," Gideon claps his hands, "that's enough fun for one evening. Go enjoy yourselves."

While my men start for the door, I stand from the chair. Gideon holds up his hand to stop me.

"Except you. You're not done yet."

I groan and playfully pout as I plop back into the chair.

CHAPTER THIRTY-FIVE

As soon as the last of the three men are out the door, Gideon settles his intense gaze on me. "I have more training for you."

Only Gideon can make training sound erotic.

I freaking love it.

I nod, standing from the chair and start heading back toward the training room. "Let's get started then."

As I move past him, he grabs my hand and pulls me into him. He takes in a deep breath of my hair and hums a contented sigh as he breathes out. He turns me to face him. His eyes dark, full of desire. Holding my face gently in his hands he brings my mouth to his. He presses his satin-soft lips against mine. My heart picks up its pace as my magic fills me with the strength of my headmaster.

Kissing Gideon blows my mind.

Every. Single. Time.

His fingers become tangled in my hair as I wrap my arms around his waist.

I could do this all day. Kissing him is beautiful, blissful, *magical*.

I want this kiss to never end. But it does as he reluctantly pulls away. I'm left light-headed and feeling like I'm walking on a cloud.

He chuckles to himself as he stands from the front of his desk and tugs my hands, pulling me behind him as he walks toward his magical closet, AKA, our secret training room. Once inside, the room morphs into a mountainous escape.

My kind of paradise.

The peaks are coated with a dusting of snow of the purest white I have ever seen. Beneath the mountains, in the valley we are now standing in, flows a crystal blue stream that weaves through the thick collection of evergreens, aspens, pines, and cottonwood trees. Deer prance through the woods, stopping to take a drink from the stream before continuing on their hike.

Bald eagles soar among the clouds in the bluest skies. A sky so blue they closely rival the one above

Crimson Isles. The sun shines with a gentle warmth. The smell is that of the cleanest air with hints of the trees of the forest blended in.

"Wow." I spin to take everything in. "Can we stay here forever?"

He laughs. "I wish we could. At least for a short time. But we have a little more training to do."

I settle my gaze on him, catching him in the act of me staring at everything with a child-like enthusiasm. "What are we covering today, Headmaster?"

He shakes his head, never losing his smile. "Two can play this game, Miss Blackwood."

"Game on."

He rushes into me, pushing me back until I'm pressed against the wall of a rocky cliffside. Even as he pushes against me, he pins my hands on either side of my head as he once again drives me wild with his kisses.

My magic stirs inside me, buzzing with strength and resolve. Because that's what he does to me. I not only feel stronger, I *am* stronger. With him, I know nothing can stand in my way. I can face any obstacle and succeed.

He pulls away. "Done yet?"

I shrug, panting for breath. "Maybe. You'll just have to wait and see."

He leans his forehead against mine and releases my wrists, exchanging his hold on them for resting them on my hips. "I need to make sure if something happens to your conduit, you can control yourself."

I nod. We had practiced over the summer and occasionally throughout the school year, when he wasn't too busy. I've gotten a lot better at managing the flow of power, but I haven't quite perfected it yet. At his request, I only practice without my conduit with him. No one else. I don't pretend to know why, but I know it has something to do with his ability to see if the magic is ever going to corrupt me. As painful as that worry is, I don't let it stop me. And apparently, it doesn't stop him either. He's also one of the most powerful mages alive. If anyone can teach me how to control my magic, it's him. That thought has been a huge comfort to me in all our sessions sans conduit.

"Also, in case you miss the fact it's off." He levels his gaze on me.

"You knew about that?" I narrow my eyes at him.

He only lowers his head once in confirmation.

"Why wait to tell me until now?" I ask.

"Because I wanted to first make sure you could handle the level of hell coming for you in case I and the others aren't able to reach you in time. That was more important to me than worrying about you using magic without your conduit." His gaze drops to my wrist, where the cuff rests.

I follow his gaze, taking in the glittering sunbursts reflecting off the sunstones. Knowing good and well what he wants, I lift my hand and slip off the cuff, handing it to him. "Do your worst."

"I intend to." He settles against the wall as I walk deeper into the training simulation.

I stop as soon as a loud crack resonates through the air. Cocking my head, I listen for the tell of an attack.

There.

Deep in the woods, roughly fifty feet away, the sound of steps crunch toward me. Another sound alerts me to something else approaching from the left, across the stream. Shadows start to move through the trees, and I realize Gideon really is going to be hard on me this round.

I square my shoulders and lift my chin slightly higher. Magic fills my palms and I know with every fiber of my being, I'm ready.

Instantly, I recall all of our talks over our numerous training sessions. Each time, he gets a little more insight into my meteorite. He believes the more I can become in tune with it, the more it may grow with me and our bond could become unbreakable.

Which is something that is incredibly important to me.

If my bond becomes unbreakable, it won't matter what the Order does to me. They'll never have it. Even if they kill me.

Golems, shadow wolves, and cloaked dummies surround me on all sides.

I study each and every single one of them. My magic burns along my skin, ready to face this threat head on.

They don't charge, instead, they wait for me to make the first move.

I'm only too happy to oblige them.

"Remember to reach for your meteorite, let it know you trust in it."

Gideon's voice echoes from everywhere, and I barely nod in acknowledgment. My intense gaze is on the foes he sent for me to destroy, and damn it all, come hell or high water, I am going to do just that.

My magic builds in both of my hands as large balls of purple and blue light swell to the middle of my bicep. Taking in a deep breath, I close my eyes and focus on my surroundings, listening to the very wind blowing through the trees, the trickle of the water in the stream, the shifts of weight from my opponents.

As soon as I open my eyes, I lift my arms and release destructive blasts of magic, taking out the Golems from my left. Their destroyed bodies shoot dust and crumbled dirt into the air, and the shadow wolves on my right howl in pain as fire consumes them. The stragglers that ended up escaping the blast run away in defeat.

I smile as I step forward, inching my way closer to the cloaked dummies. I find it fitting they are wearing black robes. After all, they symbolize the Order and how dark and corrupt they are.

Ready or not, here I come…

An hour later, exhausted and sweaty, I come away with a couple good bruises and a decent gash on my right forearm. Gideon takes me to his office where he keeps a supply of first aid items. As he works to bandage my arm, he looks me in the eye. "You've made some astounding progress today."

"Thanks. I think."

I barely escaped the vast numbers of dummies he had hidden within the trees. Their skills were seriously downplayed compared to the training sessions I have been doing with my men every evening for the last few months. He got me with the numbers though. And that's how I sustained a few good bruises and the gash on my arm.

That was the most intense, mentally draining, and energy-zapping training session yet.

"You should be proud. Celebrate it. I think we'll increase the difficulty for the next training and see how you do."

"Don't take it easy on me or anything."

"You can take it." He spreads antibiotic ointment on my arm and picks up the gauze.

I nod, tilting my head from side to side. "Sure, but that doesn't mean that I want to. I'm exhausted."

"Your endurance will build. Just takes some time." He wraps my arm with a few good layers of gauze. Once he finishes, he tosses his items into the kit and faces me. "Are you working on reaching deep and mentally touching the rock?"

"Yup. All the time."

"Good. Keep doing that. If it's sentient like we suspect, it may need nurturing, which may make you stronger."

I quirk an eyebrow. "Sure, you can handle that?"

He narrows his eyes and purses his lips as he shakes his head.

I snicker. "Uh huh."

He sighs, growing serious.

I gulp as my heart picks up in pace. I'm not sure

what the shadow that crosses over his eyes mean, but I have a feeling I'm not going to like it.

"Is there any way I can get you to reconsider spending the entire break with your father?"

I stiffen and look him straight in his blue-green eyes. "No."

It's not the first time I've been asked. Each of my men has voiced their displeasure with my being gone from them the whole week. I told Soren to get over it, and Jesse will live, and Milo... well, I told him he needs time with his family so he should go home.

I should have known that Gideon was going to push the issue too.

I shake my head. "I am going to spend time with my father. I am still building that relationship with him, and after being forced from him for so long, I still have some catching up to do."

A wrinkle appears in Gideon's forehead and I suck in a deep, calming breath. He nods. "I understand."

"I'm sorry. It's not just you. It's been all of you men. It's endearing and sweet, and I adore that you guys worry about me so much sometimes, but I deserve time away too. You've all trained me to the point that I'm an even bigger force to reckon with than ever before. I got this."

He nods again. Slowly, a smile starts to stretch his

lips. "I love how independent and fierce you are. You really have tenacity. I can certainly appreciate that as being one of the many qualities I admire about you."

I smile. "Thank you. Always aim to please."

He stands and walks over to his desk. "I can sympathize with your reasoning to go and spend time with your father." He looks at me as he reaches into a drawer. "You miss him, which is understandable."

"I really do."

"That doesn't mean that I like the idea of you leaving the academy grounds for an entire week."

I cross my arms as I make my way to his desk and take a seat in a chair. "You've ensured every precaution has been taken."

He pulls out something silver from his drawer and approaches me. "Yes, the wards and protections are strong. Yes, you are capable of taking care of business when needed." He kneels in front of me and looks deep into my eyes. "I trust, you will count on me to help if you ever need me to."

A weight shifts uncomfortably in my stomach and I can't help but wonder what the hell he thinks he's doing right now.

He smiles, takes my left hand, and slips a ring onto my index finger. He rubs his thumb over the black stone with a white starburst in the center that glitters with gold. "Rub it, like this and say my name if you ever need me. I'll arrive as soon as I can."

"Wherever I am?" I ask.

"Wherever you are. I'll find you." He releases my hand and I take a good look at the ring.

It's beautiful. I throw my arms around Gideon's shoulders. "Thank you."

I pull away and stand as he does the same thing. He places his hand on the small of my back and leads me toward the door. Before I walk through, I face him and smile. "Don't have too much fun without me." I wink and walk away, knowing he wouldn't dare pull me back.

CHAPTER THIRTY-SIX

I smile as I take in Gideon's glorious estate.

I made it here all by myself, and it's a proud moment for me.

Without missing a beat, I rush into the house and it's quiet. I figure my father is out hiking through the woods, enjoying the weather as well as doing some berry picking. He's mentioned it to me once in one of the letters he shared with me. There's a message on the answering machine. I hit play.

"Hi, Little Bird, just grabbing some berries for our breakfast in the morning. Be back soon."

The message ends with a loud high-pitch tone.

With a shrug, I continue on to my room and drop my stuff on my bed. A letter rests on the mattress and it looks to me like one my father left as a backup message. I grab it and head back down to the kitchen to make myself a snack.

Within minutes, I'm at the table, eating my bag of popcorn, observing the amazing view from Gideon's back porch. After unabashedly licking the salty, buttery residue from my fingers, I clean up my mess and head to the living room to watch a show while I wait for my father to return.

Wanting to relax my slightly sore muscles, I stretch out on the couch, my eyelids grow heavy, and I drift off to sleep. After what could've been only a few minutes or a few hours, I jerk awake, startled by how dark the world outside is. I didn't intend to fall asleep on the couch. The house is eerily silent, and I realize my father isn't back yet. This isn't like him. My intuition flares as the grandfather clock chimes eight times.

Confusion washes over me.

My father definitely should have been back by now. I walk into the kitchen just to double check the fridge for signs of beer and freshly bought groceries. But on my way, I spot the letter I took from my bed earlier and approach it instead. I had forgotten all about it and must have left it on the table after I finished my popcorn.

I slide a finger through the middle of the folded page. Within reading the first words, I know that this wasn't a backup message from my dad. In fact, it's not from him at all.

If you want to see your father alive again, you will come to my house. Come alone. No men. No tricks. If you do not heed my demands, your father will be consumed with the "Anima Sanguinonte."

If you don't know what that is, then you will soon find out.

You have until midnight tonight.

Aunt Patricia. Damn her.

I crumple the letter in my hand and clench my teeth. I don't know what sort of spell the *Anima Sanguinonte* is, but I'll be damned if I don't get there in time to stop it. Anger floods through me and my magic starts to burn along my skin. I drop the letter to the table and rush outside. I'm done playing games and I'm done with my father being used as bait to get to me.

One way or another, this ends tonight.

Suddenly I stop in the middle of the dew-covered porch as I pause to consider calling on my men, despite what the letter told me.

Normally, I would go alone. I've only ever done things on my own. It has always been me, myself, and I. But now, I don't have to go alone. I don't have to handle anything on my own. As protective as my men are over me, I know they would make this job easier. They can complement my strengths and help me strategize a solid plan.

They could help me with a Plan B, if needed.

I look down at my left hand, staring at the ring Gideon gave me. I chew on my lower lip as I consider my options.

I can go in alone, likely die in the process, and watch my father get killed, which will not only break my men's hearts but destroy everything I know and love. It's a trap I would be walking into. And my aunt is still clearly displeased with how our last run-in went. She's out for blood.

Or...

I can call on Gideon, and my other men can help. I won't die, not with them at my side. And there's a very high possibility we can also get my father out alive. It's still a trap, but with my men backing me, we can counter the trap. We can outsmart my aunt and whatever plan she has for me.

Hands down, my choice is clear.

I rub my thumb over the stone of the beautiful gift from my headmaster. "Gideon Storm."

I need you...all of you.

CHAPTER THIRTY-SEVEN

In less than five minutes, the light from a portal flashes through the house from outside. Seconds later, Gideon rushes into the house and to me, pulling me into his arms.

"I was so worried." He pulls back and looks me in the eyes. "What's wrong?"

"My father was kidnapped by my aunt."

His eyes widen as I pull away from him to grab the crumpled-up letter on the table. I hand it to him, and he reads it. Once he finishes, he does nearly the same thing I did, only instead of clenching his jaws, he turns away.

I give him the time he needs to process through everything. His shoulders move with each breath, and that tells me he's as angry about this as I am.

"How did this happen!?" His voice grows in volume as he speaks. The last word echoes throughout the house.

"I wish I knew."

"Stay here." He doesn't give me a chance to argue. He's already out the door and off the porch by the time I even take my first breath.

A bright, reddish-pink flare shoots into the sky. Several different colors shoot into the sky around the property lines. I watch from the window as Gideon shakes his head. I vaguely hear the string of curses spat out as he paces in front of the porch.

Soon, men I don't recognize appear in front of Gideon.

"What happened?" I overhear.

"Sir?" One asks, his skin blends in with his clothes, which are designed to camouflage him within shadows.

"He's gone. Explain."

The men all exchange shocked and worried glances.

The man in all black states, "Sir, we haven't had movement of any kind."

"Then how did he leave?" Gideon shouts. "You know what? Forget it. Go get reinforcements. Only those I trust. Everyone you can. Understand?"

"Sir." He takes a step back, conjures a portal, and just like that, he's gone.

Gideon gives orders I don't hear to the remaining men who nod and storm off. Gideon turns around and heads inside. His eyes settle on me and the anger is still alight within them. "Stay here. More guards are on their way for added protection. Meanwhile, I'll collect the others and be right back."

I nod.

He approaches me as he sighs heavily. He runs a hand along the side of my face and gently kisses me.

I watch him leave through the back door. I head into the living room, hands trembling and heart racing as I take a seat and wait for him to return.

Flashes start to filter through the windows as the men Gideon requested show up. The additional guards line up around the house, creating a barrier. Moments following the last flash, my men filter into the house. All of them gathering around and taking seats near me.

Each of my men have some variation of expressions that range between worry and anger.

"I'm sorry about your dad, Wren," Milo says as he settles in on my right.

"Patty's playing with fire." Jesse's tone is dark and

serious as he sits on my left. "She's going to get burned."

"We need a plan," Soren says from his chair to the right of the sofa.

Gideon paces in front of the fireplace. "That's why we're all here."

"The longer this takes, the less likely she'll buy that I've showed up on my own." I settle my gaze on each of my men.

"What can you tell us of the surrounding area?" Soren asks.

His eyes are a mix of fury and calm. It's sort of terrifying. I thank the gods his anger is not directed at me.

I dig into the details of the estate that I think will help. Once I finish explaining, Soren nods, crossing his arms over his chest.

"To save your father," Milo says, "Patricia only has to believe you arrived alone."

"Keep going," I say.

"If we were to see this area on a map, we can point out a location each of us," he gestures specifically to the men, avoiding me, "can portal to. We can each make our way toward the house, scouting for guards and lookouts."

Gideon stops pacing to face the rest of us. "I like where you are going with this." He taps his chin with his finger. "We have to time this exactly right. If we show up separately, it could tip Patricia off and we can't risk that."

Gideon leaves to get a map. He quickly returns and spreads it on the floor in front of us.

I drop to my knees and point to the exact location of my aunt's estate. "Here. That's where it is."

"So, we get there, at different points, at the same time," Soren says. "Then what?"

"Then I show up?" I ask.

"Yes." Milo sits back.

"How will I know it's safe to show up?"

"That's not the point," Gideon says. "The point is to get there before you."

"I understand that. Right now, my focus is on saving my father," I say as I stare at a spot on the floor. "What is the *Anima Sanguinonte*?"

"It literally translates into, soul bleed." Milo shivers. "The worst of curses, and unsanctioned magic." He shakes his head. "The most painful way to die. Slow, agonizing—"

"Okay, stop!" I hold up my hand. "I've heard enough."

"How do we know she hasn't already done that?"

Jesse asks. I elbow him in the ribs. "What? It's a fair question."

"I don't care. I don't want to consider that." The idea of my father's soul being bled from his body is not an image I want to contend with, but now that's the only thing flooding my mind.

"We have to consider it," Gideon says. "However, going in on the assumption that he's already dead isn't going to help Wren stay focused. Let's go in with the belief that he is still alive but be prepared that he's not."

I nod, though I feel sick to my stomach.

I don't like it. But Aunt Patricia is capable of this. It is an outcome I have to consider.

"It's going to be dark, and not knowing the landscape is going to present its own set of issues," Soren adds.

"True." Gideon sighs. "No magic unless absolutely necessary. Move as quickly and quietly as possible. We want to keep the element of surprise on our side."

"It's a trap. Are we going to be enough for this?" I ask.

He smiles. "Don't worry, I have a few friends of my own I can count on."

I let out a breath I had been holding. I'm not necessarily relaxed, but with this plan of ours, at least I'm prepared.

Gideon checks his watch. "We need to go."

One by one, we all stand and head for the yard. Gideon stops by one of the guards surrounding the house. Gideon whispers a few words to the man and he rushes off, heading through a portal.

I take one last look around the estate and at my men before we set off. It's comforting to have them at my side, fighting battles with me I probably wouldn't win on my own. I adore them more and more each day and they have become a part of my heart. No one else will ever hold these men's places in my soul. Nobody will ever come close.

Sighing, I mentally prepare and conjure up a portal.

My men do the same.

"Three... two... one..." My men step into their portal. I give it a few minutes and step into mine.

Ready or not, here I come.

CHAPTER THIRTY-EIGHT

There is something incredibly imposing about the way my aunt's estate looks at night. Even with the full moon hanging high in the sky, casting silver light onto everything, it still has a foreboding feel to it.

All things considered, my opinion may be biased.

It's hard to look at this place and see any beauty or feel any sense of family after what Aunt Patricia has done. Realizing the extent of my aunt's deception, for all I know she could be torturing my father, or worse. But I can't entertain those thoughts right now. I have to focus.

The air of this spring evening is almost unseasonably icy, which adds to the warning pulsing through me. Not only that, but it's quiet. Almost too quiet.

I startle as an owl hoots nearby.

Taking some calming breaths, I clear my mind of all pretenses and focus on the one thing that matters.

My father.

He's in there. And I need to get him out.

As I stare at the house with glowing windows, I mentally prepare for what could be the worst-case scenario.

Although my men are making their way toward the estate, I don't know how long it will take them to get here. Until they do, I have to be clever about every move I make and hold off on taking any action against my aunt.

Somehow, knowing that my men are on the way brings me comfort. I take another few breaths and approach the gate. Just like before, it opens on my approach. As soon as I'm through, the gate shuts and locks itself with a hard clang. I pause and look over my shoulder at it, just in case there is someone I hadn't noticed before hiding in the silhouette of the wall.

There isn't anyone by the gate, but there is someone somewhere, hiding in the shadows. I feel their eyes on me, observing my every move.

Regardless, I push the heavy feeling of being watched to the side and continue on the path that leads to the door of my aunt's home. And as I approach the front door, it mimics the self-opening trick of the gate. Its slow wooden creak is high-pitched and grating. A wave of heat slams into me as I step inside, and the door softly shuts behind me.

The feeling of being watched doesn't let up here either. It's increased ten-fold and now feels like I'm carrying a fifty-pound weight on my shoulders. I take in all the darker corners and each nook and cranny for signs of an ambush. So far, I find a whole lot of nothing but plaster, walls, and shadows.

A sound echoes through the dining room area from the back of the house. I snap my head in that direction and narrow my eyes on the room, waiting for someone to round the corner and come at me.

After several, agonizingly long moments, nothing happens.

Since the back of the house is the location of where the sound came from, I decide to go in that direction first. I take each step cautiously as I edge closer to the doorway, focusing on even breathing, keeping my ears peeled for the slightest sound.

As I reach the dining room, I press myself to the wall and inch my head carefully around the corner, peeking inside.

The room is dismally empty, but I know the sound came from this direction. I press my lips together firmly and glance toward the windows on the opposite side of the room. I see myself reflected back at me and silently groan as I realize this is probably the exact area my aunt wanted me to enter.

I duck back into the foyer of the large home and rest my head against the wall. I have two choices, and neither of them are particularly good ones.

One of my choices is I can continue through the dining room, based on the assumption that I was already seen, and follow through with it. Making Aunt Patricia assume she has the upper hand. It would force me to be prepared for what could possibly be an ambush waiting for me.

The other is to go in the other direction, hoping that I wasn't seen. It's a very small chance, but it could work. However, that could blow up in my face because, if I was seen, and I don't follow through, I could be headed off in the sitting room and that element of surprise is gone.

I don't have forever to stand here making a decision.

The likelihood I was already seen is highly probable.

I don't like the first option, but it is the best one I have to go on.

Holding my breath in anticipation, I step into the

room and move along the wall, acting as though I'm not aware of the obvious staring me, almost quite literally, in the face. I resume breathing as I move along. In my periphery, my reflection moves through the room with me, and when I reach the end of the wall, the kitchen is reflected within them as well.

For appearances sake, it's empty. But I'm not willing to bank on that. There could be any number of enchantments or illusions set up to make the room only appear vacant.

A creak, like that of a wooden chair, softly squeaks, alerting me that despite what the reflection shows, someone *is* in that room.

I remove myself from the wall and step into the kitchen. Instantly my eyes fall on my father in a chair. He's tied to it, gagged, and a cut on his forehead bleeds down the side of his face. Dark purple and green bruises cover his eyes and his left cheek. His hair clumps at the side of his head. His eyes catch mine and they are full of apology. He slumps in the chair, beaten and resolved to his fate.

I shake my head, lips pressed into a firm line as anger floods through me. I wonder why he didn't fight or use magic to defend himself and break free, but those questions will have to wait.

My aunt stands in the sitting room across the hall. I

know better than to think she's alone as she stands behind a chair, staring at the fireplace as the light dances along her features.

I return my gaze to my father. "I'm going to get you out of this," I whisper.

He shakes his head and quickly glances at his sister. He's trying to tell me not to go. There's too much danger. I hold up my hand to him.

"Don't worry. It's all covered."

Questions flash through his eyes as he still tries his best to silently stop me from approaching my aunt.

I step around my father, magic filling my hands, and step into the hallway. No sooner than I reach the doorway does my aunt let me know she's aware of my presence.

"You must not understand the severity of my letter if you waited this long to respond." She turns from the fireplace and faces me, setting her brown eyes on me. "Either that, or you made a stupid decision and cost your father his life."

"He's your brother. Your blood." My voice is dark and low.

She quirks an eyebrow as she looks down her nose at me. "Blood means nothing. It is a weakness, nothing more."

"It's weak to have a family?"

"Blood connections, stupid girl. Case in point," she nods in my direction.

I shake my head. "What happened to you to make you hate him so much?"

She levels her intense eyes on me. "Delaying the inevitable won't help you."

I shrug. "It's just that when my dad spoke of you, he said you two used to be close. You weren't always like this. What happened?"

"He betrayed me." Her words come out matter-of-factly. "We were going to be great, he and I." She settles her gaze over my shoulder as she talks, her expression has a wistfulness I had never seen before. It's like she really does have feelings beneath her cold exterior, she just keeps them buried.

"With his knack for magic and science, and my knowledge of spells and lore, we were going to not only secure our futures, but we were going to bring renewed honor and prestige to the Blackwood name. *That* should have been what our family is about." She holds her head up high, a smile stretching her lips, alas never reaching her eyes.

"What made you give up on your brother then?" She wants to talk about his so-called betrayal, yet she's not the one gagged and beaten.

She settles her gaze on me once more, and within

her eyes are hate, malice, and disgust. "Your mother. He left it all. Everything. All for her."

My eyebrows knit together as confusion contorts my expression. "You hate him because he fell in love?"

"He promised me!" Her statement echoes throughout the room, an octave higher than her usual tone. Her eyes widen, as if she didn't expect herself to make such a forceful retort. She takes a moment to calm herself and smooth her hair pinned tightly into a French bun. "The Order is my family now."

"That's a harsh second choice."

She takes a step closer to me. "Child, they gave me what I wanted. They've rewarded me for my sacrifices when your father abandoned me. I clawed my way to the top, and I will be damned if that is ripped away from me because of you."

"I have done nothing to you. Nothing!" I square my shoulders.

She lets out a dark laugh and the shadows in the room increase. "Oh, you have done plenty. You have magic when you should not. A problem I plan to rectify now. You killed my second in command, Deacon Lawrence." She nods once. A creak sounds behind me, and I chance a glance to see what I'm up against. The two men from Crimson Isles step into the doorway, closing off my escape to my father and the front door.

"I've been wondering when I would see you two again," I say sarcastically.

With my aunt on the other side of me, the door near her is not an option. She's powerful, and with her tenacity to lift me in the air on a whim, I would likely make it no farther than the sofa before I'm pulled back.

Shit.

The magic filling my hands grows and I narrow my eyes at my aunt. She'll be first. I dip even deeper into my magic as I prepare for what is promising to be a very painful fight.

"Don't you dare think about damaging my house."

Instantly the two men are on either side of me, gripping my arms firmly in their hands. I struggle against their grips, kicking and jerking. They tighten their hold until I wince in pain. But it doesn't stop me from struggling.

"Careful," my aunt warns. "It will only take but a snap of my fingers and your father is as good as dead."

I narrow my eyes on her. "You so much as split a hair on his head. I'll kill you."

She huffs and holds out her hand toward me. A painful shock enters me, starting in my stomach and spider-webbing out to the rest of my body. It's agonizing. I feel like my nerves are set on fire and the burn courses through me as though I'm being consumed by flames from the inside out.

Within seconds, my aunt releases me from the pain. I pant to catch my breath.

"The next one goes to your father if you do not stop." To prove her point, she holds her hand out toward my father.

That does it for me. But I don't intend to make it easy for them. I'm still going to struggle, but only enough to keep them wondering if I wisened up to their way. I don't want to be responsible for my father getting hurt. I just have to figure out a way to delay this plan of theirs, whatever it is, until my men arrive. Slowly, I nod.

The goon on the right digs his sharp fingernails into my arm as I'm half dragged toward the back door leading out of the kitchen. I hiss in response to the searing pain in my bicep, promising that after my aunt, he will be the next to die. My gaze then focuses on the back door, which I don't recall ever being there. It makes me wonder just how many enchantments the woman has on this house.

I still struggle against the two men as they drag me with them, but not vigorously enough to get another arm squeeze or a punch. I'm too busy thinking of a plan and delaying as much as possible. How the hell am I going to get out of this before my men get here?

As we step through the door, my aunt leading the way, I'm blasted with cold, icy air. It's a shock to my system. I suck in a breath of air but my lungs revolt against the cold and I cough instead. Aunt Patricia looks at me from over her shoulder, a satisfied smirk stretching her lips.

I glare daggers at her.

I really despise killing, but I'm willing to make an exception for my aunt.

Pretending to give up, I relax my body, putting my full weight on the two goons dragging me along. Meanwhile, I take in my surroundings. The shadows in the trees are moving, but they're too many and too erratic to be my men.

Oh good, we have more friends.

Fan-freaking-tastic.

A figure emerges from the woods. As I focus on him, taking in his ugly green face and thick arms and frame, a sense of dread enters the pit of my stomach.

Gnars.

I had hoped to never see him again. Yet, here he is, standing in the field, watching as I'm getting dragged closer to him, smiling triumphantly.

"What are you doing here?" Aunt Patricia asks.

"To make sure you hold up your end of the bargain this time."

"What?" I ask, glaring at both Gnars and my aunt.

She faces me and pauses as though she's really considering letting me know. But she doesn't. Instead, she rolls her eyes. "You'll find out soon enough."

Oh, lovely. Another surprise.

I just *love* surprises.

My aunt waves her hand through the air as a small shelter appears not twenty feet ahead of us. The goons edge me closer to the small building, and I amp up the struggle big time. Whatever is planned for me, I fully intend to break them. Because if it's one thing I'm not willing to do, it's go back to the trolls.

This. Ends. Now.

I reach for my magic and beg for it to help. Dropping my arms, I blast the two goons on either side of me with a nice ball of white light. That does the trick.

They groan as they release me, and I don't waste a moment as I spin and face them again. Using fire, I disintegrate them into ashes.

Mages flood onto the lawn from the shadows of the trees, and I start blasting the ground with magic to ward them off as much as possible. Recalling every scenario of training I've had with my men, I move quickly and fluidly, using my magic to push back and smash when needed. I turn to face my aunt and square this issue of ours, but she dashes into the collection of moving shadows. Gnars stands off to the side, observing my every move with a hungry look in his eyes that sets my stomach rolling with nausea.

I know that look well, and it definitely means a whole lot of pain is coming my way.

I shift my attention to the moving shadows, looking for my aunt. "Coward."

She probably didn't want to break a nail.

My heart soars when I see my men finally rush in, fighting off the multiple moving shadowy forms of mages with incredible magic and brilliant moves.

Gnars roars into the night air and faces me, closing the gap between us.

A collection of war cries fills the air… a call to charge.

A call to kill us all.

CHAPTER THIRTY-NINE

Magic is erupting everywhere.

Gideon rushes into a group of six mages and trolls, spinning his magical staff and taking out half of them with one hit. Soren back flips from an attack with a troll and blasts him with a torrent of fire. Milo works diligently to manipulate the elements, keeping them far enough away so Jesse can leverage an attack with lightning. The crack of thunder shakes the ground.

They're surrounded, but they are capable. I have faith in them to make it out of this fight with little injury.

A few stragglers edge their way carefully and cautiously toward Gnars and I as we circle each other in a three-foot diameter ring. They're several hundred feet off, taking their time, waiting for their turn to be next. But I don't focus on them. Gnars is doing the same thing I am, and I don't even care. He's gauging my weaknesses and assessing my skills.

Good luck, asshole.

The last time he and I faced off was when Professor Lawrence found me. We fought the village off together, until the chief called a surrender and threatened death if we returned. I've improved a great deal since then. Not only in strength and magic, but in my self-worth.

I still remember the sting of his mocking.

Weak.

Stupid.

Ugly.

Slave.

I smirk. "Long time, Gnars. You got fat."

He chuckles. "You think your words can hurt me?" His black eyes follow me as I move in time with him. He doesn't break from my gaze, and neither do I. I'm not who I was back then. I'm better.

And it's a lesson I'm willing to give him.

"Meh," I shrug, "I don't care if they hurt you or not."

Two mages charge forward, magic pools in their outstretched hands. I pause in my face-off with Gnars to demonstrate just how far I've come by easily taking the two mages out with a blast of fire.

I face him again. "Where were we?" I tap my chin. "Ah, yes. I was about to kick your ass."

"Still think you are better than me? Very well." He cracks his thick neck and charges.

I stand my ground, dipping into my ready stance and pulling my hands up by my face. As soon as he lowers himself to try and tackle me, I dodge to the right. He crashes against the ground with a groan. Facing him, I wait for him to stand up as I start to circle again.

"Come on, Gnars. All those berries went straight to your hips." I make a tsk-ing sound with my tongue. "I'm not impressed."

I'm goading him. I know this. But he has to know how far I've come. How much better I am, stronger, more confident. He can't take my thunder from me anymore. And he has another thing coming to him if he tries.

He growls.

I smile. "Awww, struck a nerve?"

I glance around and find my men fighting off the trolls, who were in the process of fighting off a group of mages. Some of them I don't recognize, but it doesn't take me long to realize those are Gideon's men who've joined the fray. I smile, grateful for the help. The trolls are being pushed back and forced to split up and fight my men and their allies.

"Looks like your ugly green warriors are cowards," I say with a gesture in the direction they are fleeing from.

He looks over his shoulder. "What?"

Arrogant and stupid.

I kick out his knees, sending him to the ground. It's an unfair move, I know, but he cheated against me so many times. Just giving him his just desserts.

Gnars growls again, his black eyes narrowing at me.

"Let me guess… I'm going to pay for that?"

He glares at me. Spittle flies from his mouth as he tries to intimidate me with a war cry.

"No. I'm not. Let's get something straight. I'm not your property. I'm not your slave. And I'm far from weak."

He reaches for me and I kick his arm out of the way and blast a bolt of flame next to his head.

"Go home. And never return."

I smirk to myself as that was similar to what I was told the last time we faced off. I'm not exactly thrilled about being constantly hunted by vengeful troll tribes. They let me go when I fled with Professor Lawrence.

I'll give him and his ilk the chance to flee now and call it even. But, if he ever shows his ugly face again, all bets are off.

"You're letting me go?" His voice is doubtful, slightly confused.

"My bullet isn't for you."

My gaze locks with his, and he inclines his head. His sneer tells me that he dislikes and even distrusts what I just said. However, his physical gesture indicates that he accepts my terms. When I'm certain that he won't try to lunge for me, I turn and run off to join my men, leaving Gnars baffled on the ground.

I can't help the pride and joy I feel with that. I could have killed him, but I chose the higher road, even though he would have surely tried to kill me.

I slow my steps as five mages flank me and cut off my path to my men. I square my shoulders and face down each one. They attack.

This is what I've trained for every single day for the last few months.

I conjure my shield and use it to deflect all the magic attacks and resort to my punches and kicks for those closest to me.

Keeping in mind where they are comes easy to me, being aware of my surroundings, searching for the tells of an illusion, all while defending myself at the same time. I pull my shield behind me and deliver a pink lightning bolt to the mage to my right. He flies back, landing on the ground as a pillar of smoke rises from the hole in his chest. I side kick the guy to my left as the third mage, in front and to my left fires a blast of light at me.

I twist, shifting my shield to the side as I drop to my knees. The hit knocks me back an inch, but I manage to keep my balance. I jump to my feet in one fluid move and face the mage that was behind me with a front kick and fire ball to the face.

Rotating to face the next three, I disperse my shield and blast the two at my sides with white light, incinerating them to nothing and front kicking the mage about to throw fire at me.

He flies back, landing on his rump, and I don't miss a beat as I approach and kick the bottom of his chin. His face snaps upward, spraying blood into a wide arc as he lands on his back. I circle him as he groans and tries to get to his feet.

"Are you really sure you want to do that after I just took out your buddies?"

He ignores me as he climbs to his knees. He spits on the grass in front of him as he straightens up and touches his mouth with the tips of his fingers. Pulling them back, he sees the red and sets his angry gaze on me.

I hear rushing footsteps and judging by the way my magic rushes through me, it's my men. So, I allow the mage in front of me to glare. I quirk and eyebrow and cross my arms just for added measure. I'm not afraid of him, and I never will be.

"You're a disgrace!" Blood-filled saliva shoots from his mouth.

Cocking my head to the side, I drop my arms and land a solid kick to his head. He falls to the ground, out cold.

"I would've killed him," Soren said.

"Impressive," Jesse adds.

I face my men. "We have to find my aunt quickly."

"I saw her running back inside the house," Milo says.

A cold lump forms in the pit of my stomach. "The curse!"

I take off in a dead run back into the house. As we draw closer, I hear my father's screams. I push myself to move faster and slam into the door, breaking it open. As it hits the wall, the glass inside it shatters, littering the floor with shards. I suck in a breath as I find the kitchen empty. My father's screams are so loud, I can't tell if they are coming from the sitting room or the dining room.

Jesse rushes to the dining room. "In here."

I run into the room and find my father lying on the table, writhing in agony as my aunt is actively performing the *Anima Sanguinonte* curse on him. I don't stop running until my body collides with my aunt and we fall to the floor. I sigh with relief as my father's screams cease.

I've broken the curse.

If only for the moment.

Aunt Patricia growls and tries to cast the curse on me. Pain ripples through my body. It feels like my very soul is being ripped from me. Before the pain really sets in, I slam a fist into my aunt's face. The pain stops and it feels like my organs and muscles move back to their rightful place.

I stand and yank the woman to her feet and force her to face me.

I'm done playing games. This ends now.

The men move to join me, but I hold up a hand and they pause. "No. I'll handle this. Cover my dad."

I glare at them in warning.

My aunt punches me in the gut with a magic-infused fist. I bowl over in pain. Quickly recovering, forcing my lungs to pull in air, I play her game. Gripping her shoulders, I ram my knee into her gut. She bends over, moaning in pain. I clench my fists, filling them with magic and deliver an uppercut to her chin. She flings upward and stumbles back a few steps, almost falling to the floor again. She catches herself on the back of a chair and levels her gaze on me.

But I don't give her a chance to retaliate. I point at her. A bolt of pink lightning shoots from my fingers, aimed right at her chest, where her non-existent heart is. It bounces off, ricocheting into the windows along the far side of the room, shattering them. The house shakes with the force of the boom.

She sends a stream of fire toward me. I conjure my shield, but it's almost too late. The heat from the fire sears my arm and I scream as my skin boils. The shield falters just as the fire ceases.

I throw a fire ball at her, ready for this to be over.

She dodges the blow, and the far wall ignites. The wallpaper chars and peels from the plaster underneath as the flames consume the wall, licking the ceiling. She charges me, lifting me into the air just feet before she reaches me. My throat feels like it's closing in on itself. I can barely suck in a breath of air as my vision becomes rimmed with black.

"You should not have magic." Her lips curl in disgust. "That rock inside you is not meant for you."

"Come and take it then." I force out the challenge through gasps.

She pulls me closer with an invisible force as she reaches for my chest, almost like she could pull the meteorite out of me. As soon as I'm within range, I kick her square in the nose. The force holding me in the air by my throat is immediately released and I fall to the ground. I hear a snap as sharp pain radiates up my arm. The wind is knocked from me, and I once again gasp for air as I struggle to climb to my feet.

My men are still with my father, Milo and Jesse propping him up, and Soren trying to hold Gideon back from stepping into the middle of my fight. As much as I love them and their strength, right now this is just that—my fight.

Although they still hover near, ready to intervene at a moment's notice. I appreciate the chance to avenge my father who is lying still on the table, and I'm not even sure if he's breathing. The fire consuming the wall roars and pops as it begins feasting on the next wall. Black soot covers the ceiling, and I know we don't have much longer before the house is aflame.

"Wren, we have to go," Gideon calls out. Milo and the others are already carrying my dad outside. Thick smoke billows toward us and we cough.

"Not yet." I motion for him to join the others and

leave. I clear my throat and face my aunt crawling backward on the floor, eyes wide with shock and blood dripping from her nose as I slowly step toward her. She scoots on her rear closer to the fire, and she looks back at the burning, crumpling wall. "The meteorite is mine, Aunt Patricia. You and the Order can chase me to the ends of the Earth, but you will never have my power."

"Deacon should have killed you when I told him too." Her gaze is defiant.

"Yes, I know. He was your lackey."

"He was my second in command and my lover, you selfish bitch!"

Oh, interesting. She can love? Shocker.

"Ah, but he became greedy and it ruined him. And you're following in his footsteps. You chose the wrong family."

"It won't matter." She shakes her head as I stop at her feet, staring down at her like she's a bug that needs to be squashed. "Someone will replace me. We will never stop until we have what belongs to us."

"Surrender, and I'll let the magusari take you. I'm sure there's a nice dark hole they can shove you in for the rest of your life."

A slow chuckle escapes her bloodied lips. "I'd rather burn."

Incredible. Even when faced between a chance of life and certain death, she stands by her misguided morals and beliefs.

I step back, covering my mouth and nose with the crook of my arm. My eyes sting from the smoke and flames.

She lifts a trembling hand, and at first it seems she's reaching out to me. Maybe she finally decided she didn't want to die in a house fire. But then this is Aunt Patricia. Conniving, cold, and calculated to the very end.

I'm ready for her just as she extends her fingers for a final attack, the dark magic swirling around her hands. Before she can cast a spell that's surely meant to kill me and take me along with her, I hold my palm out toward her.

"Goodbye, Aunt Patricia."

With all the strength I can summon, I blast my aunt with my magic. Bright, blinding light fills the room. It's a quick flash that dies out as soon as it begins, like the blink of an eye. But nothing of my aunt is left. Not even ash.

CHAPTER FORTY

Another flash occurs and Savannah stands in the dining room, staring at the fire consuming the room with fury.

"What happened?" She takes in the burning house and shakes her head. "Never mind."

"We have to go now." I pull on her hand and drag her behind me.

We make our way out of the back of the house and stop a good distance away on the property. My men are with my father, still watching over him. Gideon's hand glows as he holds it steady over my dad. He must be gauging how much damage was done. I can still see my father's chest slowly rise and fall. At least we have that.

I turn around and look at the burning home that

had been in my family for hundreds of years. The fire made its way to the second and third floor, working its way from the front corner of the house outward. I scan the surrounding area. Aunt Patricia's mages were either disposed of or dispersed by Gideon's men.

"I tried to get here sooner," Savannah says, "But the wards kept preventing me from portaling in."

That makes sense that she arrived right after I killed my aunt. Her death must have dispersed the wards.

"She was casting the *anima sanguinonte* on him before I stopped her."

Her eyes widen. "You stopped her in the middle of the cast?"

I nod.

"Impressive." She turns and rushes to my father. She kneels next to him and checks for a pulse. I approach and crouch beside her, watching her face screw up in concentration. Finally, she sighs. "He's alive, but barely. We need to get him back to Blackbriar."

"I'll make sure all the wards are down." Gideon starts to check the perimeter, holding his hand out in front of him, eyes closed, moving in a slow circle. Once finished, he nods. "We're good."

He conjures a portal as shouts start to echo from

the woods around us. Soren picks up my father and walks in first. Savannah goes second. I stand from the ground and stumble. Gideon's face fills with concern as he concentrates on the portal. Jesse catches me and between him and Milo, they walk me into the portal. Just before walking through, I look at the burning house one more time.

I sit in the chair next to my father's hospital bed. My leg won't stop bouncing as the seconds turn to minutes and the minutes bleed into hours.

Daylight breaks across the horizon and starts to lighten the window behind me.

Savannah had worked most of the night trying to help my father, with Gideon's help. They exhausted themselves until there was nothing else they could do. They addressed their own wounds and went to bed while I stayed up all night at my father's side, waiting for him to wake up.

"It's up to him now," Savannah had told me with a soft, sad smile on her lips. She had spoken from the doorway of the infirmary.

I nodded and she left my sight, heading to bed.

Sighing, I replay the conversation Savannah and I

shared before she went to bed, over and over again in my head. I want my father to wake up, but really, we did the impossible anyway.

Soren told me that it is very difficult to stop the curse once it begins. The fact that I had done so not only speaks volumes about my power, but my strength as well. I shouldn't have been able to break the curse, but I did.

Thank the gods.

Soren shifts in his seat, sleeping in an uncomfortable upright position in one of the hard desk chairs sitting along the wall at the foot of my father's bed. His right arm is covered by thick gauze and a healthy slather of special balm. His arm got charred during the fight. Underneath his white t-shirt, an old blood stain shows where a hole was blasted into his torso from a cheap attack. Jesse and Milo went to bed shortly after we arrived here.

I scratch at my arm, bandaged and healing from being broken and burned. My ribs ache like hell as a couple of them were also cracked. I also sustained a bruised diaphragm. Luckily Jesse's potions are powerful, or I would be in too much pain to even breathe.

My eyelids start to close, and I force myself to change my position in my seat, shaking the drowsiness from my head. I can't sleep. Not until I know my father is okay. I settle my gaze on him as I prop my head up in my hand. His breathing has evened out. That brings me hope.

He's going to be okay.

He has to be.

A tapping sound jolts me awake. I chide myself for falling asleep. Milo is standing in the doorway and walks in, limping because of the wound on his right thigh. He also has a bandage taped above his left temple. A dot of blood stains the center. Despite his obvious discomfort, he still smiles softly as he approaches and stands next to me.

"Sorry to wake you," he says.

I wave off his concern as I yawn. "I'm glad you did."

"You need to go get some rest."

I quickly glance at him. "I'm fine."

Soren stirs and stretches his arm over his head. "Any changes?" He stands from the chair and walks to the foot of the bed. He limps a little too. My eyebrows knit together with concern, but he waves it off.

Frowning, I shake my head.

"Go, get some rest. I'll take watch." Soren shoves his hands into his pockets as he levels his gaze on me.

This is not a request. I know better than to think that.

I shake my head and keep my rear firmly planted in the chair.

He sighs. "You're no good to us exhausted. You'll also heal faster."

"He's right," Milo adds.

"No. End of discussion."

We settle into a somewhat uncomfortable silence that doesn't shift until Gideon and Jesse walk in. Jesse smiles at me and stops at my father's side. He gently rubs the side of his ribs and winces. "How's the old man doing?"

"No changes," Soren says.

I glare at him as I had my mouth open to respond. He ignores me. I'm too exhausted to care.

"Have you rested?" Gideon asks. He's the one with the seemingly fewest injuries. His knuckles are covered in light gauze. Not much else stands out. To be honest, I'm not surprised. Gideon is a force to reckon with.

I meet his gaze. "I've had enough."

He doesn't seem to buy it, but he doesn't push either. And I'm grateful for that.

"How are you feeling?" Gideon asks me.

I shrug. "Fine, I guess."

He levels his gaze on me. "Fine?"

Jesse chuckles. "Warrior."

I chuckle under my breath even though I don't have much humor in me. Most of my focus is on my father waking up. "I don't know yet."

"Knock-knock!" Savannah's sing-song voice arrives just before she steps into view. "How are all of you doing?"

She receives a collection of shrugs and mumbles in response.

She sighs and moves to my father to check his vitals. "Well, I suppose not everyone is going to be in a celebratory mood after a fight like that."

I snort. "That was a battle."

"You know what I mean." She glances at me briefly before turning her attention to me. "So, what happened? I want details."

"What all did you see?" I ask so we don't cover what she already knows.

This is Savannah, after all.

"Your aunt was killing you." Her amethyst eyes darken into a deeper purple and her lips pull down at the corners. "That was the most helpless I have ever felt. I kept trying to get to you, but I couldn't. I couldn't find any of the guys." She gestures to them with a shrug and squeezes her eyes closed. She opens them and takes a deep breath. "Whoever the Order is, they're dangerous. I can try to make visions come to me to find out more about them, but they are less reliable then."

"Don't stress on it," I say. "But you are right, they are dangerous. They're after me because of my meteorite."

"They want to take it from you?" Savannah asks. "Why?"

"They think she doesn't deserve it because she is born of a human and mage," Soren answers, bitterness filling his words.

"So?" Savannah shakes her head.

"She's also more powerful than most mages," Milo adds. His eyes slip out of focus like he's recalling every detail of the fight. "I don't think she realizes what she did back there."

"What?" I ask looking between Milo and Gideon for an answer.

"That blast you emitted takes a great deal of power," Gideon says. "The fact you did that, controlled the blast, and disintegrated your aunt into virtually nothing but air, says a lot more about the power you wield than what we previously understood."

"Oh." I think about that for a moment and wonder if I should be proud or worried. "Is that... bad?"

"We don't know," Soren answers.

"Oh."

This sucks.

"Now what?"

"We will need to prepare for retaliation from the Order over the next few months." Gideon's attention shifts to the subtle movement on the bed. I caught it too.

My dad opens his eyes and instantly looks for me. As soon as his gaze lands on mine, he lays his head down and sighs. "Thank the gods."

"How are you feeling?" I stand from the chair and take his hand in mine.

"Better, now that I know you're safe." He smiles weakly. "Feel like I've been hanging out with death though."

"Dad, what happened?"

"I want to know how someone managed to get past the wards, the guards, and the gryffons," Jesse says with a curious glint to his eyes.

"Yes, that is curious." Gideon's gaze settles on my father and I hold my breath. I know I'm not going to like what is about to be said.

He closes his eyes and takes a few measured breaths. "Someone disguised as Savannah came to me, explaining you were severely sick with something she couldn't figure out. She had never seen it before, and judging by what she was talking about, it was something unnatural and unheard of by even me."

Gideon nods. "That explains the gryffons. They know her appearance. And nesting inside the woods on the property, the probably only saw that it was her and went back to sleep."

"It could also explain the guards," Soren adds. "They know she is on the list."

My father squeezes his eyes closed and my hand at the same time. "I immediately took a portal with her, expecting to show up here. But when we arrived, I knew it was a trap. First, I saw the gates to my sister's estate. Second, the sheer number of people waiting for the moment I showed up. I couldn't leave, and I was outnumbered. That's when Savannah's disguise wore off to show a man instead."

Milo leans in a little more, as though he's getting more of the conversation. "There must have been an illusion as well."

He shrugs and settles his gaze on me once more. "I took out a good chunk of the men Patricia had there, but a cheap shot got the better of me. I woke up tied to the chair." He takes another few breaths. "My conduit was taken."

I nod. I am so proud of my dad. He was out

numbered and still continued to fight anyway. "We'll get you another one."

"My own sister used me as bait to get you there. She was going to torture you until I finished the machine, then hand your lifeless body to the trolls under the guise that you were under a sleeping spell that would wear off a few days after they got you back."

I huff out a breath as I close my eyes, thankful that didn't happen. Dead or no, that's just wrong. It would have started a war between trolls and mages... maybe even humans.

"When I continued to refuse, she sent the letter to you. She was determined to get you in her clutches once and for all."

I shake my head. "I'm safe now, Dad."

"And the same goes for you." Gideon gently cups my father's shoulder. "It will be a while before you are up on your feet again. But as soon as you are, you can stay in the spare room of my suite."

My father frowns. "No. I can't burden you anymore. I need to get on my feet. Get a place of my own."

"I insist. It won't be any trouble at all. If all goes well, you'll have a position here at the school." Gideon meets my gaze and quickly winks. Barely noticeable.

But I saw it, and it makes me want to hop over the bed and kiss him on the mouth.

I resist, but later, it's happening.

"For now, no one can know you are on the grounds. Lady Alene can help with a disguise so you can get exercise."

"Why didn't we just do that before?" I ask.

"Disguises are not a failsafe," my father says. "They are temporary and temperamental. It's difficult to keep one up longer than an hour or two." He turns his attention to Gideon. "I'll do it, because I know your personal estate is no longer safe and I have nowhere else to go. However, I'll stay long enough to get my strength back. After that, I'll be on my own. I can't endanger you anymore than I already have."

"How about a compromise," I say. "Wait until your name is officially cleared. I don't want to have to rescue you again."

He chuckles. "No, twice was more than enough."

"As long as you're safe, that's all I care about." I smile.

We slip into a lighter topic as we recount the highlights of the things I did during the battle. Jesse made it sound much better than the first time and I smile, blushing from time to time, at his way of talking about my genius in fighting Gnars and my aunt.

It's in this moment that I observe my family and take it all in. The looks on their faces as they each add their own little nuggets to the story, sharing their worries, their exhilaration, and their dedication to me. They leave no doubt in my mind that they'll always have my back, and the same goes for them.

I feel whole. Complete in the sense that I now know what I had been searching for has been on this island. My team. My family.

We're going to be okay.

Hell, we're going to be better than okay.

We're going to be *great*.

CHAPTER FORTY-ONE

I'm smiling so big, my cheeks hurt.

I'm so proud of my father as he walks on his own, using a cane for support. We quietly stroll through the halls, in the middle of the night, moving him to Gideon's suite.

It's a warm, tender moment that I absorb every second of, because I know, soon enough, these moments are going to be what pull me through the darker times waiting over the horizon.

And this is going to be one of my favorite moments. Getting along, laughing, and carrying on casual conversation as we arrive at Gideon's door. He unlocks the door with a wave of his hand and holds the door open to let my father through.

We step inside, and I'm in awe.

I didn't even know there are rooms this big in the castle. This is by far, the best part.

Lavish doesn't even begin to describe the beauty of the room as I take in the gold trimmings, blended in with cream walls, marble fireplace and floors, and burgundy seating. Long windows with their golden drapes pulled open, reveal a private courtyard, and view of the ocean. Gnomes move about between the trees and bushes with their lanterns, collecting flowers and berries before disappearing from sight.

It's warm and inviting with lots of light and I can only imagine the beauty and serenity that fills the rooms with the warmth of sunlight.

Absolutely enchanting, and extremely fitting.

There are bookshelves built into the walls on both sides of the hall, leading to what I assume is the spare room, filled with a nearly endless array of tomes I would expect to see kept under lock and key. They're old, almost testimonial of the time that's passed, with the outlines of the words along their spines nearly indiscernible from age. Housed with the books are a few ceremonial masks held inside glass cubes. Paintings of creatures I can only guess at fill the hall.

A smoky grey cat the size of a large dog jumps into the room and makes a sound that's not quite a meow but more reow-reow. Gideon walks up to greet him with a scratch on the top of his head. "Well, hello, Maximus."

"He's a cat?" I ask, staring at the creature and his magnificent crystal blue eyes that seem to glow with knowledge and magic.

"Yes." Gideon faces me. "He's been with me since he was a kitten. He's a rare breed called a sapphilix."

I smile. Gideon's heart is so big for such a fearsome warrior. It's endearing. "He's beautiful."

Maximus' eyes instantly take in mine, he appears to bounce to me and stands on his hind legs stretching his body to place his front paws on my shoulders. He's looking into my eyes almost as though he can see my soul. I take a moment to take in the beautiful magnificence of the sapphilix in front of me. His face narrows toward his nose, with a bright white "W" between his eyes and darker shade of grey at his cheek bones. His mane is fluffy with a bright white collar of fluff at his shoulders. He reow-reow's at me and blinks his crystal blue eyes almost as if he is examining me too.

I chuckle. "Yes, you are smart." Maximus drops to all fours and I scratch his ears and pet the top of his head.

"Let's get you laying down," Gideon says to my father.

He nods. "That would be nice."

Though he doesn't show it, I know he's in some pain. He insisted he wouldn't take anything for pain until he was settled into the new room. This way he could sleep and relax and heal.

Maximus takes his leave, rushing out the door with a small look back over his shoulder as Gideon leads us to the spare room on the opposite end of the suite, and it's large enough to fit four of my rooms in. My father even has his own private bathroom. He stands in the middle of the room as he takes it all in with a nod. I join him at his side and cross my arms over my chest.

"What do you think?" he asks.

I shrug. "It'll do." I'm playing at being overly critical.

My dad laughs. "Yes, indeed." He hobbles to the bed and lays down. "Ah... like a cloud!"

I walk to the other side and lay parallel. My body sinks into the mattress and I feel like I'm floating in a sea of soft cotton. "It really is. Gideon, you've been holding out on me."

He chuckles. "You think so, huh?"

"I know so." I grunt as I force myself from the bed. Truth be told, I could spend my life on this bed and be totally okay with that.

In a perfect world, of course.

The Order is after me. My meteorite. They won't stop until they get it.

Well I don't intend to ever give it up easily. I intend to fight until the bitter end. With my family by my side, nothing can stop me.

Wren, Soren, Gideon, Jesse, and Milo will be back in *The Blood Oath of Blackbriar Academy,* available now!

Join the exclusive, fans-only Facebook group to get release news & updates.

Read on for a special note from the author.

AUTHOR NOTES

Hey Babe!

Well another year has come to a close for Wren and her team, and I can't be more happy that you are sharing this world with me still. It means so much to me that you cherish this story as much as I do. I am so gonna hug you tight if we ever meet in person. Promise!

I hope you continue to stick around because there is so much more in store for our badass heroine. I can't wait to dig into the next story with you.

This year has been quite a rush for Wren. We not only see her really grow into herself, but she starts to learn to not only fight for herself but for her team as well. She has her father back, yay! And just when she thinks she has this daughter thing down, she's faced with making a difficult decision that really tests her merit and the person she is. Most importantly, she learns the true definition of family.

After all, blood isn't always thicker than water, and Aunt Patricia shows this quite well.

Personally, watching Wren grow from book one has been such a treat! She's my hero.

Milo and Wren's relationship really blossoms in this book and comes to such a delicious climax (hehe). He belongs to Wren and she isn't afraid to show it. I mean who does this Agatha chick think she is messing with Milo?

Soren as a professor? Whoa. That went down in a delightful way. Hot for teacher? Yes, please!

Gideon's sheer drive to protect his woman really shows in this book as she faces off with her aunt and faces the most tragic details of her past. A lot of secrets are unfolded, and there are still more mysteries yet to uncover.

Jesse… sigh! I have to fan myself each time I think of him. He definitely knows how to tantalize every single one of Wren's desires. He's not afraid of sharing his own secrets as well. So long as it works in his (ahem) favor. I love him so hard.

Now that Aunt Patricia has been dealt with, Wren

can move forward with her classes and enjoying her four amazing, hot men, right?

Maybe.

You'll have to keep reading to find out.

Until next time, babe!

Keep on being your beautiful, badass self.

-*Olivia*

PS. Amazon won't tell you when the next Dragon Dojo Brotherhood book will come out, but there are several ways you can stay informed.

1) **Soar on over to the Facebook group, Olivia's secret club for cool ladies,** so we can hang out! I designed it *especially* for badass babes like you. Consider this as your invite! We talk about kickass heroines, gorgeous men, our favorite fantasy romances, and... did I mention pictures of *gorgeous men*?

2) **Follow me directly on Amazon**. To do this, **head to my profile** and click the Follow button beneath my picture. That will prompt Amazon to notify you when I release a new book. You'll just need to check your emails.

3) **You can join my mailing list by going to** https://wispvine.com/newsletter/olivia-ash-email-signup/. This lets me slide into your inbox and basically means we become best friends. Yep, I'm pretty sure that's how it works.

Doing one of these or **all three** (for best results) is the best way to make sure you get an update every time a new volume of the *Blackbriar Academy* series is released. Talk to you soon!